CHASING MY SUNSHINE

A YORK BEACH NOVEL
THE CAPPELLI FAMILY

NICOLE VIDAL

COPYRIGHT

TABLE OF CONTENTS

KEEP IN TOUCH WITH NV

Visit me on social media or online to learn about my newest releases:

Facebook (http://fb.me/NicoleVidalAuthor)

Instagram (http://instagram.com/nicolevidal_author)

My website (www.nicolevidal.com)

Goodreads (https://bit.ly/NVGoodreads)

Amazon (https://amzn.to/2XCLSlR)

Pinterest (http://pinterest.com/NicoleVidal_Author)

CHAPTER ONE

FRANCESCA

It's so early the sun isn't even awake yet. I slam my alarm clock and toss my legs over the edge of my bed. A moment later, I rise and pad to the bathroom to brush my hair and teeth. I pull on some jeans and a tee and rush out the door. Perhaps I should consider moving closer to the office. But... I love my townhouse. I bought it a few years ago, mostly for the gorgeous kitchen with waterfall countertops and stainless appliances. The rooms are spacious, and my furnishings have modern lines but are comfortable. My home is colorful and airy with hints of texture on the couches with pillows and a blanket over the arm of the chair.

York Beach, Maine is a quaint town with a cute village, which includes a store that pulls taffy in the window, souvenir shops, and even an amusement park. There are two popular stretches of beach as well as numerous tourist sites, like the Nubble Lighthouse and the Wiggly Bridge located in nearby Kittery.

This is my home. I only left the area to pursue my degree in landscape architecture. Now I run my own successful business, Sunshine Landscape and Design, in a neighboring town. I hop into my truck, send in my order to the coffee shop near my office, and head toward work. Thankfully, I don't have an installation today, but my crew has one. I try to supervise as many as I can, but today I need to focus on my plan for the Cooper project. A mutual friend told my sister-in-law about a bid to landscape a new hotel in Portsmouth. It would be a huge contract for my company to earn. The summer season just ended. Fall means cleanup and maintenance, and winter is planning for spring. I spend most of my workdays during the fall and winter at home. This project will give me plenty to do over during that time.

I pull up against the curb in front of the Sweet Face Pastry Shoppe and wave to my bestie, Talia, who is the owner, as I step inside. She's my antithesis. Tal is average height, blonde hair, and green eyes with flawless skin. She hates everything outdoors. I've known her since grammar school when Jimmy Delano slid his desk forward and caught her hair. I flattened him with one shove. I received detention for a week, and Talia became my bestie the very same day.

"Hi, Talia."

"Hey. Your order isn't ready yet. The espresso machine is having a tantrum despite the early hour. Here, take your muffin and a water, and I'll get your coffee as soon as I can." She shoves an apple cinnamon strudel muffin and water in my hand, then she scurries away.

I take a seat near the window and pick at my favorite muffin. No offense to Talia and her yummy creation, but the coffee is more important. I glance up when a tall, lean man with dark hair and light eyes steps into the bakery with a young girl, probably his daughter. If I had to guess, given her tall frame and awkwardness, she looks about twelve. I recall that feeling very well. As casually as I can, I watch them. Not true, I'm watching him. He moves gracefully as they approach the counter.

Jenny, one of the other baristas, steps up and takes their order. Once she finishes ringing them out, Tal shouts, "Joey, your coffee."

Seriously, Tal! She has been making fun of my nickname since we were kids. My family and close friends call me Frankie. The first time I ordered a coffee from her, she labeled it with a typically male nickname that can be for a female.

I shake my head, take the cup, and give her the side-eye. "Call me later." I raise my cup as I walk out the door. After settling into the driver's seat, I pull into traffic toward the office.

My work office is boring. I have a large, sturdy, wood desk and a comfy chair. There are two armless client chairs, which are from my dining set at home. I refuse to buy more chairs when I have two extra at home. There's a table along the wall with photo books of previous jobs. On the other wall is a small window and some plants. When I arrive, I plop down in my chair and boot up my laptop.

Once it wakes, I open the Cooper file and set out the requirements on my desk again. I refuse to fail due to a technicality. The bidding sheet sets forth the specifications for the landscape design, including the height of the shrubbery and which colors would be allowed for flowers.

By the end of the lunch hour, I have reviewed my plan numerous times. I have two more days to perfect it before the presentation. When I finish my review, I shut everything down and drive to today's jobsite.

When I arrive, I'm surprised at the progress the crew has made in one morning. "Hey, Eric. How's it going here?"

Eric is my foreman. If I'm not in charge of a site, he is. I hired him after I was in business for a little over a year. I couldn't handle the work on my own any longer. Eric is a few years older than me, but we are clear on boundaries and responsibilities. He has a wife, Amy, and two young boys named Dylan and Declan.

"Afternoon, Frankie. This job is moving smoothly. The shrubbery along the pool is complete. I'm hoping to get this portion done before it rains later this week." He indicates the tree line near the edge of the yard on the schematic.

"Good plan. Mind if I take a look?"

"Not at all, you're the boss." Most of the men in this industry aren't a fan of a female boss. The irony isn't lost on me; landscaping is about making the outside of a home or business beautiful, yet it's a male-dominated field. I follow the path around the house and wave to the rest of the crew. Jamie is a young kid, fresh out of high school. He's a great worker, punctual, and overall pleasant guy. Manuel is his complete opposite in looks and age. He's an older man who is set in his ways. I have learned a few old-school tricks from him, but thankfully he follows my plans as I set them out.

The shrubbery along the pool fence line is perfect, and the immature trees the client requested are being placed right now. Content with their progress, I return to the front of the house where Eric is consulting the plans again.

"Hey. Everything looks perfect back there. I'm heading back to the office and then home. Call me if you need anything," I inform Eric.

"Thanks, Frankie. I'll let you know."

As I sit in my seat, my phone chimes with my sister Lia's dedicated notification.

Lia: Hey, sis. Can you come pick me up?

Guess I'm not going back to the office.

Me: Sure, but it'll be a bit longer. I'm near the office. Where are you?

Lia: I'm at work.

Me: I'll be there in thirty. Can you order me a burger and fries to go?

Lia: Sure can.

I hurry to meet Lia, at least it's her family nickname. Her full name is Amelia, and she's the youngest of my siblings. Along the way, I hear my phone chime with more notifications from my siblings. I even gave my sister-in-law, Willa, her own notification. Willa married my brother Luca about six months ago. She's perfect for him. They met after my brother was shot negotiating with my ex-brother-in-law. Thankfully, my oldest sister, Lina, and her two kids were able to get out of the house safely. Willa was his nurse at the hospital. It took them a few years to finally go on an actual date though. Now Luca is a crisis negotiator with the state police. In fact, their fates changed at Hops and Barley where Lia now works. I also have another sister, Lily, who is a hedge fund manager. Her hours are almost as crazy as mine, although today I got lucky.

I park at the curb and step inside the brewery. Lia is near the bar with her friend from school, Scarlett. They met at the beginning of the semester when Scarlett transferred here from NYU. Her sister, Savannah, is friends with Willa. Lia hugs Scarlett and moves toward me with my dinner.

"Hey, Lia. How was class and your shift?"

"Hi. Thanks for picking me up. Luca got called to a hostage scene about an hour ago." We head outside and hop into my truck.

"No problem. I was going to need dinner anyway."

"To answer your question, class was fine, and the shift was dead. What about you? How is the plan for the Cooper project?"

I shake my head. Our family is super close, and we share almost everything. "The plan is great. I incorporated everything the bid requires. Now I need to land the job."

"Of course you'll land the job."

"I appreciate your confidence in me, Lia, but this is a big deal. This bid is for the Portsmouth hotel. The overarching plan consists of ten hotels in the northeast."

"Frankie, you're a Cappelli. All of us are strong, gorgeous, and badass. You've got this!"

Literal sisterhood for the win right there. I pull in front of her apartment complex. Lia leans over and hugs me. "I'll see you on Sunday unless I pick up Scarlett's shift."

"Why does she need you to pick up her shift?"

Lia shrugs. She doesn't want to share, but I know if I simply wait her out, she will. "I think she has a date with a local cop."

Interesting. Before Luca took his position with the state police, he was YPD. "Do you know who it is?"

"Nope, she didn't divulge his name because of Luca. Love you." She hurries inside without hearing my reply.

"Love you most."

After a quick ride home, I curl up on my patio and eat my burger. Thankfully, it's still warm. I hope to get some sleep tonight. The presentation is on Friday, and my nerves are already on edge. When I'm nervous, sleep typically eludes me.

CHAPTER TWO

THOMAS

"Come on, Ellie. We need to go if you want a muffin from Sweet Face before school," I call upstairs for the second time in the last fifteen minutes. Honestly, I don't like to rush her. She might be late for school, but my mornings with her are in short supply. Her mother, Tess, and I have been divorced for six years. Initially our shared custody arrangement was simpler. We lived in the same city, and neither of us had moved on to a new relationship.

I would like to say the end of our marriage was completely her fault. That isn't completely accurate. I was unhappy in my lucrative job in Boston, but Tess was blissfully happy spending my salary while caring for our daughter. She was supportive when I changed jobs, even acknowledged her spending was out of control, and she even offered to look for a job to help with the pay cut. However, no help came. Instead, Tess became angry my choice to change jobs forced her to curtail her spending and refused to find a job. I was at my current position for about six months before she asked for a divorce. We have a shared custody agreement, which was going well until she married Michael.

"I'll be right there." Ellie's response pulls me out of my head.

I have nothing against Michael, at least from the information I know. He's good to my daughter, and Tess seems perfectly content spending his old money left and right. The most recent issue is Tess wants to move to western Connecticut and take Ellie with her. We're trying to come up with a plan on our own that doesn't uproot Ellie. We haven't made any progress and are set for mediation next week.

I haven't been lucky in the dating department post-divorce like Tess. Unlucky may not be accurate. At the beginning, I was hesitant to put myself out there. Who would date a single dad with a six-year-old and a difficult ex-wife? The dating pool in this area is small. At least in Boston, the number of potential dates would have been higher.

"Eleanor, now!" My voice louder and more forceful this time.

"Geez, Dad. I'm right here."

I follow her out to the car, and we head to the bakery. After parking, we approach from the far side of the shoppe. There's a beautiful woman sitting alone at a table near the window. Her dark hair is piled on top of her head in a topknot, her skin is flawless, and she appears lost in thought. After noticing her, I continue inside with Ellie. She places her order, and I add a coffee and muffin for myself.

The barista takes our order and disappears into the back. Another blonde barista returns and calls out, "Joey, your coffee."

The woman from near the window simply shakes her head, grabs the cup from the barista, and then says, "Call me." Clearly they know each other personally, but I've never met a woman named Joey before. I can only think of one name it could be short for—Josephine. It's old-fashioned and wouldn't fit a woman like her.

I mentally chastise myself. I know nothing about this woman other than she frequents this coffee shop, knows the barista, and is beautiful.

"Dad, let's go. I'm going to be late," Ellie mumbles.

I follow her out of the bakery and back to the car. She makes it to school with five minutes to spare.

"I'll see you on Friday after school, Ellie. I love you more."

"Bye, Dad. See you then. I love you most." Most girls of her age won't share their feelings, especially at school drop-off. Luckily, Ellie understands how difficult sharing time with Tess is for me. I never had to tell her, she simply knows despite her age. I would never have chosen for my marriage to end, but it did.

I park in my assigned spot and slip into my office unnoticed. I have worked here for the last seven years. I manage the commercial properties for the Hayward Group. Currently, I'm handling two large accounts, including the Cooper Hotel and Omni Park. The Cooper Hotel is a new build, and I coordinate all the contractors from the electricians to the painters. Omni Park is a large complex with indoor and outdoor space, including a ropes course, water slides, and even a mini golf course.

My assistant, Melissa, set up presentations for tomorrow and Friday for the Cooper project. Along with the committee, I plan to select the winning bid by the end of next week at the latest. My focus today is on Omni and scheduling a permit review for each aspect in time for opening day in about a month.

I spend my entire day on the phone being shuttled from underling to supervisor and back again between departments at city hall. This shouldn't be this hard. After a draining day of phone calls and skipping lunch, I head home just after five. I didn't even have time to check my texts until I sit in the driver's seat of my car to go home.

Remi: Hey, bud.

Remi: Dude, we're going to the brewery tonight. Join us.

Remi: I know Ellie went to back to Tess's.

Me: I'm drained. Not tonight, maybe on the weekend.

Remi: I'll hold you to that.

I shake my head at my best friend and turn over the engine. I hate going home on Wednesdays. At the beginning of the day, it's me and Ellie, but she isn't there when I get home. Co-parenting royally sucks. As much as I despise Tess not putting in the work for our marriage, I never show it in front of Ellie. Until her petition to move Ellie to Connecticut, everything was fine except for the need to share time with my daughter.

Grabbing a beer from the fridge, I flop down on my couch and flick on *Sportscenter*. Preseason football is the main storyline. Despite where I live, I root for the New York Giants. Last year the team certainly had a decent season, especially considering they have a new head coach. I finish my beer and tackle a show on my DVR with a stop in the middle to chat with Ellie on the phone about her day.

"Hi, Dad."

"Hey. How was your math test?"

She sighs. Math isn't her favorite subject. "It wasn't terrible. I think I did okay."

"All right. I'm proud of you."

"Thanks. I have to get going. Mom is sending me upstairs to get my reading done."

"Okay. Love you more, Ellie."

"Love you most, Dad." I glance at the clock and wonder why Tess is sending Ellie upstairs so early. Generally, I don't question Tess when Ellie is with her and she doesn't question me. It seems odd my daughter is relegated to her bedroom. Their house has six bedrooms, and only three people live there.

I make a note to keep it in mind to ask Ellie on Friday. Otherwise spent, I turn in early myself. If I'm lucky, I might be able to see Joey in the morning.

CHAPTER THREE

FRANCESCA

At this rate, I may need to enlist Lily's help before my presentation. She has the skill set to cover the bags under my eyes from not sleeping. Dressed in my usual workday wear—jeans and a tee—I head out to my truck and drive toward my coffee dealer.

"Hi, Tal. Please tell me your espresso machine is working. I need a double today."

The shoppe has a bunch more patrons today. I'm later than usual. There's more staff near seven thirty than near seven.

"Worried about the presentation?"

I nod. My usual seat near the window is taken, so I opt for one near the back corner. I'm staring blankly at the pictures on the wall when I hear Tal call, "Tommy."

Rising from my chair, I round the counter toward the pickup area and reach for the cup that has "Tommy" written on the side.

"Excuse me, I think that's mine," a deep voice rumbles behind me. His voice sounds… Arousing is the only word that springs to mind.

I turn and find myself face-to-face with my eye candy from yesterday.

"I thought your name was Joey?" He was paying attention to me yesterday. Interesting.

I laugh. "No, it's not Joey or Tommy. It's Frankie. Pleasure to meet you, Tommy." I extend my hand to him. His hands are surprisingly rough for someone who wears a suit to work—a tailored suit that fits very well, just like my hand in his. I wonder what causes the callouses.

His brow wrinkles. "I'm confused. Do you have a few minutes to talk with me and explain why you have three commonly male first names?"

Tal calls, "Tommy," again. Her head is bobbing up and down enthusiastically. I wave her off behind my back so Tommy doesn't see me.

"Sure. Does one of the tables outside work?" I suggest.

He finds the other cup labelled Tommy and follows me to the door. "After you." He opens the door for me.

I step outside in the early fall sunshine and take a seat at one of the Sweet Face bistro tables. Once seated, I recheck the label and note I indeed have his cup of coffee instead of mine.

"This one is yours." I pass it across the table, and he exchanges it for mine. I note his order, a double shot of espresso with cream, one sugar, and a shot of cinnamon.

"So, Frankie, why does your barista friend label your coffee with commonly male names? Although I must admit, I'm glad she chose Tommy today."

I'm grateful myself. "Talia is the owner, the barista, and my best friend. She has been picking on me about my name since we met in third grade. I stood up to one of our classmates who was tormenting her.

When I told her my name was Frankie, she complemented my warrior mentality for shoving Jimmy. We've been best friends ever since."

"Do you have a bunch of older brothers who taught you to stand up for yourself?"

I smirk and wonder if he's worried they might be overprotective. "I have three sisters and one moderately overprotective brother, and he's enough. Tommy, is that what you prefer to be called? What about you?"

His smile is breathtaking. "I have two brothers and a sister."

"Where do you fall in the birth order? I'm the literal middle child."

A hearty laugh slips past his lips. "I'm the oldest. As far as my name, it's what people call me because it's also my father's name. As much as I would love to stay here and talk with you, I have a meeting at nine thirty. Can I meet you here tomorrow, say around seven?"

"I'll be here. Have a good day."

"It was a pleasure to meet you, Frankie. I'll see you tomorrow at seven. Bye."

It isn't until I turn to watch Tommy walk away that I notice Tal casually and purposefully cleaning the tables near the windows to spy on my impromptu coffee chat. Before I acknowledge her, I need to process how my assessment yesterday fell short. Tommy is tall, but the tailoring of his suit hides what appear to be buff arms, given they stretched the jacket when he leaned closer to me. His eyes are a gorgeous shade of blue, and the cleft chin is disgustingly attractive too.

Once she's sure he is gone, Talia joins me outside. "Oh, girl! He's hot!"

I shake my head. "Ya think?"

"You're kidding, right?"

"Yes, Tal. He's hot, in case my sarcasm wasn't clear." He has a large family too. Hopefully, they're close like we are. A boisterous family can be off-putting to someone who isn't close to theirs or has none or one sibling.

"Did you get his number?"

I chuckle. "No, but we're meeting here tomorrow for coffee."

Concern mars her face. "Why here?"

"It's what he suggested. If I had to guess, he's been out of the dating game for a while. Slow is fine with me."

"I love you, Frankie, but you need to get laid—hard, fast, and very, very soon."

Blunt as ever. I love her for it too. She probably knows down to the day the last time I had sex. "Maybe so, but I have to worry about tomorrow before anything else." She isn't wrong. It's been way too long since I've met a decent guy, forget the sex part.

Tristan was the most recent date. He works at another landscaping company. We met at the garden center where I was pricing items for the project Eric installed yesterday. The same night we met for drinks. When I shared the company was mine, he was suddenly protective of his company's name and his bosses. As if I need to steal his clients to be successful. The one before Tristan was a blind date set up by my older sister, Lina. I didn't even get through drinks with him. As soon as he learned Luca was my brother, the date was over. I love my crazy, overprotective brother, but I can handle myself. Hell, he taught me.

"Yet you agreed to meet him before your big presentation."

"I'll be here anyway. Don't crush my hot-guy flush please, Tal."

"Not trying to at all. He seems nice. He comes in here a few times a week. Only on Wednesdays is his daughter with him. He has seriously sexy single-dad vibes written all over him."

He does. "I gotta get to the office, Tal. Thanks for choosing the right name today. See you in the morning."

"Bye, Tommy." She winks at me and finishes clearing the table. Talia hasn't had it easy in the dating department. Her ex-husband is currently serving time for involuntary manslaughter stemming from a bar fight. Ever since then, she hasn't been with the same guy more than once. I don't blame her one bit.

I note Eric is already in the office this morning as I park in the lot. "Hi, Eric."

"Morning, Frankie. Finishing up my notes for yesterday's install. We were able to get the immature trees planted so the timeline won't be affected by this afternoon's predicted rainstorm."

"Great. Thank you. Is your schedule still clear for tomorrow after lunch?" I ask him.

"Yup. I'll be here to answer the phones while you land the lucrative contract with the Hayward Group."

"I appreciate your confidence, but it's a huge step up for this company. I was happy to capture the opportunity to present my bid."

"You'll land the contract, boss lady."

I shake my head. "Don't call me that."

"Why not? It's completely accurate, not offensive, and politically correct. Amy would have my head if I called you 'boss babe.'"

I laugh and retreat to my office. I boot up my laptop and field today's inquiries. There's a confirmation for my presentation tomorrow at two from Melissa at the Hayward Group. I forward the request for a fall cleanup estimate to Eric, who is typing away in his office. Even though I know it inside, outside, forward, and backward, I review the presentation repeatedly. Before I know it, it's past one and I haven't eaten lunch yet.

I sigh and rummage through my desk drawers for a cup of noodles or granola bar to tide me over until dinner. I pull out my phone and check my texts from this morning. I was so focused, I didn't hear it chime.

Lina: Hey there. I need to talk when you have a few minutes.

Me: Text or call?

Lina: Call. Then I know who to blame if this gets out before I'm ready and there's no record of what I said.

I dial Lina. "Hey, sis. Is everyone okay?"

"Yes, Antonio and Emilia are fine. It's about me and a guy."

Generally, Lina goes to Luca or Lily for advice about dating. I'm intrigued why she chose me. "What's up?"

"There's a guy who keeps coming into the bank when I know he doesn't need to. It isn't stalkerish, but he wants to talk with me. I would go out with him, but with the kids and Luca, I don't know."

"He's a cop with YPD?"

"Yeah."

"You're afraid Luca won't approve, right?" I question her.

"That's disturbingly spot-on."

"Aside from the fact Luca probably knows this guy, what else?"

"He's younger than me by a decent amount."

Even though she can't see me, I roll my eyes. "How much younger? Never mind, it doesn't matter. If you're interested and his age doesn't bother you, say yes. Accepting a date with a guy won't necessarily lead you down the aisle again." Lina has been divorced from Derrick for over six years now. If the right guy came along, I could see her marrying again.

"What's his name, Frankie?"

"How?"

"It's in your helpful advice." Lina snickers.

Ugh! "I met him this morning. There isn't really much to tell, other than he's genuine and I think he has a daughter."

"What do you mean 'think'?"

I mentally slap myself for saying too much. "I saw him yesterday with a young girl at Sweet Face. She's cute but tall and awkward. I quite literally remember being in her shoes. Anyway, this morning I accidently grabbed his coffee instead of mine and we started talking."

"Good for you. Is he hot?"

Always to the point. "Yes, he's hot." Disgustingly so.

"Thanks for listening, Frankie. Please don't share with our siblings yet. I have to decide if I'm willing to not only put myself and my kids out there, but with someone who I know Luca will be against from the start."

"I won't, but keep in mind, this is about your happiness, not Luca's. He'll get over it… eventually."

"Good luck tomorrow."

I smile. "Thanks, Lina. See you on Sunday." I hang up and head home in the pouring rain. After drying off, I prepare a meal and curl up with a book in my granite fireplace. A few hours later, I clean up and stand in front of my closet to select an outfit for tomorrow—both my morning coffee date and my presentation. *Is it a date? I'm not sure.* Once complete, I fall into my bed and hope Tommy shows up in the morning.

CHAPTER FOUR

THOMAS

I haven't been able to think about much else other than Frankie since I first saw her two days ago. It makes absolutely no sense. Not only is she beautiful, but she's real. She wasn't wearing any makeup either time I saw her. She doesn't need it. Her skin is flawless. Frankie is tall and thin with enough curves to imprint with my fingers.

I grab my keys and hurry out the door to the pastry shoppe. I haven't been excited to spend time with anyone in a long time, especially a beautiful woman. When I arrive, she's in her spot near the window again. She's as stunning as I remember, even in jeans and a thin sweater. Her long brown hair is down and reaches almost to her waist. It's the first time I've seen it down. Her gorgeous hair only adds to her appeal. It also gives me ideas that have no place in my head yet, like twisting it around the palm of my hand and tugging.

The shoppe doesn't really have a theme except it's cozy inside. The prints on the walls are seasonal. Summer scenes from the area fill the frames. There's one of the Marginal Way, the Nubble Lighthouse, Wells Beach, and even the Hartley Mason Preserve. I suppose Talia changes them with the seasons.

"Morning, Frankie." I stop by the table before ordering my coffee.

"Morning," she replies. "You should order some coffee, or you won't be in compliance for our date."

"Is this a date?" I hope she thinks it's a date.

"Maybe pre-date is more accurate."

Her bestie approaches the table. "What can I get for you, Tommy?"

"Can I have a large dark roast with cream, two sugars, and an apple strudel muffin, please," I request.

"Coming right up."

I don't miss the second glance she gives to Frankie as she walks away.

"Do you always get that flavor muffin?"

"If it's available, why?"

"It's my favorite of her creations too," she shares. "How was your day yesterday?"

"Work was busy, but it made the day fly by and closer to seeing you again."

A faint blush creeps onto her skin. "I agree our coffee chat yesterday was too short."

"What would you say if I asked you on a real date? One where we don't have to rush off to work?"

"I would like that," she answers.

Talia brings over my coffee and muffin and leaves silently. I'm confident she overheard me ask Frankie on a date and her response.

I have learned the hard way to ask before I get too involved with someone after my divorce. "Please don't take offense to my next statement and question. I have a daughter, and I share custody with my ex-wife. Do you have an issue with dating a single dad?"

She doesn't seem offended at my question, at least not for herself. "Are the women around here truly awful?" Her question is refreshing.

I tilt my head forward slightly. "I have come across more than a few since my divorce who stop responding when they learn I'm a father."

"When do you normally share you're a dad?"

"Initially it was after a few dates. Now I'm completely upfront about both my divorce and Ellie."

She sets her hand over mine on the table. "Your daughter won't be an issue for me."

Her skin is incredibly soft. Some of the weight lifts off my chest. "Can I have your number? I'll call you tonight to schedule our date."

She reaches her hand out after I fish my phone out of my pocket. "I'm going to text myself from your phone, so I have yours too. I don't answer unknown numbers." She texts herself and returns my phone to me.

"Once again, this was entirely too short. I'll call you tonight."

"I'm looking forward to it." Her smile makes me hopeful I won't be starting over after two dates.

After I step out the door, she waves again through the window and her bestie takes my seat. I shake my head and continue to work. From ten until three, my day is jammed with project proposals for the hotel landscaping. Everything is moving along smoothly until reality slams into my workday immediately after my ten-minute lunch break.

My assistant buzzes the intercom. "Mr. Thornton, Principal Mulier is on line two for you. She indicates it's urgent."

I steel myself for what's going on before lifting the receiver to my ear. "Good afternoon, Principal Mulier. How can I help you?"

"Good afternoon. I apologize for the interruption. Ellie is fine. However, there's a Michael Spears here to dismiss her for the day. He isn't on the access list, and Ellie insists she's slated to spend the weekend with you."

Tess has never pulled something like this before. She adheres to our visitation schedule to the letter. Also, Michael is there to pick Ellie up, which is odd. I'm torn what to do. I have two more presentations this afternoon. Rescheduling them would be unprofessional, especially given the short notice.

"Can I speak with my daughter, please?"

Principal Mulier replies, "Of course."

I hear standard hold music while I wait and wonder what's going on. Tess did file a request to relocate Ellie, but we haven't been to mediation yet. I spoke with my attorney briefly and indicated I'm completely against uprooting Ellie.

"Hi, Dad. Michael is here, but I know it's your weekend." Ellie is typically steadfast and calm. Now she sounds nervous, anxious even.

"Hi, Ellie. Did you see Michael?"

"No, Principal Mulier told me he was here to pick me up."

"What do you want, Ellie? There is no right or wrong answer." Lying to my daughter is not something I do often. In this case, I make an exception. There's a wrong answer, but I can't share it with her. I cherish my time with Ellie, and I don't want to give up what I'm scheduled to have. It's a definite drawback to co-parenting.

"I want to spend the weekend with you, not traipsing to Connecticut to look for a new mansion. Plus, I have a game tomorrow morning." Her answer surprises me, though I'm ecstatic it's what she wants as well.

I make a mental note to ask my attorney if Ellie's opinion matters in where she lives. "Okay, can you put Principal Mulier back on the phone?"

"Sure."

"Mr. Thornton?"

"Yes. Thank you for handling this matter delicately. Ellie doesn't want to leave with Mr. Spears and this weekend is my designated parenting time. Please inform him Ellie is to remain in school and I'll pick her up as usual after the day ends."

"I'll let him know. Thank you for promptly taking my call."

The list of people Melissa can interrupt a meeting for is brief. It includes Ellie, Mrs. Mulier, Coach Spencer, Coach Cole, and Tess. "I always will. Thank you for calling."

I end the call and prepare myself for my next meeting. Focusing will be difficult considering now I'm worried Tess might try to pick Ellie up herself since I thwarted Michael's attempt.

CHAPTER FIVE

FRANCESCA

"Girl, spill the details of your coffee date I didn't hear," Tal plops into Tommy's not-even-cold chair.

"You heard everything of importance, except he was upfront about his divorce and his daughter."

Tal smiles. "Clearly, he isn't aware you were ogling him on Wednesday morning when he was here with his daughter."

"Ellie, her name is Ellie. No, he doesn't know, and I didn't share. It doesn't matter right now. I need to hustle and hurry to the office, clear my inbox, and then get to my presentation."

"Okay, I won't push. I'm genuinely excited for you. He's hot and seems like a nice guy. Good luck!" Tal pushes back from the table as a group of customers file in.

"Thanks, Tal." I rise from my chair and hustle to my truck.

I would prefer to have an installation this morning. The physical work soothes my nerves. Instead, after completing my morning office tasks, I'm drawing circles on the floor of my entire office suite with my feet until it's time to get ready.

After brushing out my hair, I pin it away from my face but leave it down. I shimmy into the red sheath dress and low slingbacks Lily recommended. I skip the stockings, even though my sister feels they're necessary. Once I'm dressed, I review the summary again and leave for one of the biggest proposals of my life. A flood of text messages started coming in since I left Sweet Face.

Luca: Good luck, Frankie. You've got this!

Lily: Go get this account, sis! Wear the stockings! Love you.

Dad: I'm proud of you! Love you.

Lia: Good luck, Frankie.

Mom: In bocca al lupo. *Love you.*

Willa: You've got this, Frankie.

Lina: Rock this presentation. Love you.

I thank them all, set my proposal in the well of the passenger seat, and head to my presentation. This is the largest job I've ever pursued. I opened my company four years ago. I handle everything from securing jobs, ordering materials, invoicing, and payroll. If I land this project, I'll need to hire an administrative assistant, preferably one with payroll and invoicing experience. I simply won't have enough hours in the day.

I park in front of the modern office building that houses the Hayward Group and calm myself as best I can. Upon entering the building, I introduce myself to the receptionist.

"Miss Cappelli, Mr. Thornton is ready to see you now. I'll give you ten minutes to set up your proposal." She leaves me in the sleek conference room.

"Thank you." I boot up my laptop and throw the slides onto the screen. I also have renderings of my plan on large canvases. I move toward the large window and take in the water view.

"Miss Cappelli, it's a pleasure to meet…."

I know that voice—deep and sexy. I turn toward him. "Tommy?"

He extends his hand to me. "Frankie is short for Francesca."

It's a statement not a question. Now what? The warmth from his hand around mine shoots up my arm. I worked so hard on this presentation to let my attraction to him get in the way. "Mr. Thornton, yes, it is. Is this going to be a problem?" I mean not only for the presentation but for our pending date, although I'm not confident I convey it to him.

"No, not for me. Will it be for you?"

I shake my head outwardly, but internally I'm skeptical. "No."

"Miss Cappelli, please begin when you're ready." He takes a seat halfway down the side of the large conference table.

I inhale and exhale a few times before beginning the summary of my presentation. "I've taken the parameters set forth by the request for proposals and incorporated each aspect into this design. In addition, my flower and plant selection will allow for color year-round. Specifically, these plants illustrated here are evergreen, while these interspersed between them are a dark maroon color which will provide contrast to the light-yellow flowers from the azaleas."

I continue outlining my plan and the required maintenance that could be handled by my company or in house if the owner so chooses. Tommy asks pointed questions about the placement, timelines, and the budget. *Mr. Thornton. Ugh!*

Forty minutes later, I conclude my presentation and ask if he has any more questions.

"No. Thank you, Miss Cappelli. There's one more presenter. A decision will be made by the end of next week."

"You're welcome. Thank you." My mind is spinning while I gather my materials. I nailed this presentation, but the fact we're supposed to schedule our first date tonight gives me pause. I want this job because I earned it, not because he wants to date me. Although he wouldn't be involved after the contract is awarded. I suppose it's a plus. I wouldn't have luck if it weren't bad luck.

"Would you like some help?" His sexy voice creeps into my inner thoughts. *Seriously, does it have to be so arousing?*

"No, I can handle it. Thank you for the offer." I refuse to look into it. He's simply being polite. It means nothing. With my materials and laptop packed away, I move toward the door. "I look forward to hearing from you, Mr. Thornton."

He acknowledges my words as I walk away. Normally, I can tell if a client is interested in hiring my company before I walk out the door. Not this time. As I round the corner to the elevator, I see the next presenter waiting in the lobby. I've bid against Liam Samuels before and lost but not on anything this significant. The smug look on his face tells me he saw me too. *Exactly what I need to add to this miserable afternoon.*

Was it though? I'm not so sure. I did my best not to allow my attraction to him alter my focus. Hopefully, my assessment of my presentation is the same as Tommy's.

I don't even have to look at my phone to know it has numerous unread messages. I'm not ready to handle them though. The next thing I know, I'm parking near my reflection spot. I slide out of the driver's seat, considering I'm still wearing a dress, and walk beneath the iron arch for Hartley Mason Reserve.

The area overlooks the ocean and is sought after for wedding ceremonies due to its beautiful grounds. It's stunning. The view of the ocean is spectacular even in winter. There are eight statues in all types of leisure activities atop a large stone. I remove my shoes and wander down near the shore. Luckily, the spot that I have deemed mine is free. I have no actual claim to it, but I clear my thoughts here on this flat stone near the edge of the water.

The salty spray and whoosh of the waves are exactly what I need. I was born and raised here. The only time I left was for college. I was home almost every weekend, mostly for my mom's cooking. Rosalie Cappelli is a force of nature. She's tenacious, and I'm proud to have the same trait, at least when it pertains to my business. She cooks like no one else and raised the five of us with love and firm discipline. She and my father, Luciano, have been happily married for thirty-seven years. They met in seventh grade and have been inseparable ever since. I want a similar partnership for myself. A partner is someone to share not only my hopes and dreams but my failures too. Today isn't a failure yet, but it still might be. I would appreciate someone to share it with other than the sea.

I push my thoughts out with the receding waves and clear my mind. My presentation met each requirement the bid request set forth, and it was under budget. All I can do now is wait and hope my pre-date coffee with Tommy doesn't mess up my personal or my professional life. Or both. He's a virtual stranger, and yet I'm upset I may not be able to learn more about him. I appreciate his forthcoming nature about his daughter. His concern was genuine and hard won. It irks me there are women who could walk away from an innocent child. I'll find out tonight if I no longer have a date to schedule, won't I. I sigh, slide my fingers through the slingbacks of my shoes and wander slowly to my car. I have messages to return.

CHAPTER SIX

THOMAS

My attraction to Frankie—Miss Francesca Cappelli—has skyrocketed. The sheath dress skims over the curves she has and showcases them flawlessly. Even dressed casually, Frankie grabs my attention. I wasn't expecting professional Frankie. Focusing on her presentation was more difficult than I anticipated. More than once, I force my gaze to the screen instead of the cascade of her long, chestnut hair falling in waves down her back or the nip of her waist. Thankfully, the candidates provided a copy of their presentations for review by the rest of the hiring committee. I insisted on the actual interviews, which is the reason I'm the only person in attendance. The committee felt it wasn't necessary but gave me the time to hold them anyway.

I need to review her presentation again to make sure I didn't miss as much as I think I did. My attention was more on her than the presentation. Hopefully, I appeared to be fully engaged in her words and not the movement of her pouty lips. Lips I have wanted to kiss since I saw her earlier this week. I plan to review her bid proposal before I call her later, even though we shouldn't discuss her presentation or the job. All I know is I can't wait to call her, a feeling that only increased since she left here.

The last presenter is Liam Samuels. He has been angling for one of our projects for at least the last two years. From the instant he starts to present, I know his plan doesn't meet the same level as any of the other candidates. In fact, only two from yesterday are still in the running for the job. I maintain my focus until he completes his presentation. After sending him off with my thanks and an indication I'll decide by the end of next week, I return to my office. I have a solid hour before I want to leave for dinner with Ellie.

I open the file provided by Frankie and review it again—twice. Her proposal is thorough and extensive. Despite not giving it my full attention earlier today, I feel better about focusing more on her than work. If the committee awards her the position, it'll be based on merit, not my interest in her, a fact I should probably convey to her.

With thoughts of Frankie floating in my mind, I drive home. Like Wednesday mornings, I love coming home every other Friday knowing Ellie will be there. "Ellie, I'm home."

During our divorce, I bought Tess's share of this house. It was my grandparents' house, and I refused to let her have it. Petty, maybe a little, but she truly wasn't interested. It's a four-bedroom craftsman with original molding and hardwood floors. I've updated the kitchen and the bathrooms because the pink tile that was there didn't work for Tess. Honestly, I would've upgraded either way. One bedroom is set up for guests and one as an office I rarely use. I use the master suite, and Ellie has the room at the top of the stairs. My style is comfier than most bachelors, but that's because of Ellie. She adds pillows, blankets, and other décor whenever we shop. I want her to be comfortable here, so I don't stop her.

She hurries down the stairs and hugs me. Ellie is tall for her age, but given my height and Tess's, it's expected. Tess is fond of saying Ellie is in an awkward stage. I don't recall if my sister, Tamara, went through it, but I wasn't paying attention either. My daughter is growing up too fast, and if I could slow things down a bit, I would.

"Hi. I'm sorry Principal Mulier had to call you today."

"Don't be. I'm glad she called. You know I don't like giving up my time with you."

"I know, and I'm glad. Did Mom already file the paperwork?"

Ellie is old enough to know what's going on between her mother and me or, more accurately, between her mother and Michael. "She did."

"I don't want to move, Dad."

"I know. I'll make sure my attorney knows and you're heard."

She throws her arms around my neck and hugs me again. "Time to order, I'm starving. School lunch was gross today."

I laugh and pull out the menu once we reach the kitchen.

"How was your science test?"

"Not too bad. Oh, do we have any plans tomorrow afternoon into the early evening?"

"No, why?"

"Kylie is having a few friends over to hang out around four. Can I go?"

I shrug. "Sure your game is at ten. I need to know which parent's house." Kylie's parents are divorced too. Ellie and Kylie bonded over their shared experience.

"Thanks. I'm going to tell her I can hang out."

As she scampers away, I place our pizza order and head upstairs to change. I exchange my suit for shorts, a Dave Matthews tee, and a light zip up. An image of Frankie in her red dress and heels floats through my mind. Before I think better of it, I text her.

Me: I'll call you after pizza and a movie with Ellie.

Surprisingly, she replies immediately.

Frankie: Okay.

I'm not sure how to take her expeditious reply or the single word response, but either way, I'm calling Frankie later. Ellie opts for *She's All That.* My daughter loves older movies, and I'm grateful she's still interested in movie night with her dad. I'm sure it will pass. The pizza and mozzarella sticks are gone before the first half of the movie passes. We take a break for clearing and drink refills. After Zack and Laney have their dance in the backyard, Ellie hurries off to talk to Kylie on the phone again.

I consider waiting until Ellie goes to bed but decide I don't want to any longer.

"Hi. I didn't think you would call," Frankie answers.

"I wasn't sure you would answer." My answer is honest and unnecessary at the same time.

A soft sigh comes through the phone. "Should we be talking to one another considering this afternoon?"

"I'm not sure, but the decision doesn't rest solely with me. I insisted on in-person interviews. The rest of the committee is willing to decide solely on the presentations the bidding companies provided."

"Oh, I wasn't aware."

"Honestly though, I don't care. My ability to narrow down the candidates won't be impacted. I wasn't aware you're the owner of a bidding company when I asked you on a date." I hear her breathing, but she doesn't respond to my statement. "Frankie?"

"Yeah."

"What are you thinking?"

She exhales sharply. "I'm sure this breaks all kinds of unwritten dating rules, but could you turn on your video?"

"Of course, but why?" I press the video button and her gorgeous face fills my screen. She's no longer wearing the red dress from earlier. Now she's comfortable. Her hair is twisted on top of her head, and I can see a hoodie. It also appears she took off the little makeup she had on earlier.

"I'm better with this type of conversation face-to-face."

"Okay. What are you concerned about?"

"Aside from earlier, I'm considering how much to divulge about the opportunity or if I should simply skip it and we should talk about other things."

"Does your appearance have anything to do with earlier?"

"Meaning what?" The edge to her question wasn't what I intended.

"Let me try again. Is every aspect of earlier off the table?"

She tilts her head, a small smile curls at the corner of her mouth, and she shakes her head slowly.

"I have seen you three, well, now four times. Casually dressed Frankie is beautiful and real while professionally dressed Frankie is a knockout. Both are insanely attractive to me."

A blush creeps across her cheeks. It's even noticeable through the phone. "Thank you. Wait, four times?"

I see her mind working. Now it's my turn to blush. "I noticed you on Wednesday through the window when I arrived with Ellie."

"If we're making admissions, I saw you as well. I—"

"I... go ahead," I offer.

"Getting back to this afternoon, I want to avoid talking about the bid until after a decision is made. I don't want to share more than I should, and I don't want you to either."

"Okay, but does our current predicament mean you don't want to go out on a date with me anymore?"

"Should it?"

I shake my head. "I certainly hope not. Frankie, are you free tomorrow night?"

"Yes, but I would prefer to wait until after the committee decides."

"Sure, makes sense. Are you free next Saturday night?"

She smiles. "Yes."

"Perfect. I'll pick you up at six. Tell me more about you."

"Other than my job?"

I shrug. "If we need to avoid work altogether for now, that's fine. As you already know, I'm divorced. We have been for the last six years. My daughter, Ellie, is twelve."

"What about your siblings? You mentioned you had two brothers and a sister."

"After me is my brother Tobias. We call him Toby. He's a plumber and rehabilitates abused dogs. Tim runs the community center with a focus on at-risk youth. Last, but certainly not least, Tamara, my sister is a real estate agent. You mentioned you have three sisters and a brother?"

"Yes. Rosalina, Lina for short, is the oldest. She's divorced with two kids, Antonio and Emilia, and is a bank manager. Next is my only brother, Luca. He's a crisis negotiation officer with the state police. He married Willa about six months ago. Then there's me." A small smile blooms on her face. "Lily, short for Lilianna, runs a hedge fund, and then finally Amelia is a college student at Southern Maine."

"Your family sounds amazingly like mine. Do you have family dinners as well?"

She attempts to speak but fails. After regrouping, she says, "Yes, we do on Sundays."

"We have ours on the last Sunday of the month." I look over toward the hallway as Ellie appears. "Could you excuse me for a minute?"

"Sure."

I turn the phone over my shoulder. "Everything okay?" Usually, Ellie just falls asleep, and I check on her before I go to bed.

"Yeah, I'm going to turn in. Night, Dad."

"Good night, Ellie. Please make sure you're prepared for your game before you go to sleep."

"I will. Love you more."

"Love you most." She shuffles down the hall and turns out the light.

When I return to my call, Frankie is patiently waiting. "Thank you."

"Of course. I should turn in too."

"Sure. Can I call you tomorrow?" I would prefer to have our first date tomorrow, but I understand her concerns about the bid.

"I would like that."

"Will I see you at Sweet Face in the morning?"

She shakes her head. "No, I have auntie duty tomorrow."

"Have fun. Good night, Frankie."

"Thanks. Good night."

I end the call and turn to find Ellie standing beside me. "Who was that?"

I don't hide much from Ellie. Clearly, she knows her mother and I won't be getting back together considering Tess already married someone else. "Is everything good?"

"Yeah, I guess. Mom texted me a link to a house in Greenwich. I told you already, but I don't want to move to Connecticut with Mom and Michael. Can't I live with you?" Ellie takes a seat beside me on the couch and twists to face me with her knee bent in front of her.

"I understand this is tough for you. Ideally, we'll create a fair agreement where everyone is happy."

"I don't want to change schools and lose my friends or my teammates. Is it even possible?"

"All I can promise is to do the best I can and make sure Attorney Kramer knows you want to be heard."

"Thanks, Dad." Ellie leans forward and hugs me. Generally, she's reserved with sharing physical affection, so I'll take what I can get. "Don't think I forgot about my question. Who was on the phone?"

"Frankie. I met her at Sweet Face yesterday. Why?"

"Just wondering. It's been a while since you went on a date." My daughter isn't wrong. My last few first dates have been atrocious, and I won't share why they didn't work out. I'll find a woman who is willing to accept both of us. Maybe Frankie is that woman. The little information I know about her is promising.

I laugh. "How do you know what I do when you're with your mom?"

She smirks. "I don't exactly, but you haven't introduced me to anyone, so I assume the dates aren't going well."

"Fair enough. The last few dates weren't worth trying for a second one. I'm going out with Frankie next weekend."

"Cool. I hope you get a second one this time." She pushes off the couch and returns to her room.

"Me too," I whisper. Instead of dwelling on the fact Tess is moving to Connecticut, I search for a restaurant for my date next weekend. I narrow it down to two near the water and head to bed.

CHAPTER SEVEN

FRANCESCA

The sun is shining through my blinds. I roll over and check the time. A sense of relief passes over me when I realize I'm not late. I hurry through the shower, dress, and I'm in my truck within thirty minutes of my feet hitting the floor. Out of my sisters, I'm the fastest to get ready. Second only to Willa who unseated my three sisters soon after marrying Luca.

I take the short drive to Lina's and pull into the driveway. Newman and Bogart rush over to my truck. Why are they here? The dogs belong to Willa and Luca. I hop out and pet them both on the head.

"Hi, Auntie!" Emilia shouts from the porch as Lina steps out with her bags in hand.

"Hi, Em." I make it to the bottom of the steps. Emilia is my seven-year-old niece. She's a carbon copy of Lina when she was young.

"Antonio is finishing his breakfast. Warm-ups start in forty minutes. Thanks, Frankie," my sister shares as she passes me.

"Anytime. Have a good day," I call after her and enter the house with Emilia and the dogs close on my heels.

In the kitchen, Antonio is putting his bowl and spoon in the dishwasher. He's ten and loves soccer and reading pick-your-own-mystery books. "Hi, Auntie."

"Hey, bud. Why are the dogs here?"

"Uncle Luca surprised Aunt Willa with a weekend at Acadia."

That sounds like something my brother would do. "Are you ready to go?"

"Yup."

I scan him from head to toe and note he's missing his jersey and shin guards. I won't make the same mistake again. This season started three weeks ago, but last year, he forgot his ball and his cleats. "Are you sure?"

"Yup," he replies again.

"Bud, you're missing at least your jersey and shin guards. Hurry up or you'll be late."

He pulls his jersey and shin guards from one of the tops of the chairs. "I was testing you."

I shake my head. "Em, are you all packed?"

"All set." I corral the dogs in the kitchen and shuffle the kids to my truck. Once we arrive at the field, I escort Antonio to his coach and move to set up our viewing spot on the sidelines. "How was school yesterday, Em?

"Fine, except Janie said my dress was ugly, so we aren't friends anymore."

I don't know who Janie is, but I have a beef with her right now and Emilia isn't even my daughter. "How do you feel about what she said?"

"I don't want to be friends with mean girls."

"Good for you."

Lina deserves credit for her attitude. Lina handled some mean girls in high school, one of them was particularly awful. I don't recall her name though.

"Thanks. Can we go to the bathroom before the game starts?"

"Sure."

We meander over to the concession and restroom area. Emilia runs ahead, and I wait outside for her to finish.

"Frankie?"

A shiver caresses my skin as his sultry, smooth voice rolls over me. Turning to my left, I'm face-to-face with Tommy. I've seen him wearing a perfectly tailored suit, but dressed in causal sideline clothes, he's equally attractive. "Morning, Tommy."

"Dad, let's go." The same young girl from Sweet Face, wearing a club jersey rather than a rec jersey, stands beside him.

"Ellie, you have a few minutes. This is Frankie." His voice is strong and authoritative but not harsh.

She extends her hand to me. "Hi, nice to meet you." She attempts to discreetly check me out but fails. I'm not offended. I would too if I were in her position. She's merely looking out for her dad.

"I'm done." Emilia comes around the corner from the restroom and slides her hand into mine.

"You have a daughter too?" Ellie questions.

In true Emilia form, she flat-out corrects Ellie. "She's my aunt, not my mom." She's a sassy spitfire even at seven years old.

Ellie crouches down. "What's your name?"

"Emilia, but my friends call me Em."

"Nice to meet you, Em. I'm Ellie." Ellie rises to her feet.

I feel Tommy's eyes on me when I address Ellie again. "What position do you play?"

"Midfield. Do you know a lot about soccer?"

I can more than hold my own. "I played from when I was six through high school, including club."

Ellie's eyes light up. "Cool. What position?"

"Mostly midfield or defending mid."

"Maybe you can catch one of my games sometime and give me some pointers?" Ellie suggests.

I'm sure it's an entry-level test. Again, I don't mind at all. "I would be happy to. We're here for her brother's game on field two. Where is yours?"

"We're on field four. It was great meeting you, but I need to get to warm-ups." Ellie takes off toward her game.

Tommy verifies Ellie is out of earshot. "I appreciate you offering to help her out, but you don't have to."

I lean in close so only he can hear me. "I wouldn't have offered if I didn't want to."

"Thank you."

"Well, isn't this cozy." Liam Samuels appears behind Tommy.

I jump back as if I've done something wrong. I absolutely didn't. Tommy's cologne lingers around me while the unwanted party joins our conversation.

"How long have you two been seeing one another?" Liam asks aloud.

Tommy's hands clench and unclench. "We simply ran into one another here."

"She doesn't have any reason to be here." Liam points at me.

"While it—" Anger flares in my belly. Liam is so smug.

"It's none of your concern why she's here. However, she has a nephew who plays soccer. A fact I learned when I ran into her this morning. This town isn't large, Mr. Samuels. I could ask you why you're here as well, but I'm sure the answer is one of your children plays soccer," Tommy defends me.

"It was a pleasure chatting with you, Mr. Thornton, but I need to get to my nephew's game. Liam." I turn on my heel and walk away with Emilia holding my hand.

"You too," he calls after me.

It takes significant restraint not to turn back. It was nice to run into him this morning despite my request to hold off on our date. The more I see him, the more I want to see him.

"Who were those guys, Auntie?" Emilia asks as we approach our chairs.

"The first guy is someone I work with and the second one is someone I'm competing with for a job."

Seemingly satisfied, she plops down in her chair, pulls out a coloring book and crayons, and prepares to color. "I like the first guy better, Ellie's dad. He seems nice and very tall."

"I agree with both of those things, sweetie." If she only knew Tommy lied to Liam about the nature of our relationship. Technically he didn't, but he wasn't honest either. My phone vibrates in my hand.

Tommy: Turn to your far right.

Confused, I do it anyway. Apparently field four is over there, and I find Tommy looking in my direction.

Me: Hi. Thank you for thinking more quickly than me.

Tommy: We haven't done anything wrong, Frankie.

Me: I know, but he's my...

Tommy: You're what?

Me: Not an ex, if it's what you're thinking. If I don't earn this job, I don't want him to land it either. Never mind, can't talk about the job with you yet.

Tommy: I won't push. It was a pleasant surprise seeing you.

Me: For me too.

Tommy: I'll call you later.

I keep my gaze on him a bit longer before focusing my attention on Antonio. He plays center defender.

"Auntie?" Emilia looks up from her coloring page of princesses and unicorns.

"Yeah, Em?"

"Do you like him, Ellie's dad?"

"I only met him a few days ago, but I like what I know so far." *Not bad, Frankie.*

"Are you going to kiss him like Uncle Luca and Aunt Willa do? It's really gross."

I laugh. "I don't know. Maybe." *I want to, if I'm being honest with myself.* "Where is this coming from, sweetie?"

She looks away at the game, and once her brother sends the ball back to the goalie, Emilia twists to face me head-on. "I heard Mom talkin' on the phone last night after I was supposta to be sleep. I could only tell it was a guy because... what is it when you can hear the other person?"

"Speakerphone?" I suggest.

Em nods.

"Okay. What are you concerned about?" The last thing I want to step into is Lina's love life any more than I already am. I've been sworn to secrecy, at least for now.

"What about Daddy?" she mumbles.

Damn! Derrick has been out of her life since she was almost four. They divorced when she was three. Applause pulls my attention back to the game. It gives me time to consider my response. "Do you know why your daddy isn't living with you anymore?" I'm treading lightly here.

"Mommy and Daddy were fighting a lot, and then he moved out, at least that's what Tonio says. I don't remember a lot. When he came to visit me and Tonio, Daddy fought with Uncle Luca and shot him."

It's an oversimplified synopsis, but most of the basic facts are there. She's missing the part where Derrick wanted to take the kids on Thanksgiving when it wasn't his turn, showed up unannounced, Lina refused, and he barricaded himself in her house with them. Then again, she's only seven. "I can't answer that for you. Is this more about seeing your daddy or mommy dating?"

"I miss my daddy more."

I nod. "You should tell your mom when she gets home today."

"Okay, can we go watch some of Ellie's game when Tonio's is over?" She's going to be an amazing wing-woman someday. In fact, she already is.

"I don't see why not."

CHAPTER EIGHT

THOMAS

As much as I don't want to, I understand why Frankie wants to wait until the team decides about the bid. Yet I see her at my daughter's game, and she willingly watches most of the second half after her nephew's ended. I've never met anyone like her. Then again, she's the first woman who didn't run the other way when I shared about Ellie.

Ellie's game ends in a loss, but Frankie offers her some tips as we walk toward the parking lot. I'm not really listening to the specifics. Even though Ellie has been playing soccer for the last seven years, I still don't fully understand some of the rules, like offsides or when a direct or indirect kick occurs.

"Thank you, Frankie. I'll try some of those tips at our next game," Ellie states.

"Anytime."

Emilia tugs on Frankie's sleeve. She looks down at her niece. "Can we have lunch and see Auntie Lia at work?"

"Yes, please. Please, please," Antonio begs.

"Sure, why not?" Frankie answers.

"Do you want to come, Ellie?" Emilia asks.

My eyes snap to Frankie's. Her expression is hard to read.

"Do we have enough time before I go to Kylie's?" Ellie asks.

Of course Ellie wants to go. I don't want to put Frankie in a position to compromise her decision to wait until after the board determination. "Ellie, can you take Emilia and Antonio over to the picnic table so I can talk with Frankie?"

"Sure, come on." She guides them away.

With a bit more privacy, I ask, "What do you want to do? Don't worry about Ellie. I can say she doesn't have enough time before Kylie's and explain to Ellie about the bid later."

There's a wrinkle in Frankie's nose and her lips are pursed. It's adorable, and I can't wait to learn more of her tells. "I want to, but I don't think it's wise. I can't even share everything I feel because it pertains to the bid. It's a tangled mess in my head."

I set my hand on her forearm and immediately remove it. I want her to share, but waiting makes more sense. "I understand."

"I…." Frankie starts to add more but stops.

"I get it. I'll call you tonight." I move toward the kids, but she doesn't follow. When I turn back, her head is hanging forward. It isn't until I turn around I notice Liam Samuels lurking nearby. *Damn!* We may be doing our best to wait, but we're failing, and I'm sure Liam agrees. As much as I want to go back to Frankie and comfort her, I don't. When I reach the kids, I break the news to them and watch Emilia and Antonio walk back to Frankie. I don't like the look of defeat on her gorgeous face.

"What's going on?" Ellie demands after I settle into the driver's seat. "She's super nice and gave me some helpful tips. She's beautiful too."

Frankie is all those things, and I want to learn more. I hope the more didn't get shoved away by Liam. "I met Frankie on Thursday, and we talked more on Friday morning at Sweet Face."

"I'm not seeing a problem," Ellie interjects.

"Her company is bidding on the Cooper project. I was completely taken aback when she arrived for her presentation."

Shock materializes on my daughter's face. "So you can't date her?"

I shake my head. "Not exactly. She wants to wait until the committee decides, which is why our date isn't until next weekend. It was pure luck we ran into each other today."

"That stinks, Dad. I like her, and I met her a little over an hour ago. I know you do too." Ellie is on point.

I like Frankie, and there's nothing I can do about it right now. I exhale. "Fast food or grilled cheese?"

"Grilled cheese. I'll never pass up your specialty." A smile breaks on her face.

I nod and head home. While Ellie showers, I send a text to Frankie.

Me: I wanted to comfort you, and then I saw Liam.

I don't know if she'll answer right away, so I start lunch. Grilled cheese somehow became my specialty when my daughter was younger. Even though Tess didn't work outside of the house, Ellie wanted me home with her if she was sick. I used cookie cutters to make crazy shapes to get her to eat when she wasn't feeling well. Now I'm more creative with bacon, tomato, or ham in the sandwich.

Ellie joins me as I plate the sandwiches. Today I add tomato with a side of her favorite chips.

"Thanks, Dad. Delicious as usual," Ellie offers after her first bite.

My phone vibrates on the counter, but I don't move to check it.

"You can answer her."

"Thanks, Ellie. I appreciate the offer, but we're eating." I'm walking a thin line here. Truthfully, I want to check my phone and answer Frankie, if it's who messaged me, but I also want Ellie to know my time with her is important to me. "What time are you going to Kylie's and what time is pickup?"

"Drop off is at four and pickup at eight."

"Who else will be there?"

Ellie shakes her head. "As far as I know, Kylie, Sam, Jules, and Jessie will be there."

I want to ask if they're all girls but decide against it. Kylie's mother will be present, I already confirmed. "Thanks."

She washes her plate, puts it in the dishwasher, and returns to her room. I clean the pan and the rest of the dishes before checking my phone.

Frankie: Thank you for telling me. Waiting is harder than I thought.

Me: You're welcome. For me too.

I sigh and read the next text from Tess.

Tess: I wanted to let you know our offer was accepted on a house.

Me: Great. We need to create a plan that works for Ellie.

Tess: She's moving with me, end of discussion.

Fury boils in my veins. She's my daughter too. I know Tess can't simply take her, but it doesn't have to be this difficult.

Me: Tess, moving isn't what Ellie wants.

Tess: I'm her mother. She needs to be with me.

Me: I don't want to argue about this here.

Tess: Fine. We're meeting with the mediator soon enough.

I grip my phone when a new message comes through.

Tess: I won't let you keep my daughter from me.

Me: That isn't what I want or what she wants.

Tess: We can give her a fresh start at a private boarding school.

As if I wasn't angry enough. My ex-wife is fighting to have our daughter live with her so she can ship her off to boarding school with her new husband's money. Not happening. Is there something going on I don't know about with Ellie? I doubt it. Ellie is open with me about her friends, teammates, and school. Surprisingly, I keep my cool in my response.

Me: Tess, we should talk about this with the meditators present.

Tess: Fine, but we can give her more than you can.

Me: Have a good evening, Tess.

I don't get a response from her, nor do I expect one. I'm reeling. Why is she fighting me for residence and relocation if she isn't even going to be living with them? I take a screenshot of my texts, email them to my attorney, and request a call next week. I consider going for a run, but I don't have enough time before drop-off. Instead, I step outside and collect my thoughts on my back patio. It's my second favorite part of my home. There's a stone patio with a firepit in the center and plenty of comfortable seating. I sort through my thoughts while I stare blankly into my yard.

"Dad?"

I didn't realize how long I was stewing in my thoughts until Ellie's voice filters through the screen. "Out here."

"It's time to go to Kylie's. Everything okay?"

I refuse to put any of this on Ellie. "Yeah, of course. I need to grab my keys."

I drop Ellie off at Kylie's. I intend to go home to hang out, but instead I go for a drive and end up at the beach. It's a bit chilly, but I don't care. The beach is calming for me. It always has been. I found myself driving toward the cape more than once when I lived in Boston with Tess.

The bombshell about boarding school is a lot. Surprisingly, I got an email response from my attorney almost immediately, setting up a call for Tuesday after lunch. I don't see the point if Ellie is being shipped off to boarding school. Thinking about it makes me even angrier, which isn't helpful right now. All my conversations with my attorney indicate Tess can't relocate Ellie to another state without my consent. Knowing she doesn't even plan to have our daughter living in her monstrous new mansion Michael is set to purchase, I don't see why relocation is even necessary. I'm perfectly willing to have Ellie live here full time and visit her mother on a set schedule. The driving won't be fun, but I'll do it for Ellie.

Without any progress in my thoughts, I head back home. After making myself some dinner, I settle on the patio and wait until it's time to pick up Ellie.

CHAPTER NINE

FRANCESCA

Lunch at Hops and Barley is a good plan. The three of us request a booth in Lia's section, and we hang out for a few hours. I tip my little sister well, knowing we likely kept her from turning her table to another set of guests.

"I love seeing you guys here. How was your game?"

"Not bad. We tied," Antonio shares with my youngest sister.

"That isn't the 'portant part of today, Aunt Lia," Emilia shares.

"Important?"

Em nods furiously.

Lia continues, "No? What is?"

"Auntie Frankie has a boyfriend." Em giggles like an old lady who shared juicy gossip.

I shake my head. Lia raises an eyebrow at me. "I have to get to my other tables. Apparently, we need to chat, big sis."

I wave her off, and we finish our food. A call with Lia will commence once she finishes her shift, I'm sure. It isn't even fair to say Tommy is my boyfriend. We haven't even been on an actual date yet. When we arrive at their house, we play catch with Bogart and Newman in the yard for a while before I send Antonio to shower. Once he's done, I assist

Emilia. I don't really have to do anything except make sure all the shampoo is out of her hair.

"Are you going to marry Ellie's dad?"

Sigh. "We met a few days ago, Em. I can't answer your question."

"Oh, okay." The sadness in her response is noticeable. I don't even know if Tommy wants to get married again. I can't answer her question when we haven't even kissed yet. I want to kiss him, but waiting for the decision about my bid is more important right now than a budding new relationship. Besides, it's only a week.

I have no doubt Liam will make waves about seeing Tommy and me speaking to each other this morning. Hopefully it won't impact the bid or Tommy's job.

"Auntie."

"Yeah, Em?"

"I'm ready for you to check my hair."

I slide back the shower curtain and check her hair. "Great job, Em." I shut off the water. "Dry off and put on some clean jammies. Mommy should be home in less than an hour."

"Okay."

I leave the bathroom and locate Antonio drawing in the living room. "All good, Bud?"

"Yup." Normal kid answer, check.

"Mom should be home in a little while," I share with him as well.

"Okay," he replies without ever looking up.

I grab a water and take a seat on the back porch, watching the dogs bask in the fading sunlight. Lina arrives sooner than I expect.

"Hey, Frankie. How did it go today?"

"Hi, Lina. They were great. We went to soccer, then lunch to see Lia. They both showered but haven't eaten dinner yet."

"Thanks. Will you be at dinner tomorrow?"

"Yeah, why?"

"Just checking. Please don't say anything about…."

"Did he stop into the bank this morning?"

Lina nods. "I'm leaning toward saying yes, Frankie."

"As you should. You deserve to find happiness outside of the kids and work." Lina has put everything else before herself as long as I can remember, even more so after Derrick shot Luca.

"Thanks, but I'm still not ready to share with anyone else."

"No, worries. I have my own stuff to deal with."

"Want to talk about it?" Lina offers.

"Thanks, but I need to talk to him." I have hashed this out enough and shared as much as I plan to with Emilia and Lina for now. Even Emilia sees our attraction to one another.

"Go call him," Lina urges.

"Have a good night, kids. Love you," I say while walking through the house.

"Bye, Auntie," Emilia shouts.

"Bye," Antonio mumbles and barely looks up from his drawing.

I shake my head, pet the dogs, and bound down the stairs to my truck. The only way to sort through this is to talk to Tommy. My phone buzzes as I drive home. I step inside, toe off my shoes, drop my keys in the bowl, and head straight for the wine rack.

With a healthy pour, I settle on the master balcony before checking my phone.

Lia: Spill the beans, sis.

Me: Nothing to spill right yet. We met, I said yes to a date. We ran into him at soccer this morning.

Lia: How old is his kid?

Me: She's twelve and a skilled soccer player.

Lia: I won't pry more, except when is the date?

Me: Next weekend.

Lia: K, love you.

Me: Love you most.

I sigh and take a heavy gulp of my wine. I'm all twisted in knots, and I barely know him. I don't know whether to embrace it or run the other way. I decide to embrace it and text Tommy.

Me: Are you free?

Less than a minute later, my phone is ringing.

"Hi."

"Hi. How was lunch?"

"Pretty good. Yours?"

"Ellie chose my specialty. We came home to eat."

I smile. "What is your specialty?"

"Gourmet grilled cheese."

"I'm intrigued."

"Are you a foodie?" His question is more like a prayer, as if saying he is too.

"I might be." My response comes out unintentionally coy.

"Sweet."

I exhale, knowing we need to discuss Liam. "How well do you know Liam?"

His response is not what I expect. "Well enough to know he'll lodge a complaint against me before I get to work on Monday."

Defeated, I mumble, "Do I need to withdraw my bid?"

"No, absolutely not! There must be a better way to handle this."

I'm heartened by his fierce defense of my work. "Thank you."

"We didn't do anything wrong. We met before the presentation and innocently ran into one another afterward."

"Yet there could still be repercussions for both of us."

"Only because Liam isn't capable of seeing he isn't the only landscape architect in the area. I'm probably breaking some unwritten rule, but Liam has been a consistent applicant for numerous projects for the last two years. He hasn't been successful yet."

Even though it shouldn't, the information does make me feel better. My silence echoes along the line. I have been walking a razor-thin line avoiding sharing how much this project would mean to me and my company. It took gumption and courage for me to submit a bid for the Cooper project.

"Frankie, did I lose you?"

"No, I'm here. I'm… wrestling with how much to share about my dealings with Liam."

"You don't have to share anything right now. He doesn't have the best reputation. His references say he's difficult to work with but the result is worth it."

"All right. Tell me more about this gourmet grilled cheese." We spend the next hour talking about grilled cheese and other ordinary dishes Tommy makes gourmet.

"I'll talk to you tomorrow. Good night, Frankie."

"Good night, Tommy."

I end the call, throw my phone on the cushions, and polish off my wine. Nothing else for me to do except try to get some sleep. I may have given my presentation, but the nervousness hasn't ended.

CHAPTER TEN

THOMAS

Near eight on Sunday, Ellie strolls out of bed. She's never in a good mood when she's slated to return to Tess's. It doesn't help Tess refuses to hear our daughter when she indicates she doesn't want to move. As much as Tess would like to say I brainwashed her or spoon-fed her the answers I want, that isn't the case. Ellie simply would prefer to stay in Maine where she has been her entire life.

Since the divorce, I've learned to let Ellie decide how Sundays go. Today we're making a big breakfast with pancakes, sausage, and homemade hash with coffee for me and juice for her. After eating, Ellie throws in a load of laundry so it'll finish before Tess arrives to pick her up. It's great Ellie is capable of washing her own laundry. However, Ellie's need to make sure she always does it at my home gives me pause.

"I'm going to read on the patio," she informs me.

"Okay, maybe I'll join you."

Minutes later with a book, blanket, and a bottled water in hand, Ellie steps outside. I consider reviewing the bids again for the Cooper project but decide against it. I have already narrowed it down to Fister and Sons, Happy Lawns, and Sunshine Landscape and Design.

I pull out the files for Omni and join Ellie. She's curled into the corner of the rattan couch with a blanket over her feet. I settle into the chair. We stay outside until lunch. After lunch, Ellie retreats to her room with her clean laundry. Not long after, I receive a call from Tess.

"Hi, Tommy. Can I speak with Ellie?" Curious why Tess called me when Ellie has her own phone, which was given to her earlier than I would have liked but necessary given our family dynamics.

"Hi, Tess. Of course."

I walk down the hall and knock on her door. "Ellie, Mom is on the phone."

She opens the door and takes my phone but stays right next to me.

"Ellie, I'm not going to be able to get back to Maine tonight. Something came up with Michael's new job, and we need to stay here a bit longer than anticipated. I wanted to let you know before I spoke with your dad."

"Thanks, Mom. I'm fine here."

"I appreciate your understanding. I love you. Can I talk to your dad?"

Ellie hangs her head and hands me back my phone.

I push the mute button. "I'll be back to talk when I'm finished."

Ellie nods as I walk away. Once I reach the living room, I unmute the phone. "Tess?"

"Thank you. I need Ellie to stay with you for a bit longer. A bigwig for Michael's new job is flying in for a meeting tomorrow morning. He needs to stay."

"It's no problem at all. Do you plan to be back tomorrow evening?" I keep my voice as neutral and calm as possible.

"I'm not sure yet." We may not be married anymore, but something is off about Tess.

"That's fine. Please let me know when you will be back," I add calmly. Nothing about me is calm right now.

"I will. Thank you, Tommy."

"Bye, Tess." I end the call. My emotions oscillate from elation to confusion and everything in between. Considering Tess is the petitioner for the relocation motion, I'm sure she isn't having second thoughts. Yet it doesn't make sense for her to shirk her parenting time, especially when we're set to meet the mediator soon. Pushing my feelings aside, I make my way back to Ellie. She's sitting on the bench at the foot of her bed.

"Hey, kiddo. Want to talk about it?"

She shakes her head yet shares anyway. "Nothing to talk about. Mom has her new life with Michael, and she wants me to move there with her. It's hard enough to spend time with both of you as it is now. I don't want to move and make it even harder. Unlike some of my friends with divorced parents, you guys seem to be civil when I'm around. You even come to my games when it's Mom's day. Even though there's a set schedule, you can watch because you're local. What if you're not anymore?" A few tears fall down her cheeks. "If she chooses to leave, that's on her. I shouldn't be forced to go with her."

I sit beside her, and she leans into my shoulder. I don't for one second believe Tess intended to come home on time, but I won't share my suspicion with Ellie. I don't like the fact Tess's motion has me withholding information from my daughter again. "Ellie, as much as I would like to, I can't doubt your mom. This has only happened one other time, and her reasons then were legitimate. Perhaps she could have made more of an effort, but she's choosing to meet Michael's new boss."

Ellie indicates agreement against my shoulder.

"Do you want me to find someone for you to talk to other than me?"

She lifts her head and looks at me. "You mean like a therapist?"

"There's nothing wrong with needing a therapist to sort through your feelings. When talking to Uncle Remi didn't help enough, I had one for about a year after the divorce." Remi isn't really her uncle, but we have been friends since middle school, so it's respectful. Remington Garner was assigned the seat next to me in homeroom in fifth grade, and the rest is history. He's been dating the girl who sat diagonally from us, Evangeline Smith, ever since then—at least as much as you can start dating someone in middle school.

"I'll think about it," she mumbles.

"I'm willing to listen if you want to talk more about anything."

"Thanks, Dad. I'm going to watch a movie. Want to join me?"

"Sure." I'll never say no to an extra movie night with my daughter.

After watching a movie with fresh, buttery, homemade popcorn, Ellie turns in for the night. As much as I shouldn't, I want to talk to Frankie.

Me: Are you free to talk?

Frankie: Sure, I'll call you in a few minutes.

I peek in at Ellie, and she's sound asleep. My parents are still married and have been for the last thirty-six years. I'm trudging through divorced parenting as best I can since I don't have a perfect frame of reference for Ellie.

Within days of Tess filing for divorce, I replaced everything in the master bedroom except for my clothes. The walls are now a light gray. I exchanged a massive Victorian-style bedroom set with a more masculine mission set I built myself with navy and black linens. The floor isn't covered with a fluffy area rug anymore and has been resurfaced. I replaced the wingback chairs by the fireplace with a small love seat in a dark gray. Ellie added a chunky knit blanket and some patterned pillows to add texture. I sit on the love seat as my phone rings.

"Hi."

"Hi." A myriad of emotions runs through me. We probably shouldn't be talking until after the committee decides, but I'm drawn to her. I don't say anything else for a solid minute.

"Are you there?"

I nod as if she can see me. "I'm here."

"This was a bad idea, wasn't it?" she murmurs.

"Yes and no. Yes, because of the bid and Liam, but no because I wanted to talk with you too."

"I can't explain it. I want to talk to you and get to know you despite those things."

"I do too." *More than I should.* "Shall we start with the basics?"

She laughs. It's higher pitched than I would have thought but lovely. "Sure. Like what's my favorite color?"

"You don't have to tell me. I already know it."

"You do?" Her voice rises in anticipation.

"It's yellow." My reply is confident. I imagine she's shaking her head because I'm that sure.

"How?"

I smile, proud of myself. "You're a trained landscaper, you create lush gardens for a living, the name of your company starts with sunshine."

"Impressive. I couldn't even hazard a guess unless it's navy based on the same logic you used from the color of your suits."

Now I laugh. "It is actually, but that isn't the reason. When we were young, we needed to choose a color because our monograms are identical."

"Practical. Where would you travel if money and time were no object?"

"Digging deep, Frankie. I would travel around Europe by train and then relax in Fiji for a few weeks to recover from my travels. What wrong assumption do people make about you?"

"Nice. I've never been outside of the United States. That's easy. Once people learn I own a landscaping company, they assume I don't like dressing up."

Note to self, our date should be fancy enough for Frankie to wear a dress and heels. "It isn't really surprising. Is it why you stick with Frankie for work?"

She sighs. "Frankie has been my nickname since childhood, as you already know. It was helpful when I first started my company, but my potential clients forget about my gender once I show them my plans for their yard."

"Do you dislike being called Francesca?"

"No, not at all. Who, besides your parents, taught you the most about life?"

"Ellie, without question. When you're solely responsible for the well-being of a tiny human, everything is magnified. I learned to enjoy the little things more, especially after my divorce. I'm not a perfect parent, but I'm present when I'm with my daughter and I cherish the time I get with her."

"If you're willing to share, why are you divorced?"

I inhale and collect my thoughts a moment. "The easy answer is money, but it isn't the whole story. I had a lucrative job in Boston, but I was miserable. Tess stayed at home with Ellie and had no issue spending my salary. When I shared with Tess I wasn't happy with my job, she encouraged a job search. She didn't realize a job where I would be happy wouldn't allow her to maintain the lifestyle to which she grew accustomed. When I found my current position, Tess was supportive and even offered to curtail her spending and look for a job in marketing.

Instead, she grew frustrated with a job search of her own and within six months filed for divorce. It took me some time and therapy to realize Tess and I weren't a team. Our goals didn't align as far as our marriage was concerned. Tess wanted to be a stay-at-home mom and corporate executive's wife, throwing lavish dinner parties while dressed in the latest fashion trend. I had no issue with Tess not working, but the executive lifestyle, at least in Boston, wasn't for me. I want what my parents have."

"Which is?"

"A partnership based on mutual respect and love with a lot of fun mixed in."

"You want to get married again?"

"To the right woman, yes. What about you?" I take the moments of silence before she answers as a positive.

"I agree with you. My parents met in seventh grade and have been inseparable ever since. It sounds as if they have the same type of marriage as your parents. After thirty-seven years of marriage, they go on dates and enjoy each other's company. I want to get married and have a family as well. Do you?"

"Want more children? Yes, I wanted a large family like mine. Is it still possible? Sure, except Ellie will be significantly older than her siblings."

"I didn't mean for this to turn heavy. This certainly isn't pre-date conversation."

"Maybe it should be."

"Maybe you're right. We seem to be adept at breaking the boundaries we've set."

I laugh softly. "Yes, we are. Can I call you tomorrow?"

"I appreciate your attempt to adhere to our rules, but don't set us up for failure. Feel free to call or text whenever you want."

I smile at the thought. Even though this may cause strife for us with the Cooper project, she isn't willing to walk away. "I will. Good night, Sunshine."

"Good night."

I plug in my phone and burrow deeper into my bed with visions of a gorgeous landscaper in my head.

CHAPTER ELEVEN

FRANCESCA

The first thing I need to do this morning is get ahead of Liam if I can. I consider my options: withdraw my bid, approach the committee, or talk to Liam. Withdrawing my bid won't necessarily make a difference. I won't get the contract, but there's no guarantee Liam will. Maybe I should talk to Tommy before approaching the committee. Probably something we should've discussed last night. *Sigh.* Liam is the last thing I want to discuss when I talk to Tommy. I'm kicking myself for choosing to wait until after the contract is awarded for our date.

When I park in my spot, there's an unfamiliar car a few spaces over. His voice surrounds me as I step into my office. Tommy. As discreetly as possible, I catalog Tommy from head to toe. It doesn't matter what he wears, he's gorgeous. For work today, he chose a black suit with a sage green shirt and matching paisley tie. *Damn, he looks hot!*

"Morning, Frankie."

"Hi, Eric. Hi, Tommy."

"Morning, Frankie. I apologize for dropping in," Tommy states.

"No problem. Would you like to chat in my office?"

"Sure, lead the way."

After ushering him inside, I drop my breakfast on the desk, turn around, and find my mouth is mere inches away from Tommy's. Not only does he look hot, but he smells amazing too. This is the first time we've been alone since my presentation. The room temperature increases exponentially, and my desire to kiss him is unbearable. A million reasons not to fly through my mind, among them the bid and my reputation. Before I can process even those two reasons, his surprisingly rough hand threads into my hair and his soft lips brush against mine. Heat and tingles prickle through me from the gentle touch of his lips on mine. He pulls back enough for me to lift my eyes to his.

"Tommy."

"Sunshine."

That is all it takes for me to give in to my desire for him. "Sunshine" echoing around me in his deep sexy voice, I slide my hands up his chest, which is harder than I expect, and draw my thumb over his lips. His arm snakes around my waist, pulling me flush against him. Our lips meet in the middle and dance across one another. I melt against him as we move from light, friendly pecks to deep, sensual strokes of our tongues. I have kissed enough men to know the difference between good and bad, but also between casual and committed. We may not have been on a date and this is our first kiss, but Tommy wants it to be the first of many. I'm completely on board. We continue exploring each other, fully clothed for a while. The tenor of our lip-lock changes from tender to demanding and back numerous times before I realize he's at my office on a workday. As much as I don't want to, I capture his lower lip between my teeth and pull back. A low growl flows from his body.

"Good morning to you too," I whisper.

"I came to talk to you, but I'll happily take kisses first."

"What do you want to talk about?" I'm not sure I want to hear the answer to my question though.

"It isn't bad. I almost texted you near one in the morning for your address to talk to you then, but I felt it was a bit over the top."

"I would've given you my address and gotten out of bed to answer the door. Please share what was keeping you up."

"You."

"Me?"

"Yes, you. I decided you deserve to be considered for this contract and the fact we met beforehand shouldn't matter. Nor should the fact I like you and want to date you. While I don't have the final say, I want to make sure Liam doesn't mess it up. I don't know all the details as to why you and Liam don't get along. Truly, I don't care since it was professional not personal. I'm going to share with my boss this morning the circumstances of how we met, hopefully before Liam can make any accusations. I emailed my boss right before texting you."

I shake my head simply because we seem to be on the same page. "I thought the same and wondered if I should reach out to the committee myself. Please don't lose your job over this. It's only one bid."

"One you deserve to land."

I let out an audible exhale and shift my gaze out the window. Tommy sets his fingers beneath my chin and forces my eyes back to his. "Thank you. One of my options was to withdraw my bid."

"No, we already discussed withdrawing your bid. It isn't a viable option. Look, I know you want to do the right thing, but until those spectacular kisses, we haven't done anything wrong."

I feel my skin heat from his correct assessment.

"Not wrong. You know what I mean." He's flustered. I like it, a lot.

I nod. "I have no appointments on my calendar. If you or the committee need me to come in today, I can after I run home for appropriate clothes."

"You look hot just the way you are."

"Compliments on my jeans and graphic tees will get you far. However, my outfit is still not appropriate, especially when you wear a suit to work."

A smile breaks across his gorgeous face. I never noticed the dimple in his left cheek before now. It makes him even more attractive.

"Your red dress was even hotter than these tight jeans."

A fierce blush streaks across my face. "Thank you."

"It's completely true. I should get going. I'll call you after I talk to Linda."

I'm speechless. All I can do is nod. He drops a kiss to my forehead and walks out the door. I'm frozen in place. His faith in me is appreciated and scary at the same time. The mere fact he's willing to publicly share what little has transpired between us says a lot about him as a man. Clearly, Tommy doesn't do anything halfway. He came here first before throwing himself at the mercy of his boss. He's a keeper, and I'm surprised he's single, especially considering I can still feel his lips on mine and how much more I want him.

"Hey, Frankie," Eric's voice comes through the intercom, interrupting my delicious thoughts.

"Yeah?"

"Your sister is on line three."

"Thanks." I round my desk and fall into my chair. "Hey, sis," I answer since Eric didn't mention which one.

"Hey. I hear you have a boyfriend." It's Lily this time.

I chuckle softly. "Let me guess, Emilia?"

"Yup. Care to share?"

"As much as I would like him to be my boyfriend, he isn't—at least not yet. Although... hold on...." I rise from my chair and close my office door.

"Although what?"

"He was just here." I explain to Lily the chance meetings, how he was the representative for Hayward at my presentation and his plan to share with his boss probably as we speak.

"Nothing has happened yet?" Lily is always good at hearing slight intonation and tells in our voices. It helps her with sales at work without question.

"Nothing until this morning."

A squeal comes through the phone line. "Please share with your younger and successful, yet painfully single sister." Lily is gorgeous and driven. Most men, especially ones her age, are pushed off by her success and confidence. I'm sure her choice to work from home doesn't help matters.

"I have never been kissed like that... ever. It was hands down the best, toe-curling, breathless kiss I've ever had. I'm surprised he didn't have to scoop me off the floor after making me a mushy pile of goo like the classic movies where the characters kiss and the heroine swoons."

"What is this you speak of?"

I laugh softly. "Lil, it was perfect, and I want so much more." I've been pining for a kiss since we talked at Sweet Face. Tommy more than made it worth the wait, even though it wasn't as long as it felt.

"You're smitten."

"That's a good way to put it for now. He has serious potential. I'm scared to chase it, Lil."

"Everything worth having is worth the chase especially love."

"Damn, sis. When did you become profound?"

"When I realized the perfect man will chase me when the time is right."

"The perfect man has been standing beside you since elementary school."

"Ugh! He's my best friend, Frankie. Nothing more." Leo and Lily have been friends for as long as I can remember. She may think there's nothing more, but I see their connection when they're together. They can't seem to get on the same page. When he's single, she isn't and vice versa.

"You're fooling yourself if you think you don't have real feelings beyond friendship for the smoking-hot, tall, broody, tattooed bar owner you call your best friend."

"But—"

"No buts, you know I'm right."

"Maybe," she grumbles and ends our call. After another moment to revel in kissing Tommy and our potential, I tackle payroll and administrative tasks I loathe. At the same time, I worry about how the meeting with his boss is going.

CHAPTER TWELVE

THOMAS

My intentions were honorable before her lips were a breath away from mine. I couldn't help myself. The reward for jumping was worth it. I've never felt so much from a kiss before, not even with Tess. Even more than before, I can't wait for our date, which seems so far away.

I park and head straight to my office. However, my assistant stops me before I step foot inside.

"Tommy, Linda asked me to send you right in when you arrived."

"Thanks, could you find me the number for a local florist with same-day delivery."

"Sure. I'll take your bag."

I hand my bag to Melissa, rebutton my jacket, and head down the hall to Linda's office. I knock lightly on the glass because her assistant is not at his desk.

She waves me in. "Good morning. I got your email first thing this morning and a request for an appointment with Liam Samuels. What do I need to know before I call him back?"

"I met a woman at Sweet Face Pastry Shoppe. We chatted twice last week. I didn't—"

Linda interrupts, "Let me guess, Francesca Cappelli."

I nod curtly and continue. "Nothing unprofessional happened. I didn't know who she was until she showed up for her presentation on Friday. On Saturday, I ran into her at the soccer fields and Mr. Samuels saw us talking. I—"

Linda raises her hand to indicate she's heard enough. "The committee has narrowed down the candidates early, and Mr. Samuels isn't one of them. Miss Cappelli is still on the short list for the contract."

The knots in my stomach loosen a bit. I truly didn't know how this would go. Also, I'm not sure if I should be upset I wasted my time listening to Liam's presentation or the committee truly didn't feel the presentations were needed.

Linda continues, "As previously requested, please provide your narrowed list to the committee by the end of the day. You will abstain from voting on the awarding of the contract if necessary." Linda pauses. "Is there anything else?"

Sheer glee courses through me. At a minimum, I didn't screw this up for her. I compose myself and focus on right now, not the softness of Frankie's body against mine. "About the Cooper project, no. A reminder I have mediation on Thursday and may not be in."

"Fine. You have plenty of unused personal time. Thank you for coming in, Tommy."

"You're welcome." I leave Linda's office and walk outside to the break area in the back of the building. Inhaling the fresh air soothes me a bit. All I want to do is hop into my car and hurry back to Frankie, but it isn't reasonable or possible. My mind is turning with possibilities as I slowly stroll to my office. I accept my messages and the florist's number from Melissa wordlessly. Not even her interested look about the florist is going to bring me down.

I fall into my chair and send a text.

Me: Are you free for lunch? I can have it delivered.

Frankie: Yes. Is lunch a good idea?

Me: The meeting with my boss was fine. I'll explain over lunch. I want to see you.

Frankie: I'll be here. I want to see you too.

I smile and send my top three choices for the Cooper project to Linda and the rest of the committee. I place an order for flowers for Ellie. Hopefully, delivery will occur late this afternoon before I get home. I push my concern away regarding Liam for now and focus on the other pile of work on my desk.

After noon, I place our lunch order and head to Frankie's office. When I arrive, no one is at reception. I walk down the hall toward her office. The door is slightly ajar, and Frankie is dancing around her desk with a huge smile on her face. I knock on the doorframe and wait.

"Hey," she swings the door open.

"Hi." I surround her with my arm and set my lips on hers. With two steps, we're inside her office and I close the door with my foot. My memory is perfect. Her lips are soft and supple, and she tastes like cherry right now. Satisfied for the moment, I set her on the floor and add some space between us.

"Why are you dancing, Sunshine?"

She smiles even wider. "I'm still in the running for the Cooper project!"

I eliminate the space I gave her and pull her close. "Congratulations."

"You didn't have anything to do with it, did you?"

I shake my head. "No. Linda had a message from Liam and me when she arrived this morning. I spoke with her before she returned his call. That isn't the important part. The committee narrowed down the candidates early. They were waiting for me to give them my remaining candidates so they could inform the bidders."

"Okay, but what about us?"

"Say that again."

She looks away from me. With my fingers under her chin, I turn her gaze back to mine.

"It's presumptuous. Please forget what I said."

"Not a chance. Our chemistry is off the charts. The only reason we haven't been on a real date is the Cooper project. Your reasoning was sound, and I agreed. Living in this quaint town provided more opportunities for us to run into one another. I'm grateful for small-town closeness. Truthfully, I didn't want to wait until Saturday for our date. In the strictest definition, perhaps we aren't an 'us,' but we could be and I want to find out."

She nods and brushes her lips across mine.

The slight touch sends my mind to places it shouldn't be right now. A flash of her in my bed, her hair spilling onto my pillow, and the outline of her silhouette beneath my sheets crashes through my mind. A strong knock pulls me out of my lustful thoughts. "I'll get lunch. Do you have a break room?"

She shakes her head and moves to clear the workspace in her office.

When I return with the food, there's plenty of room for us to eat. "I ordered a bunch of options for us." There are four sandwiches, an array of chips, and more drinks than the two of us could possibly need.

"Thank you. I'm not picky." Of the four choices, she opts for my favorite.

"Why that one?" I'm curious.

"It's my favorite." She chooses a turkey on rye with provolone and honey mustard. Then she grabs a bag of Fritos and a raspberry iced tea. She smiles and takes a bite.

"Another food we both like."

"Oh, I'll share." She hands me the other half of the sandwich.

"It's fine. Now I know chances are high if I pick a favorite food of mine, you'll love it too."

We polish off our lunch in record time. Neither of us feel the need to fill the silence. It's comforting. We clean up the table and separate the trash from the leftover food.

"As much as I would prefer to stay here, I have to get back to the office."

A frown briefly graces her face. "Okay."

I slide my hand to cup her jaw and kiss her lightly. Anything more and I'll be late getting back to work. "I'll call you tonight."

I leave her office before my thoughts consume me again. Walking away is the last thing I want to do right now.

CHAPTER THIRTEEN

FRANCESCA

Honestly, I didn't want Tommy to leave either, but it was necessary. I refocus on my bid. Pride and elation flow through me. I'm so excited, but I'm trying not to get ahead of myself. All I know is I'm in the top three for this project and the final decision will be made in the next few days. After a few too many moments enjoying my progress, I plop into my chair and finish the stack of plan reviews on my desk. A little past four, I stop for the day and drive home. My phone indicates new texts along the way. The notification is generic, so it's either work or Tommy. He deserves a dedicated one.

As I park, a familiar though unfriendly truck pulls up to the curb. Just want I need right now—Liam.

"How did you pull it off?" he shouts. He may tower over me despite my height, but I'm not afraid. Luca made sure his sisters could protect themselves if it were ever necessary.

"I didn't do anything, Liam. Please leave," I respond calmly.

"How long have you been sleeping with him to get the job?"

The sheer chauvinism in his question angers me even more. "Is that what you really think? The only way someone could successfully bid on a large project is to sleep their way to the top?"

Thankfully, Smithson, my neighbor across the courtyard and friend of Luca's, pulls into his assigned spot. Liam hasn't done anything overtly stupid yet, but there's still time. I don't mind a little backup from one of York's finest men in blue.

"No, it's the only way I think *you* could beat me," Liam spews.

"Well, you have overestimated your skills or severely underestimated mine. That's on you. As I tried to explain to you, I ran into Mr. Thornton at soccer. Please leave, Liam." I take a step closer to my door and add more space between us.

Smithson, still dressed in his uniform, causally crosses the street, walks up to me, and slides his arm around me. "Hi, babe. How was work?"

"Pretty good. You?" I play along, even though the last thing I want is to date Smithson. He's a great guy and has a stable career, but he's friends with Luca. I don't want to be in Lina's shoes. If it isn't him, only Gugliotti and Davis remain as options. Considering Davis is friends with benefits with Willa's bestie, Tabi, and has been for a while, I'm leaning toward Gugliotti. It could be the newest one, Craven. I doubt she would be worried if it were him; Luca barely knows him.

"Not too bad. Sorry, we haven't met. I'm Zack, and you are?" Smithson extends his hand to Liam.

"I'm leaving. I'll prove you're still in the running for the project because of Thornton."

"Good luck." I wave, and Smithson walks me to the door. Once Liam leaves, he follows me inside.

"Who was that jackass?" he asks.

"There's a really long professional history between Liam and me. His attitude right now is because we have competing bids on an expansive project and he was cut today, but I wasn't. He thinks I slept with the project manager to further my chances of landing the contract. Before you ask, I didn't." *The more time I spend with him, the more time I want with him.*

"Wasn't going to suggest anything like that. Will he come back?" Smithson's tone sounds concerned.

"I doubt it. Thanks for coming over."

"No problem. I'm not going out, so if he comes back, call me."

I hug him and he leaves. I appreciate the charade, but I'm staying in as well. I arm my security system and continue with my evening. After eating and cleaning up, I curl up in the corner of my couch with a book. I'm dozing on my couch when my phone rings.

"Hi."

"Hey. How was the rest of your day?" Something in Tommy's voice sounds off.

"It was fine."

"What happened?"

Apparently, I sound off too. I share what occurred with Liam and Smithson. "What about you?"

"I'm glad he happened to be nearby, not that you couldn't handle him yourself."

"Thank you. What happened for you? Is Ellie okay?" Silence. I wait almost a minute. "Tommy?" My voice comes out higher than usual.

"I'm here. I don't want to burden you with my problems."

"It isn't burdening me; it's helping you. What happened with Tess?"

He pushes out a strong exhale. "She didn't come back from house hunting yesterday for her parenting time. It's odd because she filed to relocate Ellie, and our mediation is Thursday."

"I'm sorry. How does Ellie feel about it? Does it matter what Ellie wants?" I don't know Tess, but it seems counterintuitive to file for relocation and not show up.

"You amaze me, Sunshine."

Even though he can't see me, I wrinkle my nose. "Why? Ellie is the most important aspect of your relationship with Tess."

"I agree, but most women—at least the ones I've met—see drama, not my daughter. Thank you for being different and true to your word."

"You're welcome." I imagine him pacing the floor while we're talking.

"Ellie doesn't want to move. As far as your other question, I don't know. I have a telephone conference tomorrow with my lawyer. Ellie is aware of the motion, and Tess even sent her a link to the house they bought. I'm sure she offered a bedroom makeover to Ellie. However, Tess indicated she was considering sending Ellie to a fancy boarding school. If Ellie isn't going to be living in the house and Tess won't be there to parent her, why does she have to move at all?"

The anguish in his voice is heartbreaking. While I don't have children of my own, Lina had to fight for Antonio and Emilia despite Derrick's criminal behavior. "Does Ellie know or did Tess decide beforehand?"

"No, she doesn't know. Tess dropped the boarding school bombshell on me Saturday night in a text."

"What can I do to help?"

"You already are. Thank you for listening."

"You're welcome. Tell me something good from today." I urge him to focus on something other than his parenting issues for a little while. There isn't anything he can do at this time of the day. I'm sure he won't sleep much until it's resolved.

"I experienced the best first kiss of my life."

Wow! It wasn't just me. "You can't take mine!"

A soft laugh meets my ear. "Is it taking yours if we shared the kiss?"

"You have a point. I'm willing to share with you."

"I'm glad. Maybe we can top it on Saturday."

My heart squeezed. "I'm not sure it's possible. I mean, the first is always special."

"Challenge accepted, Sunshine."

Oh boy! A better kiss than earlier today, is it even possible? Of equal measure for the rest of our lives would be fine with me. I'm willing to let him try. "I didn't mean it that way."

"I know." He yawns. "I should get some sleep. Will I see you in the morning?"

"How did I not see you before last week?" I wonder aloud.

"I don't go daily. I'm later when it's only me. I adjust my time to bring Ellie to school. She uses her mom's address, so school is near there not here."

"You don't live near Sweet Face?"

He replies, "No, I don't. I actually prefer the Perk, but Sweet Face is closer to work and Ellie's school."

"My friend Kelsey, the owner of the Perk, is married to Luca's former captain. She's awesome, and their son, Ben, is super cute."

"The Ramirezes are great people. Kelsey's scones are delicious. I dare say maybe better than Talia's apple muffins. It's difficult to have two favorite pastry shops so close to one another."

I consider inquiring how he knows William and Kelsey but don't. "I agree. Please don't tell Tal. She will be offended." I chuckle.

"Your secret is safe with me. Hopefully, you'll be at your table in the morning when we arrive. Good night, Sunshine."

"Good night, Tommy." I sigh and end the call. Peeling myself off the couch, I trudge upstairs to my bed.

CHAPTER FOURTEEN

THOMAS

Her smile and demeanor, along with her aptly named business, led me to call her Sunshine. It's perfect for her. No woman has ever willingly listened to my issues with Tess without hesitation or judgment until her. We have potential. After I check on Ellie, I fall into my bed.

Early the next morning, my phone is chiming with notifications. Nothing about texts this early in the morning is a good thing. After waking Ellie and a half a cup of coffee, I check my messages.

Frankie: Good morning. I won't be at Sweet Face. My sister needs help with the kids.

Me: Morning. I'll miss seeing your gorgeous face. Have a good day.

Frankie: Compliments this early in the morning? I'm flattered.

Me: It's true.

Frankie: Thank you. Have a good day too.

I smile and continue scrolling. There's a text from Remi.

Remi: Good luck with mediation today.

Me: Thanks, but it's on Thursday.

Remi: I'll message you again then, mate. Ellie would be lucky to have you full time.

Me: Thanks, man. I would love to have Ellie full time.

We hustle out the door, grab a pastry at Sweet Face, and go about our days. The call with my attorney doesn't allay my fears but doesn't make me feel worse either. The general gist is it depends on each situation. The only bright spot is Ellie is of an age where if we can't come to an agreement in mediation, a judge *may* listen to her opinion.

Right after four, I rush out the door and back home to get Ellie to soccer practice.

"Ellie, are you ready to go?" I call out as I step inside our home.

My daughter turns toward me from the hall ready for practice. "Hi. I'm ready except for some water." She returns quickly with two bottles of water in her hand.

I turn on my heel and head back to the car with Ellie. The field isn't far away. Ellie is out of the car and off to practice once I pull into the parking spot.

"I'll be right—" Her door slams before I can finish. I consider leaving to grab a coffee, but then I see Frankie walking toward me. I hop out of my car and join her and Emilia. "Hi, fancy seeing you here. Hi, Emilia."

"Hi, Mr. Ellie's dad. Auntie, can I go swing?"

"Sure, go ahead. I'll be right there."

Emilia runs off to the playground, and Frankie starts to follow. I set my hand on her forearm.

"Will you join me?" Her voice is low, and her eyes dart around us, presumably looking for Liam.

I lean closer and hear her inhale sharply. "I want to kiss you right now, but I know it isn't wise."

"I want that too," she mumbles and continues walking to the playground.

Once we reach the edge and Frankie is close enough to her niece, I ask, "Is everything okay with Lily?"

She shakes her head and laughs softly. "Wrong sister. Lina is their mom. She's fine, but a pipe burst at work, and as the branch manager, she needs to wait for it to be fixed and certify the assets at the bank before she can leave."

"She's lucky to have you. My siblings would do the same."

"Thank you. I'm not the only one who pitches in. Lily is meeting me here to take the night shift or however long it takes. How was your call?"

"Informative but not definitive enough in my opinion. As you can imagine, I'm completely against the plan to relocate, but I was willing to bend for Ellie, except she doesn't want to go."

"It makes sense. She has a life here, one she's known since birth, I assume."

I nod. Emilia falls from the monkey bars, and Frankie moves in her direction, fast but not urgently. When she reaches Emilia, she checks her out, gives her a pep talk, and lifts her back up where she fell. Glimpses of Frankie as a mom make my chest tighten. She'll be an amazing mom one day. "Maybe we should have planned our date for last Saturday."

She laughs. "Maybe we should have. Are you free tomorrow for dinner?"

I turn to face her and barely resist the urge to touch her. "Did you push up our first date and make it an at-home date?" I smirk at her.

"Never mind, forget I said anything." Redness creeps across her cheeks.

"I'm kidding. I don't really believe in fate or the universe per se, but since I saw you, our paths keep crossing. Yes, I would like to have dinner with you tomorrow. What is your—"

Emilia drops down from the monkey bars and takes off running.

"Emilia…" Frankie whips around as she passes us.

Frankie visibly relaxes when Emilia throws her arms around a woman who looks strikingly similar to Frankie. She reaches back for my hand but lets hers drop.

"It's—" I know how she feels. It irks me too. Everything is out in the open and our meeting was innocent.

"No, it isn't. We haven't done anything wrong." She reaches her hand toward me, and this time, I thread my fingers with hers.

"Hi, Lil. Tommy, this is my sister, Lily."

Lily gives me the once-over before greeting me. She pauses at our intertwined hands. "Hi, pleasure to meet you."

I watch the sisters talk without words, mostly head nods and eye movements. It takes resolve not to chuckle or ask what they're saying. I fail miserably. "Would you like me to leave so you can talk about me?"

Frankie's fingers tighten around mine. I don't want to leave, and she doesn't want me to, which I like, a lot. Both women laugh.

"No, don't mind us. We've been doing that since we were kids. What brings you to the park this evening? Frankie mentioned your daughter is older than our niece and nephew. Too old for the playground."

"Ellie is at practice on field three. Seeing Frankie was sheer luck." Amazing, fantastic, made my day better, and I'll take it considering the upheaval everywhere else.

"Oh—"

"Aunt Lily, can we go back to the swings?"

Either Emilia truly wants to swing, or she understands I want to be alone with Frankie. Why isn't important. I'm grateful because she's right.

"Of course, Em. Antonio knows we're switching off?" Lily addresses Frankie.

"Yes, he knows."

"Nice meeting you, Tommy. Perhaps I'll see you again." Lily extends her hand to me.

"You as well. Bye, Emilia."

"Bye, Mr. Ellie's dad." She all but drags Lily to the playground.

I lean into Frankie. "Hi again."

"Hi." She turns to look at me.

Everything about her is perfect. Despite her physical job, she has curves. Curves I want to mark with my fingers. Her skin is flawless, her lips are pouty, and I ache to kiss them again.

"Want to sit or walk?"

I glance at my watch. Ellie still has about an hour left of practice. "Let's walk."

Hand in hand we stroll down the narrow path between the trees. After a half mile, we're out of sight of the park. I pull Frankie into my arms and hide behind a huge tree wide enough to obscure us both. I cup her face and drop my lips to hers. A deep moan catches in her throat. Her mouth is a potent combination of passion and longing. Frankie's hands slide beneath my suit jacket. Her fingernails dig into my back. I pour every ounce of desire I harbor from the last time I was able to taste her into this kiss. Everything about her is more than I imagined when I first saw her through the window.

I travel outward from her lips along her jaw to below her ear. "I wanted to kiss you the moment I saw you."

Goose bumps rise on her skin from my words. "Me too. I love our impromptu dates."

I draw back to look at her before responding. "I do too." The flash of desire in her eyes has my lips pressed to hers again. We alternate exploring the depths of the other's mouth. Our hands search for an appropriate place to land. I settle my palm on the curve of her ass with my fingers grazing her soft, warm skin. Frankie draws her nails down my back and up the front of my thighs. The strain on my pants increases exponentially when her fingertips graze my length. As much as I would like to continue this, exhibitionism isn't high on my list of things to do.

"We should... So good... Slow...." She adds some space between us. Her reaction indicates she's reluctant to do so like me.

"I think we might have gotten a little carried away."

She shakes her head slightly. "Only because we're here. I wouldn't mind losing myself more with you in private."

I raise an eyebrow.

"Too blunt?"

Surprised but elated we're both in this. "No, just surprised you're willing to articulate your feelings so clearly."

"No reason not to."

She's refreshing. After hearing a distant rumble of thunder, I drop my head.

"We need to head back now," I add as a few raindrops start to fall. I graze my lips across hers once more and take her hand in mine. With each step toward the fields, the rain falls harder and harder. Before we make it back, we're both soaked. Frankie is gorgeous by almost every standard definition, but there's something about a wet threadbare tee clinging to a woman's curves that makes it hard to breathe. My protective and possessive instincts kick in, and I wrap my jacket around her shoulders. I'm not sharing that view if at all possible.

"Thank you."

"You're welcome." Ellie's team is wrapping up as we reach the central area of the park. "Apple muffins tomorrow?" I curl our clasped hands around her waist and draw her closer.

"Sure. I'll see you then. Good night, Tommy."

I lean forward and kiss her softly. "Good night, Frankie." As I pull away, Ellie joins us, but I don't release my hold on Frankie.

"Hi, Frankie."

"Hi, Ellie. How was practice?"

"Pretty good. Coach was impressed with the moves you taught me. I tested them out during our intra-squad scrimmage before the rain started."

"Happy to help."

"Are you free on Saturday morning?" Ellie asks.

My chest tightens. Not only do I like Frankie, but my daughter does as well.

Frankie's face brightens. "I think so. What time?"

"Her game is at eleven," I supply.

"I'll be there."

"Great, thank you," Ellie replies.

"We'll walk you to your truck."

At her truck, Frankie removes my jacket before settling into the driver's seat. It's impossible to miss the outline of her breasts in her sopping wet shirt. I close the door and walk to my car with Ellie.

"I like her, Dad," Ellie shares after buckling her seat belt.

"I do too." No reason for me not to be honest with Ellie. She didn't blanch when she saw me with Frankie, and she was bold enough to invite Frankie to her next game.

Once we arrive home, Ellie cleans up, eats, and then goes to bed. I text Frankie before turning in myself.

Me: I had a nice time on our walk.

Frankie: You mean kissing on the path at the park.

Me: Busted. I'll see you in the morning.

Frankie: Looking forward to it.

Me: I am too. Sweet dreams, Sunshine.

Frankie: Good night.

I plug in my phone, check on Ellie, and turn in for the night with Frankie on my mind.

CHAPTER FIFTEEN

FRANCESCA

We may not have started out normally, but we feel normal. I wake at five and hurry to Sweet Face. Tal will let me in the back. I knock on the door and wait.

"Morning, Frankie. You're early."

"Hi, Tal! Want some help?"

"Already set for this morning. How are you?"

"I'm great! How are you? Why are you here and ready for the day so early?"

"You like him," Tal states.

I smile. "I more than like him. I crave time with him. Every time I see him, I want more. You didn't answer my question, Tal."

"Holden is up for early release in a few months."

"How do you feel about it?" Tal's marriage was fine until the bar fight. They seemed genuinely happy. He asked for the divorce after his conviction. Holden refused to tie her down since his sentence was ten years. I don't understand how he's being granted early release after barely five.

"Honestly, I'm not sure. I only agreed to the divorce because it's what he wanted. I understood his position; now I'm not so sure it was the right choice."

"I'm here if you want to talk more, but it's time to open the front door."

"Thanks, Frankie. You're the best friend a girl could ever ask for."

"You're welcome. I could say the same for you." I follow Talia to the front of the store and take my seat near the window. It isn't long after Tommy and Ellie join me for breakfast too. Soon they rush off to work and school while I trudge to my office. No reason for the end of breakfast to be upsetting except my time with them is over for now. How quickly it happened shocks me.

After greeting Eric, I plow through my dreaded administrative tasks and then review the proposed planning calendar Eric created. My attention is pulled away when my phone chimes.

Tommy: Can I bring anything tonight?

Me: You.

Tommy: Can do. Six?

Me: That works.

Tommy: What is your address?

Me: LOL. My address would be helpful. 1200 Watercliff Terrace.

Tommy: See you then.

I sigh and force myself to focus until it's time to go home and start cooking. I eat a sandwich and some chips I brought for lunch. I meet with Eric about his proposed calendar, and after a few tweaks, it's set for the fall cleanup. Soon I'll be able to stay home most days. I'm actually looking forward to it a bit. My home office is more suited for large project work. A large project is still wishful thinking, I suppose.

After three, Eric buzzes me. "Frankie, Ellie Thornton is here to see you."

What is Ellie doing here? How did she get here? I hurry to reception, escort her to my office, and close the door.

"Hi, Ellie. Are you okay?" I barely resist the urge to check her out. She looks shaken but not hurt.

She nods, sinks into one of the chairs, and her backpack falls to the floor. I wonder if she's like Lia and will share if I wait her out. I'm racking my brain trying to recall their parenting schedule. It's Wednesday, so Ellie should be going to her mom's after school.

"What happened, Ellie?" My voice is smooth and steady despite the worry I feel.

"My mom wasn't at home. She's always home. The living room and dining room are trashed. When Dad wasn't available, I wanted you."

Oh my heart. I care about you too. "Ellie."

She doesn't look at me.

"Ellie, please look at me."

Her eyes lift to mine. It's been a while since I was a teenager, but the look on her face is unmistakable. Fear, concern, and anger stare back at me.

"I'm not upset. In fact, I'm glad you trust me enough already to come here. Where is your mom's house? How did you get here?"

She provides me with an address. Its's a little less than two miles from here. "I walked. It isn't far. I walk to Double Scoops with my friends during the summer from Mom's."

The ice cream shop is further away from her house past my office. I nod. "Did you go inside?"

"When I opened the door and saw the mess, I locked the door and sat on the front stoop for a bit. Then I tried Dad."

There's no reason for me to pry any further. "We need to get a hold of your dad."

She nods and dials while I text him at the same time.

Me: Ellie is here at my office. She appears to be physically fine. Call me please.

"Hi, Melissa. It's Ellie. Is my dad free? No, it isn't urgent." I can't hear Melissa's response, but Ellie replies, "Okay, please tell him I'm with Frankie at her office."

Despite Ellie's assurance to Melissa, it is urgent. Either someone broke into the house or Tess was involved in an altercation of some kind. Honestly, I can't say which one is accurate. Ellie's ringtone breaks into my thoughts.

"Hi, Dad. I'm fine. I walked to Frankie's office. I saw the name on her truck last night. Okay." After a deep breath, she shares Tommy's side of the conversation. "He was on the phone with his lawyer about tomorrow's mediation. He said he'll be here in about an hour."

"No problem. Any chance you have a ball in your bag?"

A small smile curves at the corner of her mouth. "It's rare for me not to have a ball. Why?"

"Come on. There's a decent-size grassy area in the back." I scribble a note for Tommy and tape it to the door. I glance at my phone and note a text from Tommy as we exit the building. The preview has *Thank you* in all caps. Once we have enough space, we start passing back and forth.

A while later, we make a temporary goal out of two garbage pails. Ellie asks, "How did you know this would help?"

"It worked for me when I was your age. I may not have experience with divorced parents, but I do remember being a teenage girl. It wasn't always fun."

"No, it isn't, especially the divorced parents part."

She tries to dribble around me, but I steal the ball, drag it back, and score. I'm quiet, hoping she'll keep talking.

"My parents are great separately, and they're civil to one another, at least when I'm around. Most of my friends can't say that. Dad goes to my games even when it's Mom's time. I hope it isn't a problem. Saturday I'll be with my mom." I shake my head, and she continues. "Even before Michael became my stepdad, I knew my parents weren't going to get back together. Now I realize Dad was protecting me. You're different, aren't you?" She stops the ball and looks up at me.

These are mature observations for a twelve-year-old. I suppose balancing between two households isn't easy and offers some hard life lessons. I'm treading lightly because I don't know how much Tommy has shared with her. "I can't speak about anyone your dad dated before we met. He was upfront about being divorced and you right after I agreed to a date. I think he was protecting both of you by sharing from the very beginning."

"Makes sense." She keeps talking as we pass and dribble the soccer ball. "I'm worried. Mom is doing some out-of-character things lately. She didn't come back from house hunting. She wasn't home when I got there, and it's trashed." Now Ellie is repeatedly rolling the ball under her feet while she talks.

"Like?" Again I try to interject as little as possible.

"Each little thing may not make sense, but overall... It started to change when Michael was promoted at work. There were more parties, which means more shopping for my mom. It also means sometimes I'm at home alone during Mom's parenting time so she can attend with Michael. She keeps trying to be younger. Her beauty regime is insane, and she has standing appointments for manicures and pedicures as well as root cover-up. It's as if the person she was three years ago when they met isn't good enough anymore."

I don't even know how to answer this one. Thankfully, I don't have to. Tommy chooses this moment to join us.

Ellie runs over to him and throws her arms around his neck. "I didn't know where else to go. I was scared. I'm still scared. Is Mom okay?" She releases him and steps back a bit.

Tommy reaches for my hand, draws me close, and presses a kiss to my temple. "I'm not angry. I'm glad you felt comfortable enough to seek out Frankie. When you went inside, was it only a mess or was anything missing?"

I see where he's going with this, and it's scary. There are so many scenarios in this situation, none of which are innocuous. Unfortunately, Luca's career rubbed off on me a bit. I tighten my fingers in his.

"I only opened the door, noticed the mess, and called out for Mom once. When she didn't answer, I closed the front door. I didn't notice if anything was missing. I'm sorry," Ellie mumbles.

"No problem. As far as your mom, I don't have any answers for you. I called her before I left my office and got her voice mail. She knows you're safe with us. I asked her to call as soon as she can," Tommy informs Ellie.

"Can we go to Hops and Barley for dinner?" Ellie asks.

Tommy glances in my direction, and I dip my head slightly. Though Ellie will likely eat the meal I planned, the romantic aspect will probably be weird for the three of us.

"I don't see why not," Tommy answers her.

"Maybe I wasn't clear. Will you come, Frankie?"

"Sure. Thank you for inviting me."

Ellie throws her arms around me and squeezes tight. "Thank you for listening," she whispers.

"I always will," I whisper back. She tightens her hold even more.

"Ellie, why don't you grab your bag, and we can head out?" Tommy suggests.

She retrieves her ball and dribbles to the office door.

"I think I should call my brother and get some insight into what happened today."

"Meaning?"

"I'm not sure what the right thing to do is right now. Tess could be injured or worse in the house, for example."

"I hadn't really considered that. Okay, please call."

I pull out my phone and dial Luca.

"Hey, sis. Everything good?"

"Hi. I'm fine. I have a question though. A guy I started seeing recently has a daughter from his first marriage. After school today, she went to her mom's and the place was trashed. When she called out, her mom didn't answer. She didn't enter, closed the door, waited for thirty minutes and then came to my office. Her father called her mother but got her voice mail. Is there anything else we should be doing? Should we call the authorities?"

"Assuming there was no evidence of forced entry or physical harm, there isn't anything else to do right now. You could call the police, but they likely won't do anything immediately given her mother is an adult."

"Okay, I figured as much."

"I assume the daughter has a safe place to go with her father until her mom is located," Luca states.

"Yes, she does."

"Okay, I gotta go. Let me know if anything changes. Love you."

"Love you too. Be safe."

I relay what I learned from Luca to Tommy. "Well, that's slightly comforting. Honestly, I'm surprised Ellie didn't call on her own when she got to the house. There are no words to explain how I feel right now. I knew you were different, but I... Even Ellie sees it. The best I can do right now is thank you for being... well, you."

I set my finger on his lips. "I meant what I said. I care about both of you."

"I believed you. Seeing it happen is entirely different."

I rise on my toes and kiss him softly. His response indicates my light peck isn't enough right now. He takes over, and his kiss is grateful, passionate, and possessive. It's all-consuming, and it takes restraint not to untuck his shirt and glide my hands over his skin.

"We should stop and get going."

A low growl vibrates between us. He pulls back and whispers near the shell of my ear, "I don't want to. I want more." His eyes meet mine.

"I do too, but now isn't the time."

"It could have been."

"I know. I'm not going anywhere. Let's get some dinner." My reply has both truth and longing threaded together.

He brushes his lips across mine, links our hands, and walks me to the office.

CHAPTER SIXTEEN

THOMAS

My emotions are scattered: anger at Tess, concern for Tess, pride Ellie handled herself responsibly, elation Ellie feels safe with Frankie, and optimism Frankie is all she seems to be. The only drawback I see at this moment is our date was replaced by dinner with the three of us.

That isn't true. Figuring out what is going on with Tess is an issue as well. We meet Ellie in Frankie's office and leave for the restaurant.

When we arrive, a tall, brunette server hugs Frankie. "Hi, I'm Lia, her youngest sister. You must be Tommy." Lia shamelessly checks me out on her sister's behalf.

"Guilty. Nice to meet another sister."

"Another?" Lia questions me.

"Yes, I met Lily at the field last night."

"You must be Ellie. I've heard so much about both of you. Follow me, I have an open table."

Ellie's face brightens a little and she replies, "Hi."

Frankie simply shakes her head as we follow Lia. I love that she has a bunch of siblings too. It's something I wanted for Ellie. Maybe it could still happen.

"I'll give you guys a few minutes." Lia leaves after sharing a few things with Frankie without words.

"Do you have a code with all of your siblings?" I ask Frankie.

She smiles and nods.

"Care to share your youngest sister's opinion of us?" I point between myself and Ellie.

Frankie leans in to answer me. "She only mentioned you, and now isn't an appropriate time to share her opinion." A pink flush graces her cheeks.

"Don't get embarrassed now," I whisper.

"Not embarrassed, I'm not used to having someone worth checking out in my sister's opinion."

I press a kiss to her lips. "I'm happy to be that guy." Our hands link beneath the table.

Lia returns and takes our order. While we snack on chips and salsa, Ellie is quiet. There's nothing else I can do about this situation right now. I've called Tess, left messages, and informed her Ellie is safe with me. I even considered calling Michael but decided against it.

"Hi, Ells." A booming voice pulls me out of my head.

"Uncle Remi. Aunt Eva." She jumps up and hugs both. "Join us. We have plenty of room." Ellie scoots further down the booth.

I catch Remi's eye and nod. "Frankie, this is my best friend, Remi, and his girlfriend, Eva. Guys, Frankie."

"Nice to meet you," Eva acknowledges Frankie.

"You as well."

Lia returns and takes their order as well.

"So, Frankie, what are your intentions for my best friend here?" Remi puts her on the spot.

Many times over the two decades, I've wanted to strangle Remi for some bonehead comment. This question might take the cake.

"You don't have to answer," I interject to protect her.

"Yes, she does," Remi counters.

I notice Ellie is listening intently but feigning disinterest at the same time.

Frankie tightens her fingers in mine under the table. "My intentions are to get to know him and Ellie and build from there."

Not bad, Frankie.

"I like you. I can work with that. Please know I would grill anyone who wants to date him after the other failed dates."

"He's telling the truth. Remi is protective of his bestie," Eva adds.

"I would expect nothing less from the almost lifelong best friend. It's great Tommy has someone like Remi in his life. Everyone needs a protector at some point. I'm not offended. Two of my sisters have already done the same."

"How many sisters do you have?" Ellie asks.

Lia delivers our food and refills our drinks.

"I have three sisters and a brother."

"Wow, like my uncles and my aunt but reversed," Ellie compares.

"It is actually. When I was younger, it was craziness, but now it's controlled crazy."

Remi and Eva take turns questioning Frankie. She handles each one with grace and comedy. Even though she answers the questions, she's parsed her response carefully. The five of us eat the delicious burgers and sweet potato fries. Frankie, Ellie, and Eva beg off dessert. After hugs goodbye, Remi and Eva hop into their car and drive off. Arm in arm, the three of us walk to Frankie's truck.

"I'll call you later."

She nods and kisses me lightly. "Good night. Bye, Ellie."

"Good night, Frankie."

I close her door and walk to my car with Ellie. My phone chimes in my pocket on the drive home. Ellie doesn't say anything until we reach our driveway.

"Thank you for not being mad at me."

Her, no. Tess, definitely. I inhale sharply and turn to look at her. "You didn't do anything wrong. I haven't said so yet, but I'm proud of you. You handled an unforeseen circumstance well today."

"I'm scared for Mom. I'm sure it's weird for you now with Frankie in your life, but it's how I feel."

"Please share how you feel regardless of how I might feel, especially about your mom. We may not be married anymore, but I still care about her. I'm worried too. The last few weeks, she has been acting…."

"Odd," Ellie supplies.

"I agree. As far as Frankie, my feelings for her are different from your mom."

Ellie nods. "Were they ever the same?"

No. "At the time, I thought they were. Now, I'm not sure."

"I knew Frankie would be there for me if I showed up, even in the short time I've known her."

"I'm glad. Let's go inside. You have school tomorrow."

As we walk to the door, Ellie mumbles something.

"Ellie?"

"Will she show up tomorrow?" she repeats.

I shrug. Truly, I don't have an answer for my daughter who I'm sure has so many more questions than she's asking. "I hope so." That's only a partial truth. If she does show up, we might be able to make progress. If she doesn't, I might be able to get her motion dismissed. "If you want to talk more after you change and prepare for tomorrow, I'm here."

"Thanks, Dad. Love you more."

"You're welcome. Love you most," I call after she turns upstairs. Leaning against the cold, granite countertop, I pull out my phone.

Remi: Was everything okay? Why was Ellie with you?

Remi: I like Frankie. I'm happy for you.

Remi: It's Eva. What he said. LOL.

I reply about what occurred today and share I like her too. It's more than like, but Remi and Eva don't need to be fully in my thoughts. Frankie embodies everything I'm looking for in a partner. She cares for me and Ellie. Tonight, she willingly gave up a romantic dinner for burgers with my daughter after pushing off the same date for her business goals. She's ambitious, smart, and has a huge heart. The rush of kissing her is more than I've ever experienced. Francesca Cappelli in my arms is unmatched. A rush I want to chase every day.

I climb the stairs and peek in on Ellie. She's curled up with a book in her window seat. "Hey, you all set for the morning?"

"Yup. I'm going to come here after school. I don't want to go back alone until everything is settled."

"Okay, I'll make sure Mom knows. I'm proud of you Ellie. Love you more."

"Thanks. Love you most."

I turn, and Ellie calls me back. "Dad?"

"Yeah."

She pauses as if she needs to share her thoughts carefully. "Is it weird for me to like you and Frankie together? Is it bad I really like her and want to spend time with her too?"

Oh, Ellie. I step into her room and sit beside her at the window seat. It also gives me some time to collect my thoughts. Half of me is ecstatic my daughter likes the woman I'm dating. Dating doesn't feel adequate, but it isn't important right now. The other half is sad she's concerned about her mother's feelings, especially given her recent choices. "I appreciate you see Frankie makes me happy. She does." *Very much so.* "I'm glad you like her as well. I hoped you would. It's completely normal for you to feel torn between your mom and Frankie. Maybe it would be helpful to think of Frankie more like a bonus mom instead of a replacement. Don't you have similar feelings for Michael?" That was harder to ask than I anticipated.

"Not really. He isn't around a lot. When he is, he's in his office or out with Mom at some fancy event." I didn't know any of that. It's what Tess wanted, the monstrous house, executive parties complete with the jewels, clothes, and spa treatments. It surprises me I didn't see her materialistic aspirations earlier when we were married.

"Your feelings are normal, and thank you for sharing."

She nods and hugs me. Getting through the divorce was hard enough when Ellie was six. This at twelve, with everything else she's going through, is a lot for both of us.

"Good night, Dad."

"Night, Ellie." I shuffle down the hall, change, head back downstairs to the patio, and place a call.

Frankie answers almost instantly. "Hi."

"Hi. I'm sorry about dinner."

"It's fine. Ellie needed you more than I did tonight."

"Really?" I'm not buying it.

She exhales sharply. "I wanted to spend time with you, and I did. Would I have preferred to be alone in a private place? Yes, without question. You have no control over Tess's actions. It isn't your fault."

"Sunshine, you're one of a kind."

"Thank you. How is she?"

"She's worried about Tess and anxious to go back there after school tomorrow. Ellie informed me she's coming here until everything is settled."

"It makes sense. Have you heard from Tess?"

"No, nothing."

"Can I pry a little?"

"Ask away. I don't have anything to hide."

She pauses a bit too long.

"Frankie?"

"Yeah, I'm here. Has she done something like this before?"

"That's prying?" I chuckle softly. "Not like this, no. She has only missed one other time she was supposed to be with Ellie in the last six years. She was at the hospital with her best friend whose husband just died from a widow-maker heart attack. However, both Ellie and I agree Tess has been acting odd lately. Nothing substantial, only a bunch of trivial things that are out of character."

"Will she be there tomorrow?"

"I hope so. I want some resolution for Ellie. Me too, if I'm being honest. I don't like the upheaval in my life."

Frankie exhales again.

"What, Sunshine?"

"Would you like me to come tomorrow?"

This moment right here is where Francesca Cappelli set herself far beyond every expectation I had in my future partner. "You have no idea what that means to me."

"I do because you would offer the same support to me if the situation were reversed."

She's absolutely correct. "As much as I would like to say yes, the mediation is limited to the parties and counsel only."

"Oh."

The sheer disappointment in her voice makes me want to go to her. "Will you be at the office?"

"Yes, for the morning at least. Things are slowing down a bit."

"I'll find you once we're through."

"Okay. I hope Tess shows up."

"Me too. Thank you for today, Frankie."

"You're welcome. Bye."

I stare at my phone until the screen goes black. Rather than ponder tomorrow any longer, I step inside, find the keys I need, and pull on some shoes. I'm out the door without my phone before I realize it.

CHAPTER SEVENTEEN

FRANCESCA

I would give almost anything to have met them sooner. If we had, I would be able to check on them in person. *Sigh.* I set my glass into the sink. My phone chimes in my hand.

Tommy: It's Ellie. I didn't have your number. Are you still up?

Me: Hi. Are you okay? Is your dad?

Tommy: We're physically fine, but I think he needs to see you.

Me: Why?

Tommy: He went into his shop. He only does goes to the workshop when he's upset.

Me: Okay. Give me your address.

Tommy: Thank you. I'm going to add your number to my phone and delete these.

Worried about Tommy but happy Ellie texted, I pull on a hoodie and some tennis shoes. Within twenty minutes, I'm walking around Tommy's house to his shop in the backyard. I wave to Ellie who said she would be in the upstairs window. I take a deep breath and knock on the door.

"Frankie. What are you doing here?"

I step inside his sanctuary. The smell of wood and varnish permeates the air. There's a large table saw and lumber meticulously organized around the edges of the large auxiliary building.

"A little birdie might have texted me and mentioned you were upset." I slide my arms around him and lift my gaze to his.

"I thought she was asleep already. I usually wait to come out here."

"This explains the callouses on your hands."

He nods.

"Do you want to talk or work?"

"Neither." He brings his lips to mine and takes a searing but oh-so-perfect kiss. In less than a minute, he pushes me against the workbench and unzips my hoodie, casting it to the floor. My nipples are taut and visible through the thin T-shirt.

"No bra?" While I'm not well-endowed, a bra is generally necessary when I leave my house.

"I was worried. It takes too much time."

His rough hands slide along my arms, intertwine our fingers, and raise them above my head. Gripping the hem of my shirt, he lifts it over my head, depositing it atop my hoodie on the dusty floor. His large hands cover my breasts and knead in turn. *That feels...* Craving his kiss is one thing, but the ache I feel extends to his touch too. I draw my hands down his corded biceps and dip my hands beneath his shirt. His abs contract beneath my fingers, and my palms warm against his skin. My first impressions of him were off, way off. Not only are his arms sculpted, but the rest of him might be too.

"Sunshine," he murmurs, moves his arm around my waist, and lifts me.

My legs wrap around his trim waist. In three strides, he sits in a wooden chair near the back corner of the workshop. He drops kisses along my jaw, down the curve of my neck, savoring the valley between my breasts before ravaging them equally.

"Tommy." The sensations coursing through me just from his talented mouth are excruciating. I can only imagine when his mouth savors other, more intimate parts of my body.

His hands curve around my shoulders from behind, supporting me as he moves lower. He nips around my navel, sending spikes of need between my thighs. My heated core inches closer and closer to his impressive length as he moves south. When he reaches the waistband of my leggings, he begins climbing upward. Containing my disappointment is impossible.

"Here is not the place to savor you properly," he says against my belly.

Well damn! "Doesn't mean you shouldn't know how I feel right now." My voice comes out unintentionally smoky.

His response vibrates against my skin as he nips along my rib cage and drags his tongue along my lips before plunging into my mouth again. We explore, stroke, and grope one another freely until we're breathless and panting. Once sitting, I tug his shirt up. *Holy crap!* The ripples and ridges of his eight-pack are droolworthy. I take too long ogling him.

"Sunshine?"

"You have been holding out on me."

He smiles. It's a shy one but panty melting at the same time. "We haven't exactly been alone much."

"True, when do you work out?"

"Every morning. I have a full gym in the basement. Is that really why you lifted my shirt?"

I shake my head, hold his shirt with one hand, and lower my chest against his. I wrap my arms around him as he does the same. A contented sigh falls from my lips. The contrast of his sculpted chest against my breasts is sheer decadence.

"You fit perfectly in my arms."

"Mm-hmm," I murmur against his neck. Even well into the evening, he smells delicious. His cologne is fresh and clean at the same time.

We're quiet for quite some time. "Thank you for coming."

I always will. It's crazy soon for me to feel this way. Isn't it? "You're welcome. Why didn't you ask me to come over?"

"I've never navigated a life with a tweenager, an ex-wife, court hearings, and a relationship with a sexy business owner at the same time. I'm unsure how to pull it all off."

I press a kiss to the hollow of his collarbone and lift my head, adding a little space between us. It's almost enough to leave me feeling bereft from the loss of his body against mine. "I'm here. I want to listen and help where I can or where it's allowed. More precisely, I want to be with you. I know it includes all of those things, but I understand."

"I want to be with you too, but it isn't as easy as I thought it would be."

"Meaning?"

"I don't like to keep bringing her up, but if Tess were acting as Ellie's mom, my schedule would be less crazy. Please don't misunderstand, I prefer having Ellie with me full time, and I miss her when she's with Tess, but I would have time to woo and date you properly."

"You're doing fine."

"Then you're a saint."

"Hardly, I'm realistic. I said yes to a date knowing you have a daughter. My response isn't going to change because it got harder. I'll happily take whatever time you have while you figure out things for Ellie." A slight breeze flows through the open door, and I shiver.

"Want to go inside?"

"No. I want to stay here in your arms."

He laughs softly. "I'll hold you as long as you want—inside where it's warmer."

I brush my lips across his before replying, "Deal." I redress while he makes sure everything is unplugged. "What do you build?"

"Lots of things: benches, planters, picnic tables, and bookshelves. I also built my bedroom set."

"That's amazing!"

"Thanks. Let's get you warmed up." He throws his arm around me and leads me inside after locking the workshop.

His home is cozier than I would expect for a bachelor. It's probably Ellie's touch. The woodwork looks original and well kept. Tommy leads me straight to the couch. He stretches out on the chaise and invites me to join him. I sidle against him with my head on his chest and one leg thrown over his. He covers both of us with a blanket from the back of the couch. Within minutes, Tommy is sound asleep. I consider whether to stay here or go home. I decide to stay, given the late hour and my desire to sleep wrapped in his embrace.

The next thing I hear is "Frankie," along with a gentle nudge.

"Morning, Ellie." *Ellie?* It takes me a moment to regain my bearings.

"Where's Dad?"

"Good question. He was right here. We fell asleep while we were talking. Working out, maybe?"

As if a lightbulb went off in her head, she says, "I didn't check the basement." She scampers away.

I take stock of myself. Still fully dressed in last night's clothes. Luckily, my braided hair isn't a rat nest this morning.

After completing the check, Ellie returns. "Success," she indicates.

"Good. Can you direct me to the bathroom?"

"Sure, use Dad's. Mine needs to be cleaned. It's the chore I hate the most. The master is upstairs, last door on the right."

"Thanks."

"Frankie?"

"Yeah?"

"Thank you for coming when I texted."

"Thank you for letting me know." I rise, drape the blanket on the back of the couch, and climb the stairs. When he mentioned he built his bedroom set, I was intrigued. Now, I'm floored. It's gorgeous. If I had to guess, I would say a queen-size, mission-style bed with matching dresser and chest of drawers as well as two night tables. This must have taken a long time. The bedding is navy with black accents.

I step into the bathroom, close the door, and freshen up. Dark gray Carrara tile mark the walk-in shower. There's a soaker tub and a large double vanity. I undo the braid and finger comb my hair after brushing my teeth with my finger. When I step out, I'm confronted with a shirtless, sweat-drenched Tommy. *Holy hell! He's...* My mouth is dry, and heat pools between my thighs.

"Morning."

I'm still pulling my jaw up from the floor, figuratively at least. True, I saw him shirtless last night, but in the light of day, his upper body is exceptional.

"Sunshine?"

"Yeah." *Get it together, Frankie.* "Morning."

He smirks and tugs on a shirt from the bureau. It takes everything in me not to pout.

"Ellie sent me here. I'll get out of your way."

He shakes his head. "She told me. No need to rush out on my account. Did you find everything you need?"

"Didn't look for anything."

"Okay. Why are you flustered?"

"Have you seen yourself in the mirror lately?" He's... built like a Greek god gorgeous.

"I could ask you the same thing."

He closes the gap between us, pushes his fingers into my hair, and kisses me breathless. I lose myself in him the instant his hands or mouth are on me, especially when it's both.

"What time do you need to leave?" I ask.

"I need to leave in about forty minutes or so. Please stay until then. After I drop Ellie off at school, I'm meeting my attorney at her office."

I smile. "Okay. I'll make some coffee while you get ready."

"Thanks. I like having you here in the morning," he whispers before dropping a kiss on my forehead.

"I like being here." I leave his bedroom and return to the kitchen before my need to strip his clothes off and have my way with him takes over—not something we have time for this morning anyway. I join Ellie in the kitchen and, with a little help, successfully make coffee. There's a mixed bouquet of flowers in a vase on the island.

"Thanks, Ellie. Do you need anything?"

"No problem. No, I get school lunch, but thanks."

"You're welcome. Your flowers?"

"Dad sent them to me on Monday."

This man is an amazing father. He might be giving his future son-in-law higher expectations than most. I sip my coffee at the island with Ellie. After I finish my cup, I set one up for Tommy. He joins us in the kitchen dressed in a pinstripe gray suit with a crisp Oxford in a light shade of pink and a gingham plaid tie. He looks hot as hell! *Rein it in, Frankie. You're not alone.*

"Morning, Ellie."

"Hi. Have you heard from Mom?"

"No, sorry, sweetie. Hopefully, I'll know more this morning."

Ellie shakes her head and finishes her bagel. He switches to a travel mug, brews his coffee, and checks his phone again.

"Time to go, Ellie," Tommy informs her.

"Okay, I'll meet you in the car. Bye, Frankie."

"Have a good day, Ellie."

"You too." She grabs Tommy's keys and heads out the front door.

"Are you ready to leave?" He slides his arms around my waist.

I raise an eyebrow.

"You don't have to leave because we are."

"I appreciate your offer, but I need to shower and get to the office for at least the morning. Please call me when you know more."

"Of course." He kisses me softly, threads our fingers, and we leave to start our day. As soon as they drive away, my chest tightens for them.

I'm not sure if Tess showing up is promising or not. I shift into reverse and drive home.

CHAPTER EIGHTEEN

THOMAS

Waking with Frankie, even on my couch, was more comfortable than it should've been given how long I've known her. Ellie is completely silent during the drive to school. I park along the curb, and she hugs me.

"I know you're kind of in the middle, but I don't want to move," she breaks the silence.

"I know. I'll do my best."

She nods, hugs me again, and says, "Love you more, Dad."

"Love you most, Ellie." I watch my daughter head into school with a heavy heart and slumped shoulders.

I'm doing the best I can to protect her, but given her age and Tess's recent choices, it's difficult. The loud honk from behind me forces me to pull away. I drive to my attorney's office and check my messages again.

Remi: Anything from Tess? Good luck today.

Me: No. Thanks.

Toby: Good luck. I'll stop by later after my morning job.

Tamara: Give her hell.

Tamara was never a fan of Tess. My sister doesn't even bother to hide it anymore, especially after the events of the last week.

Tim: Let me know if you need company this afternoon. I have office work today.

I reply to everyone, thanking them. After a moment to gather myself, I step out of the car, and my phone vibrates again.

Frankie: I'm not sure if good luck is appropriate. I'm hoping for progress for you and Ellie.

She speaks to my heart and soul on so many levels. I'm confident we can find our way together despite the current upheaval in my life with Tess.

Me: Thank you. I'll call you.

Frankie: You're welcome.

With a bit more resolve, I head inside to my meet with Antionette Kramer. She's a solo practitioner who handles business and family matters, mostly representing fathers. When I step into the reception area, she's on the phone and waves me into her office.

"Unacceptable. This is her motion. I'll call you back when I get a time to go before the judge, Pat."

That isn't good. The only reason to go before a judge is to ask for a dismissal of Tess's motion. I should be ecstatic, but it'll only prolong this process. Tess will simply file again later. I'm trying my damnedest to be cordial and polite, but her choices this past week give me pause. It's out of character for Tess, but I have no idea what's causing it.

"Good morning, Tommy. The caller was Tess's attorney. She isn't attending the mediation this morning. I already filed a notice with the clerk to see what time we can go before the judge today to get her motion dismissed."

"Okay. Did her attorney indicate why she doesn't plan on showing up?"

Antionette shakes her head. "No, merely the fact she couldn't make it this morning."

"Her behavior over the last week is unacceptable."

"Such as?" my attorney inquiries.

I recap the events of the last week and the impact on Ellie since the last time I spoke with my attorney. Antionette is furiously scribbling on a notepad as I speak. "Also, when you speak with her attorney, could you inquire if she plans to return soon? Ellie is going to need access to Tess's house to get things for soccer and other personal items. She has a key, but I don't want to go there without permission."

She makes a note. "What is your schedule today?"

"I took the day off, so let me know where you need me to be and when," I assure her.

"I'll be in touch. Ideally, the judge will have an opening right after lunch."

"What time will that be?"

"They take the bench at two."

"I'll make arrangements for Ellie."

She turns to look at me fully. Appraising me. "Can I be honest?"

I nod.

"You're my first father client who truly put his child first and wasn't trying to stick it to their ex. It's admirable, and I wish more of them were like you."

"Thank you." I rise from the chair. "Let me know when you hear back."

She replies, and I leave her office. I'm more unsettled than I was before. True, I want the motion to go away. It'll make Ellie happy to stay with me full time, and me too if I'm being honest. Yet I'm worried about Tess. It's a conflicting feeling. I'll always care about Tess as Ellie's mom, but beyond that, not so much. My feelings for Frankie are overwhelming, and I must admit, I like it. It's different from the young lust I shared with Tess.

I call Tess and leave another voice mail asking her to contact me about Ellie, not the motion. I place a call to Ellie's school and add Frankie to the dismissal list, just in case. I also text Remi to see if he is available to keep Ellie company on Saturday night in case Tess doesn't return. He replies quickly in the affirmative. I shift into drive and meander who knows where.

As usual, when I need to clear my head and I'm not near my workshop, I find myself at the shore. Since I'm dressed in a suit, I stay on the grassy area of Short Sands Beach. There's no sand beneath my feet, but it'll do for now. This time though Frankie is in my thoughts as well. She's always present even when things in her life aren't going as planned. As if on cue, she texts me.

Frankie: I hope you can agree to what Ellie needs.

Sunshine. It's the perfect term of endearment for her. She's happy, positive, and sees the world as it is—full of choices, not conflicts.

Me: Where are you?

Frankie: Home.

Me: Can I come over?

Frankie: Always.

I hurry to my car and drive to Frankie's. I park behind her truck and knock on the door. The soft floral scent of her perfume or bodywash surrounds me when she opens it. She's freshly showered, wearing leggings and a running hoodie with her hair still drying.

"Come in."

Once inside I draw her against me, my lips against the curve of her neck.

"It didn't go well?"

I shake my head but don't release her. "It didn't go at all yet. Her attorney said she wasn't showing up. Mine filed a motion to dismiss, which she hopes will be heard this afternoon." I kiss her neck, then her lips before adding some space between us.

"Oh, that's terrible. Is it usually that fast?"

I shrug. "I didn't think to ask. I guess it could be since, if we came to an agreement, we would have to go before the judge to make it official."

"Makes sense."

"If I need to go, would you mind meeting Ellie at home when school lets out?"

"Not at all. She has practice tonight too, right?"

This woman is more than I could've ever asked for. "How do you know that?"

"I realize it's fast and we shouldn't make this much sense yet, but we do. I care about both of you. Knowing her schedule is part of the deal."

"I'm right there with you despite the mess I am right now."

"It's not a mess. It's real life. You have every right to be upset. As much as I would like to try to stay neutral, Tess isn't my favorite person, and I don't know her. I can only imagine how you and Ellie feel."

"Thank you."

She rises on her toes and kisses me softly. "Hungry? I'm not a grilled cheese aficionado, but I can make a mean turkey sandwich."

I smile. "Not hungry, but thanks." I glance around and take in her home. It suits her well. It's comfy but structured. It has the same accents Ellie added to our house—a pillow here, a textured blanket draped there.

"Want to sit outside for a bit?"

I shrug off my jacket, drape it on the back of a chair at the granite island, and follow her outside. Her patio is set up like mine. Right now, the only difference is her laptop is set up on the table.

"Do you have work to do?"

"Not really. Even if I did, I would rather sit with you."

I don't miss the *especially today given what's going on* she didn't say. Like her, I would do the same. Settling into the corner, I open my arms to her. She curls against me, her head resting on her forearms across my chest.

"Do you need to talk or just be?" she asks, her eyes pinned to mine.

"Just be."

She kisses my lips lightly and rests her head on my chest. I surround her with my arms and enjoy the peace she brings to me. Shortly after midday, Antionette calls to share we will be heard this afternoon. As much as I don't want to leave, I press a kiss to Frankie's head before we move inside.

I reach into my jacket pocket, pull out my keys, and twist one off the ring. "Here, this opens the front door. It works in both locks. I think I did both this morning. I'll call you when I know anything."

"Okay. What time will she be home?"

"She gets home just before three," I inform her.

"Practice is at five at the same field, right?"

I nod. "I hope it doesn't take all afternoon, but yes."

"Just in case."

 She's different and willing to parent Ellie too. Sliding my hands to cup her face, I skim my thumb over her lower lip. A sexy sigh falls from her lips as I kiss her. Our kisses have been tender, soft, hard, and even passionate. This one is comforting, as if she will always be beside me when things are tough in life, and not only with Tess. I'm looking forward to more time with her.

"I'll see you both later." I brush another kiss across her lips and step out her front door with a bit more confidence than I had this morning.

CHAPTER NINETEEN

FRANCESCA

After Tommy leaves, I clean up my workspace and pack a bag with an extra hoodie and a blanket for practice. I want to spend time with both of them, so walking at the park suits me fine.

Near two, I leave my townhouse and make a quick stop at the Perk. I grab an iced latte for myself and a few scones for Ellie and me. I pull into the driveway and let myself inside. It feels a bit weird, but I push those concerns away. I'm here for Ellie.

I curl up on the chaise with my book and coffee to wait for Ellie. After a few chapters, I hear a key slide into the front door. Closing the book, I move to the front door, but it isn't Ellie.

"Who are you?"

A tall man with dark hair and similar light eyes to Tommy steps inside. "I'm Toby. You must be Frankie."

"Hi, Tommy's brother, right? Sorry, I was only expecting Ellie." I ignore the warning bells in my head from Luca. The man has a key to the house. He looks similar enough to Tommy, and he knows my name. I kind of dig he's talking about me to his family. No, it's more than kind of; I love it.

"Yes. No problem. Wow, he wasn't lying," Toby replies.

"About?"

"You're beautiful."

"Thank you."

"Is he home?"

I shake my head. "He went back to court this afternoon. He asked me to meet Ellie." As I my finish the sentence, Ellie opens the front door.

"Hi, Elle belle."

"Hi, Uncle Toby. Hi, Frankie."

I see concern on her face. "He asked me to meet you. He's still at court."

"Okay, so it isn't terrible news," Ellie replies.

"No news yet. How was school?" I don't plan on sharing the little bit I know. It could still go either way.

She shrugs and walks into the kitchen.

I follow her and ask, "Do you have any homework?"

"Nope."

"Want to kick outside?"

She nods and runs upstairs.

"You have any soccer skills, Toby?" I inquire of him.

From upstairs, Ellie shouts, "Absolutely none, but it's fun to watch him try."

Toby smirks and hangs his head.

"Okay then."

The three of us head outside to the backyard. Ellie pulls a goal out from behind the workshop. I team up with Toby against Ellie. She's holding her own against the two of us. To be fair, her assessment was correct; Toby is awful. Despite the goings on with her parents, Ellie is laughing and cheering while we shoot around in her yard. The smile on her face is worth the fact I'm exhausted now. Apparently, landscaping shape doesn't equal soccer shape.

"Do you eat before practice or after?" I ask while she retrieves the errant kick Toby made.

"After."

"Good, then we have a few more minutes."

Ellie dribbles around Toby, and he lands on his butt. I hear a hearty laugh from behind me. Ellie too. She stops dribbling and runs to hug her dad.

"So?"

"Let's clean up, head inside, and we can talk."

Ellie frowns. "Is it bad?"

"I'm not sure how you'll feel about it."

She nods, and Toby helps her put the goal away. I approach him, kiss him, and pull away much too soon.

"Thank you for being here. I forgot to mention Toby might stop by. I'm sorry."

"No worries. So I heard from a certain little brother of yours you might have mentioned me."

"Oh no! What did he say?"

I smile. "Nothing bad."

Relief streaks across his face, but I see his mind working on what he may have said to Toby. I'm more curious now. Ellie and Toby interrupt, and we head inside.

"Come on, Dad. Spill," Ellie urges.

"For now, the relocation motion has been dismissed. However, your mom can refile it later."

"Okay. Where is she now?"

He takes Ellie's hand in his. "I still don't have any more information than I shared with you. Mom didn't show up this morning. I learned she wasn't coming from her lawyer."

"Is she okay?" Ellie whispers as her shoulders fall.

Oh my heart. Not only does Tommy wear his heart on his sleeve, so does Ellie.

"As far as I know, she contacted her lawyer to say she wasn't coming."

Her shoulders fall further before she speaks again. "If she can call the lawyer, why can't she call me or you back? It doesn't make sense. Does she even want me around?"

Tommy pulls Ellie into a hug. After a few seconds, she pulls me in as well. I look at Tommy. His expression screams heartbreak and hope at the same time. Heartbreak from her statement but hope of her acceptance of me. Ellie releases us both.

"Still up for practice?" Tommy asks.

"No choice. I want to start on Saturday against the Renegades, except…"

"Except what?" Concern laces Tommy's voice.

"I don't have my uniform here. What if Mom doesn't come home in time?"

"I'm coordinating with the lawyers to take you to her place to get whatever you need."

"Is it still trashed?"

"I don't know. Okay?"

"Yup, I'll get ready," Ellie hustles upstairs.

"Damn, bro! That's heavy," Toby admits.

Tommy takes a few deep breaths before replying, "Yes, it is."

"I'm going to head home. It was a pleasure meeting you, Frankie."

"You as well."

Tommy walks Toby to the door, and I overhear, "Don't screw up, big bro."

"Don't plan on it."

We leave for Ellie's practice with barely enough time to get there. She hurries to the field while we walk around the park hand in hand. It's a bit brisk, so I'm glad I brought my hoodie. Plus, leaning into Tommy isn't a hardship at all.

"Do you want to talk more?"

He shrugs. "I'm torn. While my attorney got the motion thrown out, Tess can refile. Her refiling doesn't concern me as much as her failure to return from Connecticut and the boarding school threat. I may not be married to Tess anymore, but something is wrong. The problem is I don't know what. Is it her choosing Michael over Ellie or something worse like a problem with someone from Michael's job?"

"What does your gut tell you?" I urge him.

He shakes his head. "This is about Michael. Before him, she never failed to show up for parenting time. We were more communicative than we were when we slept side by side. I highly doubt boarding school was Tess's idea. Too many things don't add up."

I tighten my fingers in his.

"Let's talk about something else," he suggests.

I raise an eyebrow. "Such as?"

"I like waking with you nestled in my arms in the morning."

I smile. "I do too. What is the plan for Saturday, or is it up in the air because of Tess?"

"You're truly one of a kind. I asked Remi and Eva to hang out with Ellie."

"Okay. Where are we going?"

"We're going to dinner at *Château Franc*."

It's nearly impossible to get reservations there. "I'm looking forward to it."

He leans near the shell of my ear. As he moves closer, my body heats despite the chilly air. "So am I."

We walk in silence for a bit and reach the end of the path. Turning back toward the field, Tommy inhales sharply. "I don't have words to express my gratitude for you and Talia."

"Talia?"

He laughs. "If it weren't for her, would we be here right now?"

I smirk at him. "Eventually, probably. She did expedite our meeting though."

"I've never met anyone like you. You see me. You see Ellie. Most importantly, you see me and Ellie as a unit but separately as well. You're a rare woman, and I'm grateful Talia makes fun of you on your coffee cup."

"Me too."

We meander our way back to our vehicles. Before Ellie wraps up, we share a toe-curling, melt-into-a-puddle-of-goo kiss that is barely appropriate for our surroundings.

"You can't kiss me like that here."

A twinkle materializes in his eyes. "Why not?"

"It makes me want more."

A devilish grin grows on his face. "I want more with you—soon."

Sweet mercy! All I can do is nod, clamp my eyes closed, and clench my thighs together. Ellie joins us, and we each head home separately.

CHAPTER TWENTY

THOMAS

We hurry through our morning routine, and I barely get Ellie to school on time. It seems the morning after practice is tougher than the rest. My inbox is overflowing from only one day away from my office. Near eleven, I take a break and try Tess again. As the phone rings, I repeatedly remind myself not to get angry. Surprisingly, she answers.

"Hi, Tess."

"Hi, Tommy." Her voice sounds steady and calm. "I talked to my lawyer. You can take Ellie to the house to get whatever she needs for her game. I hope to be back soon."

"Thank you, Tess. What's soon?" I'm gathering information to share with Ellie.

"Hopefully, I'll be home by the time school ends on Monday."

"Okay. Could you return Ellie's call tonight? She needs to hear from you."

"I'll do my best."

I consider not asking this next question, but for Ellie, I do anyway. "I know it isn't my place anymore, but are you okay?"

I'm greeted with silence.

"Tess?"

"I'm fine." The signature female response that generally means anything but fine.

Yet we aren't a couple anymore. Therefore, I don't have the ability to read into her response.

"I realize you have Michael now, but if you need help, Tess, please reach out."

I would almost swear I hear Tess choke back a sob. "Thank you. I'm fine."

If I learned anything during our marriage, pushing Tess more would be a mistake. "You're welcome. I'll take Ellie after school today for her things. Bye, Tess."

"Goodbye, Tommy."

The call ends while I still have the phone against my ear. I have no idea what to make of Tess and her responses to my questions. She didn't even mention the motion or its dismissal. Her behavior is unsettling. Tess is a lot of things, but insecure and unsure of her choices doesn't fit well.

All I want right now is Frankie. It makes absolutely no sense. A call with my ex-wife ends with no definitive resolution of current issues, and I want to call the woman I'm dating. I'm drawn to her despite the turmoil in my life. She makes me happy being herself. Her effect on me is complete and rare. Before I overthink it, I call her.

"Hi. How is your morning?" Her voice is cheery and soothing.

"Hi. So-so. I missed seeing you this morning."

"Me too. Do you want to talk about it?"

I shake my head even though she can't see me. "Not really. I needed to hear your voice."

Frankie is silent a bit too long.

"Sunshine?"

"I'm here."

I can only imagine the thoughts going through her mind. What would make me need to talk to her but not actually talk to her? "I should get back to my work before I pick up Ellie. I'll call you tonight."

"Okay. Please say hi to Ellie for me." Her reply sounds resigned and slightly dejected.

"I will. Bye." For a moment, I felt better. Now I wonder if it was the right choice given how she sounded. I push my mixed feelings away for now and return to my office.

"Mr. Thornton, Linda would like to see you in her office," my assistant informs me.

"Thanks." I turn on my heel and walk to her office.

She waves me in before I can even knock. "Please have a seat."

I take a seat, and she pushes a stack of papers in my direction. "The committee has made a decision regarding the Cooper project."

I'm an idiot! She thinks it was about Cooper when it was about Tess.

"Could you give me one minute?"

"Sure."

I whip out my phone and text Frankie.

Me: I'm sorry. I'm an idiot. My morning has nothing to do with you or Cooper. I talked to Tess. Actually talked.

Frankie: So you don't have bad news for me?

Me: No, I don't know the board's choice yet.

Frankie: You're forgiven and not an idiot. You have a lot on your plate.

Me: You amaze me, Sunshine.

Frankie: I could say the same for you. TTYL.

Me: TTYL.

I return my attention to Linda. "Thank you."

"You're welcome. I don't want details, but did you make progress yesterday at mediation?"

"Only to the extent I got her motion dismissed for now."

Linda nods curtly. "I understand. I've been there. Let me know when you need more time off for court."

I wasn't aware Linda went through custody issues with her ex. Outwardly, everything seemed to be going smoothly. "I will. What can I do for you?"

"Ah, yes, here's the final decision packet for the Cooper project. The committee narrowed it down to Sunshine Landscape and Design and Fister late Monday. Given your new relationship with Miss Cappelli, we excluded you purposely to avoid any indication of impropriety."

I nod, and my entire body tenses when she mentions Frankie's company.

"After an anonymous ballot, Sunshine Landscape has been awarded the Cooper project. We made the decision yesterday while you were out of the office."

I'm so excited for her! "Thank you. I appreciate it."

"You're welcome. Please reach out to Miss Cappelli and let her know. We request a meeting with her final budget and timeline in two weeks. The plan is to open the flagship hotel for the spring. Once it's complete, you'll work with her on the plans for the remaining nine hotels in the northeast. The schedule is laid out in here."

"Thank you." I draw the plan closer.

"Once Omni is complete, your sole focus will be Cooper Hotels."

"Of course."

"It may require some travel. Will that be an issue?" She's treading lightly here given my current custody issues.

"No, it won't." I'm sure one of my siblings or my parents will be able to handle Ellie for an overnight or two if Tess doesn't refile the relocation motion.

"Excellent. Have a good weekend."

"You too."

I contain my glee a bit longer as I hurry back to my office. Behind closed doors, I place a call to Ellie's school informing her I'll pick her up today. Then I dial Frankie.

"Hey."

"Hi. Where are you?"

"At my office."

"Are you alone?"

"Yes. You're freaking me out."

I laugh lightly. "Not my intention. Please sit down and turn on your video."

Moments later, I'm staring at the gorgeous face of my girlfriend. *Girlfriend. I like it a lot.*

"Hi, Sunshine. I just left my boss's office. I'm going to be working exclusively with the landscape architect for the Cooper project on all the hotels."

"Congratulations! Don't you have another large project you're working on?"

"Yes, Omni, but it wraps in a few weeks. Sunshine, it's you. I'm going to be working with you on all the hotels."

Joy, elation, and a bit of relief splash on her face. "Wait, what? Really?"

"Yes, really. Congratulations, you earned the contract."

"Ohmigod! OMG! I'm so freaking excited and proud of myself!"

"You should be. I'm so proud of you too!"

Sheer glee is plastered on her face. "What happens now?"

"Right down to business. The work part of me likes it, but the boyfriend part thinks you should celebrate more."

She wrinkles her nose. "Boyfriend, huh?"

A sliver of worry passes through me. "Too soon?"

"No, not for me. In fact, I like it a lot."

"Me too. I'll forward you the schedule. We need the finalized timeline and budget for Portsmouth in two weeks."

She smiles. "No problem. Did you know you were handling the rest of the hotels before today?"

"No, I didn't. I need to pick up Ellie. Do you want to come over after movie night? That sounds awful. I don't want to take away—"

"Stop. I understand. You have an extra movie night with Ellie. It's your time with her. I'll see you both in the morning at soccer. Eleven, right?"

"Yes."

"Also, are you and Ellie free on Sunday afternoon?"

"We're free. She'll go to Tess's after school on Monday. Why?"

"Would you both join me at family dinner?"

"We would be honored. I'll call you later. Congratulations, Sunshine!"

"Great! Thanks. You too. Have fun with Ellie."

I end the call, pack up some paperwork, and head out. After parking, I walk to the designated area for dismissal.

"Hi, Dad. Is everything okay?"

I hate she's worried again. "Yes, I'm going to take you to get your stuff for your game and whatever else you want." We walk side by side to my car. I open the rear door and her door. She sets down her bag in the back and climbs into the passenger seat.

"Oh. Okay. Did you talk to her?"

I round the car and buckle up. The note of sadness in her voice upsets me deeply, especially since there's nothing I can do to take it away. "I did. She gave me permission to go into the house with you. She didn't say anything about the motion being dismissed."

"Is she coming back?"

I turn to face my beautiful daughter. The fact Tess doesn't see the damage she's causing concerns me. "What do you want to hear, Ellie? The truth or would not knowing be better."

"I want to know what she said even if I'll be disappointed again."

How heartbreaking. "She said she would try to call you tonight and plans to be back on Monday."

She pushes out a harsh breath, settles herself, and says, "Okay. Let's get this over with."

Shortly thereafter, we pull into Tess's driveway. I take the key from Ellie and unlock the front door. I have been inside probably two or three times since Tess married Michael. The living room has been thoroughly cleaned and sanitized as the strong cleanser scent suggests and, if memory serves, rearranged.

"Was the furniture like this last week?"

Ellie shakes her head. "No, it was trashed and not arranged this way. That isn't the same couch."

I nod. "Do you want me to come with you?"

"Yes, please." She leads me upstairs to her room. I lean on the doorframe while she gathers her things. She's moving quickly around her bedroom. She zips the bag and walks toward me in less than five minutes.

"All set?"

"Yes. Time for pizza and a movie. Is Frankie joining us?"

My daughter's heart is as big as mine. "I wanted to keep movie night just us for now. Okay with you?"

She nods in agreement, and we leave Tess's. I share about my date tomorrow, her evening with Remi and Eva, as well as family dinner.

"That's cool. Emilia is super cute."

Hours later, after the pizza has been consumed and the movie ends, Ellie turns in and I call Frankie.

"Hi, Sunshine. How are you?"

"I'm good. A bit tipsy but good."

"Are you alone?"

She giggles. "No, Tal is here. How was the movie?"

"Good. I'm going to turn in to speed up seeing you in the morning."

"Aww. You're so sweet to me."

"I could say the same to you." She has no idea how much she means to me, but I'll show her as long as she'll let me. "Congrats again, Sunshine. Thank you for understanding the importance of movie night."

"Thanks. You're welcome. I'll see you in the morning."

"I'm looking forward to it."

"Me too, Sunshine. Sweet dreams." I sigh, lock up, and fall into my bed alone, wishing I wasn't. After almost an hour of tossing and turning, I grab my keys and head to the workshop.

CHAPTER TWENTY-ONE

FRANCESCA

Even though I haven't played competitively in years, the pitch is still one of my favorite places. The shoreline and my flat rock are where I go to destress as an adult, but when I was younger, a freshly mowed grass field with a hint of dew worked equally as well.

"Morning, Sunshine." Tommy greets me with a tender kiss, one that leaves me aching for more.

I note the teams line up to start the game. I locate Ellie at midfield with a huge smile on her face. "Morning. Am I late? I thought the game started at eleven."

"No, not at all. It does, it was supposed to. They are starting early since the teams are here and the forecasted rain. Don't worry. You're here and you didn't miss anything." He slides his fingers between mine.

I hear the subtle anger toward Tess and her failure to put Ellie first even if it's for sports. Even more importantly, I hear the relief I'm here. Relief I follow through. I almost let it go until I feel a new cut on his hand. He was in the workshop last night. I look over at him. "Why didn't you call me?" I glide my thumb over the newly rough skin.

"I didn't want to bother you, and you had company."

Ellie takes the ball down the right side of the field and crosses it to her teammate who scores the first goal of the game.

Once the cheering subsides, I turn him to face me. "I understand you don't want to burden me with your problems with Tess, but it's part of being with you."

"Thank you. I don't want her to be the focus of our conversations. I knew from the moment I told you about Ellie you were different. I'll remember the next time. Maybe you can join me in the workshop again."

My skin heats up from the reminder of the last time I was there. His mouth is dangerous. "I will every time you need me."

He lifts my hand to his lips and kisses the back. A small woman with short, dark hair and red-rimmed glasses hip checks Tommy.

"Hey, Tam! What are you doing here?"

"You gave me the schedule." She notes our linked hands. "You must be Frankie."

"Hi. Nice to meet you."

She looks up at her brother, and I see the distinctive nod of approval. I refocus on the game. Ellie is playing midfield. Her ball skills are good, but her field vision is stellar. For the second time, Ellie takes the ball down the right side of the field. This time though, she shoots and misses off the post, but her teammate redirects it into the corner of the net. The rest of the game passes, and Ellie's team wins by two goals. After a short post-game chat, Ellie bounds over to us and hugs me.

"Hey, Frankie. Thanks for coming. Hi, Auntie."

"Anytime," Tamara replies.

"What did you think about the game?" Her question is directed to me.

"Overall, your team did well passing the ball and looking for the open player. Your striker was slower during the second half. Not sure if she was winded or injured herself."

"How do you know she hurt herself?"

I smile.

"She tweaked her ankle just before halftime," Ellie informs me.

"I saw you implemented my suggestion for switching sides of the field when you attack. Well done."

"Thanks." Ellie smiles and fist bumps me.

I don't miss a look that passes between Tommy and his sister. It's a mixture of shock and approval all at once. Part of me is sad the women around here are so awful. The rest is happy they stepped away from an amazing father and even better man. Tommy will go to the ends of the earth for Ellie. I wouldn't be surprised if he loves his partner as passionately too. I would be so lucky for him to choose me.

"Sunshine?"

"Uh-huh." I turn my gaze to Tommy.

"Are you okay?"

"Yup. Did you ask me something?"

He smiles, and his eyes light up. "Where did your mind go?"

I turn and note Tamara and Ellie are walking toward the car about twenty yards ahead of us. "It isn't something I should share yet."

We start walking toward the parking lot as a few sprinkles start to fall from the sky. "I'm intrigued, but I won't push. Still interested in going on a real date with me tonight?"

"Absolutely. What time should I be ready?"

We stop at my truck. "I'll pick you up at six."

"Where did you park?"

He points a few rows over. I locate Ellie and wave. She waves back.

"So much has happened since I asked you on this date. I'm glad it's tonight."

"Me too." I set my hand on his chest, grip his shirt, and pull him closer.

"If you wanted a kiss, all you had to do was ask."

I laugh and press my lips to his. "You can kiss me whenever you want."

"You can too. I'll keep it in mind, Sunshine." He opens my door and closes it.

I push out a breath to calm myself. I'm nervous for our date. I realize it's been a long time since I've been on a decent one, but still. There's only one thing to do—call in reinforcements.

Me: Can you meet me at my house?

Lily: Freaking out about your date?

Me: A little, and it makes no sense.

Lily: I'll be there in thirty.

I exhale a breath of relief. Lily will talk me down from the ledge. No reason for me to be worried about this date. We've spent more time together in the last week than I ever have with any man before knowing it was going to head south.

I park in my driveway and head inside. I grab a water and chug most of it. After a strong knock, my front door swings open.

"I'm here. Let's get your nerves settled and you dolled up for your date."

"Hi, Lil. Thanks for coming."

"Of course. What are you worried about? You have seen him every day over the last ten days or so, right?"

"I know, and he called me his girlfriend last night. At the time it felt fine, but now I'm freaking out."

"Why? You get along well. I know you have at least kissed. Has more happened since?"

I open my mouth to talk, but no words come out.

"That good or that bad?" Lily asks.

"Scary good, melt-into-a-puddle-of-satisfied-goo good."

"Did you sleep with him?" Her question is informational not judgmental.

"No, but I don't know if I'll be able to stop myself if we have the opportunity."

"Why would you?" She has a point.

"It's soon, Lil."

She tilts her head to the side. "Maybe so, but he isn't anything like Tristan or the blind date Lina set up, right? I assume you more than like him."

I nod furiously.

"You're afraid he might be the one." It's a statement, but I answer the implied question anyway.

"Yes." On point as always for everyone but herself.

"Then wear your naughtiest lingerie, sexiest dress, and fuck-me heels and find out."

"What if it's bad?"

Lily literally laughs in my face. "Is there a such thing as bad sex? Yes, but if he can make you swoon with only a kiss, I would bet he has a clue."

She isn't wrong.

"I give."

"Good, go take a shower, and I'll make some snacks for hair and makeup time."

"Love you, Lil."

"Love you more, Frankie."

I hurry into the shower and let the water wash away my concerns, at least for the date part. The afterward part, I'm still nervous about, but it's me, not him.

A little after five, Lily puts the finishing touches on my makeup after spending almost the last hour blowing out my hair. I pull on my dress and fuss over which pair of shoes. I don't want to be taller than Tommy, so I opt for the medium-height pair.

"What are you up to tonight?" I ask my sister.

"I'm going to watch movies with Leo."

"Maybe you should take your own advice. Has anything romantic ever happened between the two of you?"

She shrugs. "We kissed once under the mistletoe at a holiday party, but it was a chaste, friendly peck. We aren't ever on the same page relationship wise. He's dating someone right now, and I'm not."

"Yet he's spending Saturday night with you instead of his girlfriend. Wait, why isn't he working?"

"Danica is travelling for work. He takes off at least one weekend night a month. Something about burnout, being the owner and not the bartender anymore. Honestly, I miss my time with him when he's dating someone."

"You should tell him how you feel. I'm confident he has no clue you would be interested if you were both single."

"Would I be? I wouldn't want to ruin what we have for the possibility of something more, especially if we lose what we already have."

"I can't answer that. You should at least consider talking to him."

"I'll think about it."

I nod and turn to face her. "How do I look?"

"Hot as hell. He may faint when he sees you in this dress."

I hug her. "Thanks, Lily."

"That's what sisters are for. Do you want me to stay or go?"

"Don't take this the wrong way, but leave. Please. I'll have an out if you stay."

"Love you. I want details."

"Love you more. Broad-strokes details, maybe."

Lily hurries out the door, leaving me twenty minutes to pace the floor.

CHAPTER TWENTY-TWO

THOMAS

"Have a good time, Dad. Say hi to Frankie for me."

"Thanks, Ellie. Have fun with Uncle Remi and Aunt Eva."

"We've got this. I don't expect you back before breakfast." Remi reaches out his hand and slides three condoms into my palm.

I give him the side-eye. His expectation makes my nerves tick up a bit more. An overnight date on the first date? It's so soon. *Craziness.*

It isn't really a first date though, right? I'm nervous. I don't remember the last time I was this nervous for anything. Not accurate. It was when Ellie was born. When the nurse set her in my arms and went to tend to Tess. Which means a relationship with Frankie scares me as much as fatherhood. If being with her approaches the joy of being a dad, then it'll be worth it.

I grab my keys and head out the door. When I start down the driveway, Ellie rushes out the front door.

"I think you forgot these." She hands me the flowers I bought for Frankie.

"Thanks, Ellie."

"Stop worrying. Frankie already likes you. Love you more."

"Love you most." I take a settling breath and drive to Frankie's. I knock lightly on her door.

"Hi, come in." She ushers me inside.

The sight of her dressed for our date makes my blood pound through my veins. Frankie dressed for a date is greater than professional Frankie. Sexy siren would be an apt description. Her little black dress skims over her curves like it's tailored for her alone. As if the cut of the dress weren't enough, when she closes the door, I notice a gold zipper runs down her back from her neck to the hem of the dress. It's unzipped to the middle of her thighs. Her toned legs look long and lean with those open-toe, high-heeled shoes. She's stunning.

"You look gorgeous." I kiss her cheek and hand her the flowers. The bouquet includes mini calla lilies, scabious, ranunculus, snapdragon, and garden roses in shades of purple and ivory.

"Thank you. You look pretty hot yourself." Her voice is shaky. She sets the flowers on the credenza near the door.

"Sunshine, what's wrong?"

"I'm off-the-charts nervous right now." Her admission escapes in a low voice.

"Good."

She raises an eyebrow.

I step closer to her, slide my hand over her hip, and draw her against me. Her hands flatten against my chest. I slide my other hand up to cup her face and whisper near the shell of her ear, "I am too."

"Why?" she whispers back.

"Probably for the same reason you are—our potential." I add a sliver of space between us merely because I don't want to let her go. "You can thank Ellie for that realization."

Her lips curve up into a small smile. "You can thank Lily."

"Let's go see if they're right."

She nods.

"I need to kiss you first." I thread my fingers into her hair and tug backward, exposing the elegant curve of her neck, drawing my tongue along her skin upward before wetting her lips the same way.

She attempts to stifle a moan but fails. *I see you, Sunshine.* I dip my tongue into her willing mouth and savor her. Her hands grip my shirt. All too soon, she pulls away.

"We won't leave if you keep kissing me like—"

"Like what?"

"Like you need to devour me or you won't survive the night."

"That's disturbingly accurate." Reluctantly, I put more space between us.

The unflinching desire in her eyes has me pushing her against the front door. "I don't think I can go slow the first time with you, Sunshine."

"Don't." Her hands deftly open the column of buttons down the front of my shirt as mine glide down the outside of her thighs, gripping the hem of her dress. Thinking better of it, I turn her around, caress the curve of her ass, and draw the zipper up to her neck. I expect to find panties and a bra, but I don't.

"You're bare beneath this dress?"

"Yes." Her response is breathy and bursting with need. "Touch me, please." She begs while removing one arm after the other. Her dress falls to the hardwood.

I press a kiss to the center of her back while grazing my fingertips along her inner thighs. She widens her stance, inviting me to touch her. One finger slides forward, spreading her folds. She's dripping with arousal.

"What were you thinking about?"

"You. Us. This."

I plunge two fingers into her heat and immediately curve my fingers. As I move, the sounds of pleasure fall from her pouty lips. The instant her center starts to pulse around my fingers, I withdraw and guide her to the couch.

As we walk, she unclasps my pants and dips her hand into my boxer briefs.

"Sunshine" spills from my mouth as her soft skin surrounds me tightly. My clothes float the floor while Frankie's eyes lock with mine. I kiss her hard, grip her waist, and turn her away from me. She steadies herself with one knee bent on the cushions and her hands on the arm of the couch. I sheath myself and thrust forward into her to the root. Almost immediately, her inner muscles clench and pulse.

"Tommy, I need you to move."

I rock back and push forward with my hands imprinting on her hips. Her hand slides down her taut abdomen and rubs circles at the apex of her thighs.

"Don't stop."

Mere moments after her plea, her heated core contracts and I explode in hot bursts. Her inner walls pulse around me as I empty into her. All too soon, I withdraw and lower us to the cushion with her in my lap. I push her soft, silky hair to the side and press open-mouthed kisses along her shoulders. A soft, satisfied sigh surrounds me. Mind-blowing doesn't cover how I feel. Life-altering is more accurate.

"Frankie."

"Yeah?"

"Bathroom?"

"Down the hall, first door on the left," she mumbles and slides from my lap.

"I'll be right back. Don't move."

"Couldn't even if I wanted to."

Fear grips me, and my chest tightens. Did I misread her? No, not possible. She invited me to touch her. Panicked, I ask, "Did I hurt you?"

"No, not at all. I'll be right here."

I hurry to the restroom, dispose of the condom, and clean up. Even though it's likely a guest towel, I wet the smaller one and bring it to Frankie.

"Thank you." She takes the cloth and cleans up a bit.

"You're making me nervous. Are you sure I didn't hurt you?"

She sets the cloth down, cups my face with her hands, and skims her lips over mine. "I assure you, you didn't hurt me."

"Then what?" My concern ratchets down a few levels.

"My mother has a saying she repeats to my father frequently. It's something like, when I am with you, the only place I want to be is closer."

"That's beautiful."

"The butterflies, my nerves, and the raw feelings we just shared, I've never felt anything similar until I met you. I realize it's soon, but I know without question or reservation, our potential may be limitless."

"I do too."

I surround her with my arms and lower us both to the couch. We lie in silence with our limbs tangled for a few long moments. Her fingertips whisper over my chest while mine caresses her hip and the curve of her waist.

"I'm not sorry we missed our reservation, but we should eat something," I say into her hair.

"I'm not either. I might have fixings for grilled cheese if you're up for sharing your skills."

I grin at her and kiss her supple lips. "You mean my other skills."

She shakes her head and buries it into my chest. After recovering, she quips, "You're terrible."

"You kind of love it though."

She laughs. "Actually, I do. We'll use the first skill set again after you feed me."

With a kiss to the top of her head, I say, "Well, then let's get to it." I sit and search for my boxer briefs and pull them on. After helping her to stand, I offer her my shirt.

"Thanks." She slips it on and buttons most of the buttons. Her hair is slightly mussed, and her skin is still flush.

Damn! She's sexy! I take her hand and move into the kitchen.

She opens her fridge. "I have sourdough, rye, or white."

"Sourdough."

"Provolone, cheddar, or swiss?"

"Provolone."

Frankie sets it beside me and pulls out the butter.

I set the pan on the stove and tug her against me, setting my lips to her cheek. "Please sit. Do you mind if I rummage for more ingredients?"

A look I can't discern mars her gorgeous face. Whatever she thought to say, she quickly dismisses it. "Nope, have at it." She takes a seat and watches me.

I decide on the rest of the ingredients and get to work. Her eyes watch me intently as she considers the options I laid out: sourdough bread, provolone, apples, and a few spices.

"Are you sure about this?" Her skepticism is clear.

I smile at her and continue cooking. "Yes, I'm sure." I may not be a trained chef, but I know what combinations of foods taste delicious in my specialty. I plate the sandwiches and move beside her at the island. After pressing a kiss to her temple, I wait for her to try the sandwich.

"Ohmigod! This might be the best thing I ever put in my mouth!"

Filthy, dirty thoughts filter through my mind. *I can top the sandwich, Sunshine.* I remind myself she's talking about the grilled cheese.

The fierce blush on her cheeks and hanging head inform me she just realized her word choice given our current state of undress.

"I'm going to keep my witty response to myself," I murmur.

"Much appreciated. Seriously though, this is amazing."

I nod and continue eating. When she finishes, she takes our plates and washes them in the sink. I join her and wash the pan beside her. Seamlessly, we move around her kitchen as if we have been for years. Once I set the pan to dry, I pull her into my arms. I wet her lips with my tongue before kissing her boneless.

"What do you say to a painstakingly slow round two?"

"Nothing wrong with fast round one."

This woman owns me. Only she doesn't know it yet. "Didn't say there was, but slow exploration is preferred."

I've stunned her speechless.

"Where is your bedroom?" My words emerge measured and soft.

"Upstairs at the end of the hall."

With that tidbit of knowledge, I dip my mouth to hers and kiss her. The tips of her fingernails skim down my chest and graze my length as we start moving to the staircase. With precision, I unclasp the buttons of my shirt, which looks insanely better on her. I expose inches of her soft, ivory skin before setting open-mouth kisses downward. At the base of the stairs, I lift her into my arms and wrap her thighs around me. Ignoring the heat of her core against me takes restraint as I climb. Laying her out on the stairs isn't painstakingly slow, but I ache to feel her from the inside again. But first, I need to see if she tastes as sweet as she smells.

I shoulder the door open wider and step into her bedroom. Lowering her to her feet, I open the cuffs and push my shirt to the soft area rug beneath my feet. Frankie places kisses along my chest and down my flank. It's been too long since I've been with a woman before tonight. When I was younger, I would be perfectly content allowing her to continue her quest to give me pleasure. Not anymore. Tonight, I want her to scream my name—repeatedly.

"Sunshine."

She lifts her gaze to mine. Desire, lust, and a flash of carnal memory from earlier flare in her chocolate eyes with darker flecks. One kiss to her lips, then I take my time savoring her skin. As I kiss down the elegant curve of her neck to the ball of her shoulder and over the top of her breasts, we near the long edge of her bed. I lick, nip, and suck until her nipples are taut peaks. Despite her profession, Frankie's fingernails are manicured and score my back as she gets increasingly aroused. I wrap my arm around her and guide her into the middle of her huge bed. Dragging my tongue along the edge of her hip causes her to bow off the bed.

Following lower, I watch goose bumps skitter across her lean legs. I skim my fingertips from her ankle along the inside of her thighs. Frankie widens her legs, inviting me to touch her again. Two fingers slide between her thighs and separate her folds. Tugging her to the center of the mattress, I draw the flat of my tongue along her seam.

Frankie inhales sharply and grips her duvet. I spear her with my tongue and taste her arousal. She's as sweet as I imagined. I suck and nip until her body tightens beneath me. Her hands thread into my hair. As I tickle her swollen nub with my tongue, I plunge three fingers into her channel. Frankie convulses around my hand and against my mouth.

"Tommy, Tommy, Tommy!" she shouts between moans of bliss. I refuse to relent until her shudders of pleasure slow and subside. Excruciatingly slow, I explore back up to her mouth and kiss her precisely and deeply.

Her hands glide down my side and push down my boxer briefs. "I need you to fill me again."

"You're feisty."

"It's your fault. I wouldn't be if it wasn't so damn fantastic before."

I smirk before shaking my head.

"What?"

"Do you have condoms up here?"

"No, but I have an IUD. I haven't been with anyone since my last relationship ended three years ago."

"It's been longer for me." I haven't been with anyone other than Tess. Casual sex doesn't work for me. It's not who I am.

"That's a crime. You have some ground to make up." A sly smile graces her gorgeous face.

I arch an eyebrow at her, shuck my briefs, and push forward into her hot, wet heat. The feeling is indescribable. I savor her body gripping mine and kiss her with ardor. Being with Francesca is in a universe of its own. She wraps one leg around my waist and the other anchors behind my knee, burying me even deeper into her.

Our rhythm is demanding and deliberate. My back tightens as my release nears. I meld our mouths as she chases her decadent climax. Her arms cling to me as she trembles from the waves of her orgasm. I move in smooth strokes until I explode inside her.

Panting, I lower to my elbows and capture her mouth again. We kiss while our bodies recover. Afterwards we cuddle in sated comfort. She fits in my arms as if she were made for me and me for her. I can simply be with Frankie and it feels fantastic!

Groggily, I turn in search of a clock. It's near two in the morning; I slip out of her embrace and pad to the en suite bathroom. It's like mine, except hers has an amazing view of the woods adjacent to her townhouse. When I return to her room, she's sitting against the headboard clutching the sheet over herself.

I pull on my underwear, grab my shirt from the floor, and take a seat on the edge of the bed. I lean in and claim her mouth for a searing kiss that screams I don't want to leave but I need too. "Are you free for breakfast later on this morning, say eight?"

"Yes, I'll be there."

I smile. "Good. Do you happen to be free in the evenings and on weekends for the foreseeable future?"

"Yes, why?"

"When I'm with you, I only want to be closer. Will you spend them with me?"

Her face lights up, and she lunges forward, almost knocking me off her bed. As she peppers my mouth with kisses, she murmurs, "Yes." After I rise from the edge of the bed, she moves to get up. "Stay, I can show myself out."

"I appreciate your chivalry, but I need to set the alarm after you close the door. Also, I don't want to give up another kiss before you leave."

I finish dressing as much as I can while Frankie ties her silky robe. Once downstairs, I tug on my pants and shoes. "I'll see you later, Sunshine." Drawing her against me, my hands slide over the luxurious silk. "Leaving is harder than I thought it would be. I want to tug on the sash at your waist and take you again."

"I wouldn't be opposed, but you need to go home."

I twist the knob and open her front door. I consider the war of right and wrong going on in my mind, balancing being a single man and a dad to a tweenager. I decide to put my relationship with Frankie first at least for right now. "She's fine with Remi and Eva." I kick the front door closed and strip the robe from Frankie's body while she removes my clothes again.

CHAPTER TWENTY-THREE

FRANCESCA

Near six, I wake to the smell of coffee. I'm tired and deliciously sore in places that haven't been touched by a man in—well, ever.

"Morning, Sunshine. Your dirty coffee mugs are hilarious." Tommy is standing mostly dressed in the doorway of my bedroom with a mug in his hand that says, "Yes, I have a dirty mind and right now you're running through it naked."

I smirk. "Morning. Lina and Lily started the collection. Every so often, they find new ones." I could get used to having him here in the morning, especially if it means we spend the nights like last night. That isn't accurate. *I want to wake up with him daily.* Waking up with him daily is going to take some time. I sigh inwardly as he sits beside me and hands me the cup. "Thank you." He's sexy in the morning, even more so after a night filled with sex.

"I need to get going. Still up to coming over for breakfast? Maybe nine instead of eight?"

"Absolutely. How are we handling this?" I motion between us.

"What do you mean 'this'?"

I shake my head. "With Ellie. How open are you with her?"

"Did you misunderstand what I said last night?"

I tilt my head in question.

"No other woman has met my daughter. There were no other all-night dates or sleepovers. I have only been with you since my divorce."

Holy hell! He has some serious skills that haven't been used in way too long! *Mine.* "No, I didn't make the correlation from what you said. I'm honored to be the first to meet Ellie."

"Anything else?" A sly grin appears on his stubble-covered face.

"Yes, but it will take too long to discuss and a lot more coffee."

"Fair enough." He leans in and kisses me tenderly. Every kiss leaves me aching for more. "I'll see you in a little while. Come over when you're ready."

"Okay."

He kisses my forehead and walks out the door. I savor my coffee, which is somehow prepared perfectly, and replay every decadent touch from last night. Twenty minutes later, I drag myself into my huge shower and let the scalding water soothe the aches it can reach.

I bound up the front steps of Tommy's house, and the door flies open.

"Morning, Frankie."

"Hi, Ellie."

"Dad is in the kitchen cooking a massive amount of food." She takes off up the stairs quickly.

I smile. "Thanks." Stepping inside, I hang my zip-up on the hook and add my keys to the bowl by the front door. It feels oddly domesticated.

When I step into the kitchen, I'm assailed by the tantalizing smell of bacon and coffee. Rounding the island, I kiss Tommy hello.

"Hi, Sunshine."

"Hi. How can I help?" I ask, washing my hands.

"Coffee please."

I nod and busy myself with two cups of coffee. "Why is Ellie in a crazy good mood this early on a Sunday? And isn't this a lot of food for three people?"

He laughs. "Tess called and said she would be here soon. Remi and Eva are still asleep."

"*Oh.*" I fail to hide the disappointment and sadness in my voice, the hollowness in my chest indicative of my feelings. I have no reason to be upset Ellie wants to spend time with her mother. Yet I am. I have no right to feel rejected. Yet I do. I'm already attached to both Tommy and Ellie, deeply attached.

Within seconds, his arms are around me and his lips press to the nape of my neck. "I'm sorry," he murmurs against my skin.

"Nothing for you to be sorry for. You don't need my approval to…." I turn in his arms, and he traps me against the counter.

Concern he hurt me and a dash of joy spark in his eyes. "Either way, I'm sorry. Ellie deserves a clear schedule, and quite frankly, so do we. If you don't want me to come to dinner later, I won't. I know you invited both of us."

I shake my head. Before I can reply, Ellie and a woman I recognize enter the kitchen.

"Good morning, Tom…. Hi, I'm Tess." Reluctantly Tess extends her hand and appraises me. "I know you."

The angst in the room dials up to one hundred. Despite the time and place, she's perfectly coifed from her clothes, including a cardigan, to her red-soled shoes. I note a significant amount of makeup caked on her right cheek.

I may not have remembered her name, but I never forget a face. Tess was Lina's mean-girl bully. "Yes, you do. Lovely to see you again." As Tommy drops his front arm, I extend my hand and welcome her through gritted teeth.

Tommy looks between the two of us before greeting her. "Morning, Tess."

"Tommy. Thank you for being flexible."

Tommy nods. The inevitable question about our relationship doesn't come. I would prefer Tess ask us instead of Ellie. The awkwardness of this gathering gets worse when Eva and Remi enter the kitchen.

"Remington. Evangeline. Good morning." Intrigue and questions play out on her face.

"Tess," they say in unison.

"Would you and Michael like to join us for breakfast? There's plenty," Tommy offers. He probably wants to break the tension. Unfortunately, he fails.

"Michael stayed in a rental in Connecticut."

Sensing the awkwardness, Ellie moves toward us, hugs Tommy and then me, and waves to Remi and Eva. "I'll see you on Tuesday after practice."

"I'll be there," Tommy replies.

"Will you be there too, Frankie?" she addresses me.

"Yes." My response is clear and direct. I won't ever let her down like Tess has in the last few weeks.

Tess cringes at my response, winces, and lifts her hand up but lets it drop before touching her face. I only know high school Tess and a little of what Tommy and Ellie have shared, as well as her recent actions. However, she's hiding something. I don't like to speculate, but my suspicions aren't good.

Ellie grabs Tess's forearm and all but drags her out of the house. As she does, I notice another wince. More evidence something is wrong keeps surfacing.

The four of us take a seat with fresh coffee and eat the huge breakfast in silence, other than required pleasantries to pass food. Once the dishes are washed, Remi and Eva excuse themselves to clean up the guest room.

"We need to talk." Tommy's tone is unwavering, letting me know this conversation isn't optional.

"Okay." I step outside onto the porch and take a seat on the stairs leading down to the grass. Some time passes before Remi and Eva stick their heads out the door to say goodbye. Then Tommy sits beside me.

"I'm truly sorry about messing up our plans for later today. I was more focused on Ellie having time with her mother, especially since Ellie is supposed to be with Tess this weekend."

"I know. I'm sorry for getting upset. It isn't my place to question how you navigate what's going with on with Ellie's custody."

"No reason for you to be sorry at all. I love that you want to spend more time with both of us and you were disappointed Ellie can't join us anymore. That is if you still want me to join you."

I push out a breath slowly. "The disappointment hit me harder than I expected. My afternoon included both of you, and I told Emilia. I may not go at all now. The three of us can go next weekend. I'm not used to navigating a schedule with three adults, especially one who is... inconsistent."

"Kind of you, but I'll stay here and you can blame me if you want to go to dinner."

I consider his offer but immediately dismiss it. I won't make Tommy look bad because of Tess before they join our first family dinner.

"You may not think I'm kind after my next statement. I don't know Tess now, but Tess fiercely bullied Lina in high school. It's why she recognized me. I'm sharing only for your information. I preface my next statement by saying again, I don't know Tess well at all, but she is acting odd. Along with her failure to show up for her relocation motion, the trashing of the living room and no-show for parenting time with Ellie, she's overdressed for the weather, coverup is caked on her right cheek, and she winced when Ellie grabbed her forearm."

Tommy hangs his head. "I saw her wince too. Well, I noticed the clothes and the wincing, not the makeup."

"Have there been any other signs?" I ask quietly.

I shake my head. "Generally, I don't *see* Tess. Only Ellie does. Today was a rarity. We communicate through text or email. Ellie goes between our homes from school or practice."

"Did her behavior change after Tess married her husband?" Luca's interrogation skills may have rubbed off on me a bit. My instinct is to dig until I'm sure Ellie is safe.

"Right after the divorce, I was mostly worried about Ellie and a bit about myself, not Tess."

"Understandable."

"Her recent behavior has been strange, but it's only since Michael's promotion and then relocation came up."

"I'm concerned for Ellie if Tess is suffering through domestic violence."

He draws me closer and sets a kiss to my temple. "I know. I'm concerned too. Even Ellie mentioned she was acting differently. How do I handle this? I don't want my daughter in the middle."

"I'm not sure. I would suggest talking to Tess, but it seems you only talk about Ellie, which makes sense considering your relationship to one another. Yet if Michael is harming Tess, the next question is will he harm Ellie?"

Tommy shudders beside me.

"I'm sorry. This topic is delicate."

"Don't be sorry. The thought crossed my mind, but I dismissed it. I need more evidence to consider he may be hurting Tess. The mere fact you see signs and are concerned makes me rethink what I believe to be true."

He rocks onto his feet and extends a hand to me, leading me back inside. We curl up on the love seat in his bedroom, my head against his chest, his heart hammering against my temple faster than it should be right now.

I push off his chest so I can look at him. "What do you know is true?"

"The change in her behavior occurred since Michael's promotion."

"Ellie mentioned something similar when she came to my office but not in those terms. She was talking about her mom shopping more, increased frequency of manicures and pedicure due to more evening corporate events with Michael. It didn't seem important, but now I'm not so sure. On the surface it's meaningless, but she needs different clothes to hide bruises on her arms or back."

"I don't think there is anything I can do right now. Michael isn't here. I have no concrete proof."

"Exactly what Luca would say. You only have a bunch of things that might add up to something or, taken separately, nothing."

Tommy leans up and brushes his lips across mine. "Can we talk about something else?"

I kiss him again and set my feet on the floor. "Grab some shoes. I want to show you my workshop."

A confused look graces his face, but he pushes to stand too. Within twenty minutes, we're walking with our hands intertwined under the archway of Hartley Mason.

"This is your workshop?"

"Yes, why?" We stop and take off our shoes. It's the off-season, so this park isn't crowded anymore.

He grins at me. "Then I have two. I either build something or go to my secret spot on Short Sands when I need to think or sort through stuff. I went there after dropping Ellie off at Kylie's last week when Tess dropped the boarding school plan. So much has happened since then. At least for now, nothing is happening with our custody agreement."

My designated spot is unoccupied. Tommy hoists himself up and then pulls me into his lap. "I'm truly sorry about dinner."

"It's fine. It'll be equally as awesome next Sunday, assuming you're both free."

"Yes, we would like to join you. Please blame me with Emilia at least."

"It won't be necessary but thank you for offering to take the heat. She's feisty."

"So is her sexy aunt." He tightens his arms around me while pressing his mouth to the back of my neck.

"Sexy, huh?"

"Very much so."

I turn and kiss him hard before replying, "Thank you. You're pretty hot yourself." I twist forward, lean back against him, and close my eyes.

"Thank you for sharing your spot with me," he murmurs near my earlobe.

"You're welcome." I lose myself in his arms and my thoughts about many topics from Tommy, Ellie, and hiring an assistant.

Tommy takes a deep breath before speaking. "Sunshine, will you stay with me tonight?"

"Yes. Why were you nervous to ask?"

"You exceed everything I have been looking for, and it's scary. So much so I'm still not convinced you're real. More importantly, I'm afraid to believe we can work."

"The same is true about you." About an hour later, we head to my place where I pack an overnight bag and necessary items for work. After a simple dinner of grilled chicken and vegetables, we turn in for the night.

CHAPTER TWENTY-FOUR

THOMAS

After an easy and delicious dinner and Frankie's promise to Emilia by phone that Ellie and I will be there next Sunday, we turn in for the night. I haven't shared my space with anyone since my divorce. Having Frankie here feels right, and I want her as long as she'll have me. Early the next morning, I wake with Frankie pressed against me. I'm making an exception to my workout regime this morning.

My alarm hasn't sounded, so it's before six. Frankie is curled against me facing away. I wiggle backward, adding a sliver of space between us. My lips mark her shoulder and inward to the center of her back. A soft moan falls from her lips, but I'm not convinced she's awake yet. I continue kissing a path down her back. When I reach the dip of her lower back, a small giggle echoes in my bedroom. I drag my tongue outward and move to hover over her.

"Morning, Sunshine."

"Is it morning?" She doesn't open her eyes.

"Yes, it is."

She frowns and looks up at me. "You're one of those jump-out-of-bed people, aren't you?"

"Perhaps. Would that be a problem?" I grin at her.

"Not necessarily. You'll need to be stealth to get up for your workouts while I sleep for almost another hour each morning."

"I can work on it as long as we wake up together."

"What about Ellie?"

She's incredible. She sees the example her waking up in my bed would be for my daughter and wants to talk about it. "What about her? She has her own room."

Frankie rolls her eyes and shakes her head at me. "I mean—"

"I know what you mean, and I appreciate your concern. I need to be able to be both a boyfriend and a dad. They aren't mutually exclusive. We, you and I 'we,' not Ellie and I, need to find a respectful balance, especially since we'll be working together too."

"Okay. We should get moving to work though, right? After all, it is morning."

I lower myself on top of Frankie and kiss her before hopping off my bed. "What does your schedule look like today?"

"I need to set up some interviews for an assistant and work on the budget and timeline for Cooper. What about you?" She hangs her feet off the bed and joins me in the bathroom.

"I have to wrap up the Omni project. The soft opening is Saturday. Then I can focus solely on Cooper, which we need to schedule a meeting for next week."

"I'll check my calendar when I get to the office." After brushing her teeth, she opens the door to the shower and turns on the water. She strips off her clothes and sets one foot inside. "Are you joining me?" she asks, looking over her shoulder.

"We will be late for work if I join you."

She frowns. "You're extremely thorough."

"Is that a compliment?"

"Perhaps." She steps into the shower, and despite my statement, I watch the water running over the curve of her perfect ass for a few too many moments. I leave and use Ellie's shower, so I don't prove myself right and we're late for work.

After a few stolen kisses, we head into the kitchen. While I make coffee, Frankie throws together a few items for lunch. "Ready, Sunshine?"

"Yes." I hand her a coffee to go and follow her out the door. With another quick kiss at her truck, I hurry to my office. Before I even sit in my chair, the craziness starts.

"Morning, Tommy."

"Morning, Melissa. What is going on?"

"There are some significant issues with the Omni soft opening Saturday. Linda wants to see you about them."

"Thanks." I take a gulp of my coffee and hurry to Linda's office.

She waves me in immediately. "I received a call from the fire marshal for Omni late yesterday."

"Why did he call you?" It's my project. He has my number.

"I'm not sure. Anyway, there are issues with the allowable capacity and the type of permit the client applied for."

"I applied for the permit they requested and met the requirements of the building capacity. The error wasn't on this end."

"I'm sure you're right, but it needs to be fixed."

"I'll take care of it. Anything else?"

Linda shakes her head. "Nothing other than scheduling the budget and timeline meeting with Miss Cappelli."

"I spoke with her. She's going to get back to me with her selected time."

Linda nods. She was honest when she indicated my relationship with Frankie wasn't a big deal if the job gets done. "Let me know when you make progress with the permit issue."

"I will." I push up from the chair and return to my office. As I pass, I ask Melissa, "Can you bring me the Omni file and the contact information for Fire Marshal Dennison, as well as the owner?"

"Right away."

I finish my now cold coffee and email Frankie about scheduling her meeting next week. Once I finish, Melissa enters with the requested items.

"Thanks." I spend the next three hours with call after call to the fire marshal and the owner. Once I determine the miscommunication, I set a time to meet with the fire marshal to correct the problem this afternoon.

I leave my office and drive to the Omni site. As I park, my phone chimes with a text.

Frankie: Dinner at my place tonight?

Me: Sure. What time?

Frankie: Six-ish.

Me: I'll be there.

I join the marshal and the owner at the door and enter the indoor entertainment park. "Thank you for coming on short notice, Marshal Dennison. You as well, Mr. Peters."

"Once you pointed out the issue, the fix should be easy once I confirm the measurements."

"Good."

Over the next hour, he confirms my information and insists the occupancy issue will be corrected for the soft opening Saturday. I thank him and consider going back to the office. Instead, I head home and log in there. After clearing my work email, with the few hours I have left before dinner, I decide to lace up and go for a short run. My short run is usually about six miles. It's what some runners consider long. When I'm done, I hurry through the shower. I redress and pack a bag to have dinner at Frankie's. Did she intend to invite me overnight? I'm not sure. We can talk about it tonight. While I pack, my phone chimes a few times.

Ellie: Just wanted to say hi.

Me: Hi. How was school?

Ellie: Fine. I'll call you later.

Me: Okay. Love you more.

Ellie: Love you most.

It isn't abnormal for Ellie to message me after school when she's with Tess, but this one sounds clipped. Maybe I'm reading too much into it. I'll find out later when we talk.

I arrive at Frankie's before she does. About ten minutes after I park, a police officer knocks on my window.

I open the door. "Yes?"

"Frankie isn't home," the tall officer explains and takes a step back.

I step out of my car and close the door. "We're having dinner. I'm a little early. Are you the officer who assisted her with Liam Samuels?"

"Yes. You must be the new guy in her life. I'm Zack. I live across the street." He extends his hand to me.

I shake his hand. "Tommy. Thank you for coming to her aid, even though I'm confident she told you she could handle him."

Zack laughs heartily. "Something like that."

Frankie pulls into her driveway and hops out of her truck.

"Hi, guys." She walks to my side and kisses me softly.

"Pleasure to meet you, Tommy. Have a nice dinner. Later, Frankie."

"You as well," Tommy replies.

"Bye, Zack."

We walk up to her door. I follow her inside, wrap my arm around her waist, and draw her against me.

"Hi, Sunshine."

"Hi. How was work?"

"Busy, but I fixed the issue with the fire marshal. You?"

"I have one interview set for tomorrow at lunch and then two on Wednesday. I also reviewed the budget and timeline again. Tomorrow morning, I'm going to price the plants again while Eric does the same at a different nursery."

I can't wait any longer. I need to kiss her. I slide my hands up her back and kiss her lips. She moans against my lips, and I know without a doubt, we aren't eating dinner in the next hour. With each step we climb, another article of clothing litters the staircase. After my shirt, hers and her bra, I guide her to the carpeted step. I slide off her tennis shoes and socks, then draw her leggings over her hips. Goose bumps erupt on her legs as my hands move upward.

Apparently, I should have paid more attention when Frankie was dressing this morning. When I reach the inside of her thigh with my kisses, I notice the naughtiest panties I've ever seen. The black lace wraps around her hips, but she's bare to me already.

"Do you have an aversion to panties?"

"No. Remember you asked me what people assume about me."

I nod.

"For me, if I can't dress up, I wear sexy lingerie instead."

"You're fascinating." The facets of this woman will keep me on my toes every single day. I lean forward and glide my tongue along her folds. Her long fingers thread into my hair. I nip and suck until she writhes against my mouth. Not content with giving her only one orgasm, I plunge my curled fingers inside her and rock them while flicking her nub with my tongue repeatedly. Once the shudders subside, I kiss up to her lips.

"Keep going," she whispers. Her tongue wets a path down my chest and traces my abs while she dips her hands beneath the waistband and bunches my boxer briefs at midthigh as I climb and hover over her. Frankie swallows me to the root and moves her hand in rhythm with her tongue along the underside of my length. My lower back tightens as my release builds.

"Sunshine, I need you to stop if you don't...."

She continues hollowing out her cheeks as I explode down her throat. Once I finish, Frankie kisses her way upward and meets my lips higher up the staircase. I pull up my boxers, wrap my arm around her waist, and we climb the rest of the stairs and fall onto her bed a tangled mass of limbs.

"You were right," Frankie murmurs.

"Do tell why I was right, gorgeous."

"We would have been late for work this morning if you shared the shower with me."

"I'll get up earlier the next time we spend the night together."

She purses her lips and wrinkles her nose. It's adorable. "Is there any reason you can't stay here tonight?"

"No, I wasn't sure staying was part of the dinner invitation."

"Oh. Tommy, will you stay with me tonight?" Her voice falls off as if she has more to say. As if sleeping alone tomorrow night because Ellie is home would be the appropriate decision despite what we want. She's correct, we both want to wake up together, but we also need to consider the timing for Ellie.

"Yes. I packed a bag just in case you might ask. After we cook dinner, I'll get it from the car."

"I like a planner."

"What else do you like?" I murmur against her neck.

"In no particular order, I like you support me in running my own business. It scares some men, especially ones in the same industry."

I nuzzle down around the curve of her chin.

"Watching you with Ellie is heartening and beautiful, especially when I can tell you're scared of making a mistake. You walk a tightrope between her and Tess, and I'm sure it isn't easy."

I move up and skim my lips over hers.

"I love the callouses on your hands from when you build something, but the reasons you build concern me."

I lift my eyes to hers.

"I'm not conveying this well. I'm willing to listen if you feel like you to need build something."

"Thank you. I don't always build when I'm upset or need to sort something out. I'm willing to listen for you too."

"Should we cook some dinner?" she suggests.

I agree, partly because I'm starving, and I have all night to painstakingly explore and mark every inch of her soft, smooth skin. She pulls on her silky robe, and we cook an amazing meal that tastes like it should have taken hours, not thirty minutes. After dinner, we climb the stairs and spend the rest of the night exploring our likes and dislikes in bed.

CHAPTER TWENTY-FIVE

FRANCESCA

The last few days have passed quickly. My interviews went well, and I now have an assistant at the office. I'm going to take a week to train Macy, and then I'll be able to focus solely on the Cooper project. It seems, as long as Tess is following the parenting schedule, Tommy and even Ellie are much calmer. They know what to expect and prepare accordingly. This weekend Ellie will be with us. I'm looking forward to it. First, I need to get through this day of training with Macy.

We have gone over the phone system and created a chart for who gets which calls, Eric or me. The invoicing company is handling the training for the system this afternoon via video chat. I settle into my chair and update the budget for the Cooper project again. Eric was able to find a local distributor who can handle the order for the azaleas and evergreens at a deeper discount than the previous one.

Near eleven, I take a break and head outside for a few minutes. During my break, I review the texts I got this morning. First my sisters in a group text.

Lina: Hey there! We missed you last Sunday.

Lily: How is it going with Tommy?

Lia: Will you be there on Sunday? Luca was asking about Tommy.

Me: Thanks, girls. Things are going well. Yes, we'll be there on Sunday.

I consider updating Lina about Tess but decide the group text isn't where to do it. In person is the best bet. I would hope by now Tess has changed. I know Lina has put it behind her. They would run into one another though eventually. I leave sharing with her for another day and focus on the text from Ellie.

Ellie: Will you join us for movie night tonight?

Oh, Ellie. I have to think about the proper way to respond to her message. I appreciate she wants me to be there, but I also know Tommy cherishes his time with her.

Me: Can you talk?

Tommy: I'll call you in a few.

I finish my break and head back inside.

"Frankie, Mr. Thornton is on line two," Macy buzzes me.

"Thanks." I close my door and answer the call. "Hi."

"Hi, Sunshine. Is everything okay?"

"Yes. I wanted to talk to you about something. Please know whatever you prefer is fine with me. I know how important it is to you. I also don't mean fine as in the generic female fine but I'm really not fine."

"You're making me nervous, sweetheart."

"Sorry, not my intention. Ellie invited me to movie night, but I don't know how to answer her. I don't want to lie to her, but I don't want to interfere either."

"That's all?"

I exhale. "That's all? You're not upset?"

"I know the day will come when she chooses to skip movie night altogether. This way I get to have both of you with me. Do you want to come?"

"I do, but I didn't want to intrude. I want as much time with you as you're willing to give me. Both of you." I want all the time, but with Tess in the mix, it's going to take a bit longer. If it were only Tommy, we would have talked about waking up daily wrapped in each other, preferably naked.

"Please join us. What would you like on your pizza?"

"I'm not picky. No mushrooms or anchovies though." Sheer glee courses through me. Acceptance from Ellie is a big deal. *I'm falling for them.*

"I can work with that. Will you stay with me this weekend? Sleeping alone after practice and waking up alone was torture. I miss your skin against mine and the scent of your hair tickling my nose. I want as much time as you're willing to give us too."

"What about Ellie?"

"She called you when I went to the workshop. Ellie didn't seem bothered you were there the next morning." Everything he's saying is accurate.

My only concern is Ellie. If Tommy doesn't think it's an issue, I'm in. All in. "Yes, to all of it. Movie night and staying with you."

"See you later, Sunshine."

"Bye." Giddy and relieved, I text Ellie.

Me: Thank you. I would love to.

Ellie: Sweet. I'm going to tell Dad.

Me: See you later.

Ellie: I'm so excited.

I smile, save my progress, and clear off my desk. After a check in with Macy and Eric, I head home to pack. When I open my front door to leave for Tommy's, I find my mother and Lia on the front stoop about to knock.

"Hi. Is everything okay?" Showing up unannounced is worrisome.

"Yes, everything is fine," Lia shares.

"Hi, Mama." I kiss her cheeks.

"Are you running off to your boyfriend's house?"

I love Emilia with all my heart, but she failed as my wing-woman here. "Yes, we're having movie night with his daughter."

"Bring them to dinner on Sunday, or we will be back until you do, *capisce?*"

"Yes, Mama. I love you." Satisfied the three of us will be at dinner, they leave as quickly as they came. I throw my bag onto the passenger seat and drive over to Tommy's.

When I arrive, I knock but no one answers. It's only then I notice Tommy's car isn't in the driveway. Luca would have my head for failing to notice something with such significance. I set my bag down on the deck and take a seat in one of the Adirondack chairs to wait.

Less than ten minutes later, Tommy pulls into the driveway behind my truck. Ellie hops out of the car, hurries up the steps, and throws her arms around me.

"Hi. I'm so excited you're joining us. Thank you."

"Hi, Sunshine. You didn't have to wait. You have a key." He leans down and kisses me softly.

Oh. He's in as deep as I am.

"You two are super cute," Ellie gushes as she opens the front door. "I'll be down in a few to pick a movie, Dad."

"Okay," Tommy calls after her. He takes my bag and sets it on the floor next to his. His hands slide around my neck as he draws me closer for another kiss. Not an "it's been too long since I kissed you" type—no, this kiss is "I missed you so much I ache." The length of time doesn't matter. It's been a day, not a month. His feelings seep into me through his lips and tongue as he consumes my breath. I set a hand on his chest and add some space.

"Your kisses make me lose my bearings, along with some other things."

"So do yours," he replies. "I'll meet you upstairs after I order."

"Sure." I grab my bag and start to climb as Ellie whooshes past me on her way down.

"I'm going to search for a movie," she declares.

I shake my head and continue climbing. I set my bag down and rummage through it for a hair tie. After twisting my hair up, I toe off my tennis shoes and take a seat on the bed in time for Tommy to join me.

"That was quick."

He laughs. "We order from the same place each week." Tommy strips off his suit and hangs it in the closet. His shirt, socks, and undershirt go into the hamper right inside the door. It's fascinating. He moves to the bureau and pulls out shorts and a shirt. "Stop looking at me like—"

"Like what?" I whisper.

"Like you want to handcuff us together and have your way with me."

I smirk. "I'm not sure about the handcuffs, although I'm sure Luca has a spare set, but I would like to have my way with you."

He slides in front of me as the words tumble from my lips, his sculpted abs on full display at mouth level. I lean forward, but he backs away. "You don't have time to do that with your insanely capable mouth."

I push out a breath and rise to my feet. "Then I suggest you put on your shirt or the pizza will be cold and we will be explaining some stuff to Ellie."

He shakes his head, tugs the shirt on, and then his shorts. After an all-too-brief kiss, we curl up on the couch to wait for dinner.

"How do you select the movies?" I ask.

"Ellie picks them each week."

"Cool. My brother and his wife love classic movies. So much in fact, their dogs are named after classic movie actors. They have movie night each week too."

"Sweet! What are their names?" Ellie asks.

"Luca's dog is named Bogart, and Willa's dog is Newman."

"How does Seinfeld qualify as a classic?" Tommy asks.

"It doesn't. He's named after Paul Newman from *Cool Hand Luke.*"

"I see. What are you choosing, Ellie?"

She smiles and starts the movie, *Can't Buy Me Love.*

"Great choice," I state as the opening scene plays.

About thirty minutes in, we take a break to plate our dinner and retake our seats. We watch and eat, mostly in silence. Ellie opts for the chair, and her attention is rapt on the movie. When I finish my food, I snuggle against Tommy on the couch. As Ronald and Cindy ride the lawnmower into the sunset, I push up to sitting and take the plates to the kitchen.

Once the kitchen is clean, we settle on the porch while Ellie heads up to her room to talk with her bestie.

"Do you mind bringing Ellie from the field to Omni tomorrow?" Tommy asks.

"Not at all. I'm going to be there anyway. How early do you need to leave her game?"

"It may not be necessary. Her game is at ten. I need to be at Omni at noon. She may want to shower in between events."

"Whatever works. I'm surprised you aren't still working tonight given the opening is tomorrow."

"I fixed the only issue on Monday. Otherwise, I would be."

I shiver from the chilly air settling around us.

"Want to go in?"

"Nope, I'm just going to cuddle closer for now." I burrow deeper into his arms, and he presses a kiss to my temple.

"Love that. Thank you for calling earlier."

"You're welcome. Remember the tightrope I indicated you walk with Ellie and Tess? I'm still navigating mine with you and Ellie too. I don't mean it in a bad way. We're still learning our boundaries, at least I am with Ellie. You mentioned it was special to you, and I won't force you to choose; it isn't fair to Ellie, you, or me."

"That's one of the many reasons I'm crazy about you. We're a package deal with an extra adult to deal with, and you're willing to tiptoe the line for us. You know what you want, and I'm ecstatic it's us." I know he means both him and Ellie and him and me.

"Good. I'm crazy about both of you." I shiver again.

Tommy pushes to his feet and reaches his hand for mine. "Time for bed, sweetheart."

"Will you warm me up?"

He grins at me. "With pleasure." I follow him upstairs, strip off my clothes, and slide into bed wearing only a camisole and panties.

CHAPTER TWENTY-SIX

FRANCESCA

Tommy's ninja skills are exceptional. Even though we were awake for a few more hours after we came to bed, he's already up and he didn't wake me. Good for him. I don't work out often, but if I do, it's in the evening.

I roll onto his pillow and check the clock. It's barely past seven. He gets up early even on the weekends. As I wrestle with getting up and finding coffee, Tommy slips into the room.

"Morning. How did I do?"

I smirk at him. "Morning. Pretty well. I didn't even know you got up."

"Good, though I must admit, leaving you in bed naked and alone was difficult."

"Then I need to work on my skills."

"Meaning?" Intrigue dances on his face.

"I'm clearly failing if you aren't satisfied enough to get out of bed in the morning."

He sits on the edge of the bed. "I'll never get enough of you."

I have no words. Luckily, I don't need any. Tommy presses a light kiss to my lips and pads to the bathroom. I rise, scoop up my clothes, and step into the bathroom too. Even brushing his teeth, this man is beyond gorgeous.

"You're staring."

"Yup. You realize you're stupidly hot, right?"

His cheeks turn bright red.

"Why did that make you blush?" I wonder aloud.

"No woman has ever admitted to blatantly ogling me. I kind of… love it." He smirks at me and turns on the water.

"I am. I will. How is that possible?"

He slides his arms around me and pins his eyes to mine. "Probably the same reason as you. I never put myself out there to receive compliments or risk being hurt."

It's scary he sees that in me. His statement is completely accurate. I rise on my toes and shove him toward the shower. "I'm going to make some coffee. Please don't use all the hot water."

"You're amazing, Sunshine. You could join me instead," he suggests.

"Nope, can't be late to Ellie's game," I remind him.

He pouts and steps into the now steamy enclosure. I throw on a shirt and some shorts before heading to the kitchen. It isn't until I'm on my way back upstairs I encounter Ellie.

"Morning, Ellie."

"Morning." She's shuffling to her bathroom barely awake. Her hair is a mess, and the strap of her tank top is askew. Someone is a hard sleeper.

I set his cup of caffeinated goodness on the vanity and sip mine while he finishes showering.

"You're staring again," he murmurs while he towels off.

"Yes. You should get used to it. It isn't going to change."

"Understood. In you go, gorgeous."

I steal a quick kiss and shower. Much to my dismay, Tommy is already dressed and out of the bedroom when I step out of the bathroom. I dress and join them in the kitchen. Ellie is now dressed and ready to go.

"Ready, ladies?" Tommy hands me a travel cup of coffee.

"Yes," Ellie and I reply at once.

I follow Tommy to the field in my truck in case he needs to leave before the game ends. At the field, Ellie hops out of the car for warm-ups.

"Have fun," I offer as the car door slams.

"It isn't personal," Tommy mutters.

"I know. I was just like her. I don't take offense." Quite literally, I was like Ellie. I spent hours upon hours at this park, well before and after game time.

We grab our coffees and head to the sidelines a few minutes before the game begins. With our fingers linked, we stand on the edge of the field. The game is evenly matched, and there's no score at the half. As the second half begins, Ellie takes the ball forward down the left side of the pitch and crosses it to her teammate. Her teammate shoots but misses. Ellie takes a shot, misses, and heads in the ricochet off the goalie's hands for a goal.

"That's my girl!" I hear a woman shouting repeatedly from my right. I look over at Tommy who is looking past me to the right.

"Tess?" I ask under my breath.

"Surprisingly, yes."

The game wears on, and it appears everything will be fine until one of the rival team members injures her knee. Given the severity of the injury, a decent amount of extra time is added at the end of the second half.

Tommy repeatedly checks his watch. "I have to go," Tommy murmurs near my ear.

A rush of tingles and memories of other times with him filter through my mind. I nod, attempting to push away the dirty thoughts. It doesn't matter where we are or what he says. Tommy in proximity to my ear makes me squirm.

"Okay. We'll meet you there." I turn and kiss him goodbye.

"I'll remind Ellie you're taking her to Omni."

"Thanks."

He kisses me again and hurries away while typing. As we near the end of the game, the opponent takes a few promising shots. However, the goalie for Ellie's team is talented and blocks them both. After the game, I watch Ellie from across the field.

After the postgame talk, Ellie walks in my direction. Unfortunately, Tess intercepts her. I watch as they talk. I don't move toward them until

Ellie starts getting visibly upset. Her hand is clenching and unclenching at her side and her posture is rigid. As I get closer, I hear their conversation.

"Thank you for coming, but I have plans with Dad and Frankie."

"Come with me. We'll make a day of it. Manicure, shopping, and dinner out."

"I appreciate you want to spend more time with me, but this weekend is Dad's."

"You were with Dad last weekend," Tess throws at Ellie.

Ellie turns her head and sees me approaching. "That was your choice. Not mine. You chose to stay in Connecticut with Michael for his job."

"Don't be disrespectful, Eleanor. It wasn't a choice. It's his job." Her tone becomes agitated because Ellie won't choose her.

"It isn't disrespectful. You chose to stay with Michael for work. It's fine. I don't want to go to Connecticut anyway."

"Your father put those thoughts in your head," Tess fumes.

Ellie holds her ground. "No, you're wrong. This has nothing to do with Dad. It's how I feel. I tried to tell you so many times. I don't want to leave my school, my friends, my teammates, or my family."

"You can make new friends at the private school we found for you."

I'm sure Tess left off the boarding part on purpose.

"Mom, you aren't listening. These feelings are mine, not Dad's."

"Where is he anyway if it's his time? You're supposed to be with your Dad, not his girlfriend." Tess points her perfectly manicured finger in my direction.

Ellie grits her teeth and pauses before speaking again. "Don't talk about me being with Dad when it's his time. You leave me *alone* while you go to Michael's work parties. It's the same thing. He was here. He left to attend the opening of his latest project. To which, I'm going to be late. I'll see you after school on Monday."

I was hoping to get out of this unscathed by Tess's tongue, but it isn't in the cards.

"You aren't her mother. You don't get to make decisions or take things from me. I'm her mother. You never will be."

"I don't want to do this with you here or anywhere else. Not now or ever. I'm not trying to replace you as her mother. How you choose to handle your relationship with Ellie is up to you. However, I am willing and would like to be an extra mom if Ellie will have me. I'm also willing to be friendly with you for her benefit and Tommy's." I'm not sure what Tess thought I would say, but my words clearly weren't what she expected.

She's stunned speechless.

"I'm glad you were able to make it this morning to support Ellie. We really need to get going though. Tommy is expecting us." Hopefully, Ellie will take the opportunity to walk away from this conversation.

"I'll see you on Monday, Mom," Ellie adds before turning toward the parking lot. After two steps, she starts running.

As she approaches the truck, I unlock the doors, and she closes herself inside. I can only imagine what is going through her mind right now. I could encounter one of a few things when I reach her: rage, tears, or both. The closer I get to my truck, the more into focus Ellie becomes. She's bawling. Her face is already red and blotchy. I twist around and locate Tess who is getting into her luxury SUV. I would like to say I'm surprised, but I'm not.

"What can I do for you?" I ask after settling into the driver's seat.

Ellie launches herself over the center console and hugs me close. I wrap my arms around her as tightly as I can. Through her tears, she croaks, "How could she say all of that? I tried to talk to her so many times. Dad would never... Did you mean what you said?"

There's a lot to handle in all those questions. I add a little space between us and wipe her tears. "I can't answer how or why your mom would say those things to you or try to get you to choose. It isn't my place to share my opinion on her statements. I can say, I know you were straight with her about your feelings regarding moving to Connecticut. I'm sorry she isn't hearing you. I appreciate you standing up for me and your dad. In my opinion, she never should have put you in that position. I meant what I said. I'm here for you anytime, day or night."

"Thank you for listening."

I dip my head forward. "Did you bring clothes with you, or do we need to go to the house?"

"We don't have time anymore. Do we? I don't want to be later than we already are. We are late, aren't we?"

I nod. "It's not going to be a problem. He will understand."

"He shouldn't have to. I get it, they're divorced, but seriously, it isn't hard to be nice. At one point, they loved one another, right?"

"Yes." At least it's what I'll say to Ellie. I assume at some point Tommy loved Tess, although it isn't something we have discussed.

"I'll switch to my sneakers and wear my uniform. I want to be there for Dad."

"Okay." I hug her close again and instinctively kiss the top of her sweaty head. I feel Ellie relax in my embrace even the slightest bit. "We can talk more if you want or wait until later with your dad."

"Thank you for listening. I'm good for now."

"You're welcome. I will always listen. I may offer advice too, but you can use it or not as you see fit."

"I'm glad Dad found you, Frankie."

I smile at her. "Me too. For all of us."

The ride to Omni takes about thirty minutes. We are nearly an hour late. During the drive, Ellie composes herself. Her skin is less blotchy, and she seems to have calmed down. Yet I ask anyway.

"Do you want more time before we go in?"

"No, thank you. I won't let Dad down because my mother is being... the adjectives I'm thinking of aren't nice... I'm good for now, but I might want to talk at home later."

"We'll listen whenever you're ready to talk," I assure her.

After stepping inside, we locate Tommy quickly. Ellie gives him a quick rundown of the rest of the game and then runs to the ropes course area. We follow quickly behind her.

"What the hell happened?" Tommy whispers after a tender kiss to my lips.

"More like who. Tess happened. We can talk about it more when we leave," I reply.

The guide instructs Ellie on the harness and ropes course rules, and she climbs to the tallest point. Despite the turmoil of the last hour, Ellie has a huge smile on her face while we watch from the floor.

A tall, slender woman with angular features in a navy sheath dress and peep-toe heels approaches us. "Well done, Tommy. This is fabulous. I can't wait to get my boys here."

"Thank you, Linda. Francesca Cappelli, please meet Linda Solder."

Frankie extends her hand to Linda, and she takes it. "Pleasure to meet you in person. Your plan for the Cooper project is exceptional."

"You as well. Thank you. I look forward to our meeting next week."

Linda glances around the indoor entertainment facility. "Again, excellent job. I'll see you on Monday."

We finish our goodbyes and locate Ellie. She's focused on making the second-to-last jump of the course. Ellie high-fives us both and hurries back to the beginning to take on the advanced course. At the end, the cheerful guide gives her a medal for completing both. This business will do well in the future.

"I'll meet you both near the door in about ten minutes. I need to speak with the owner one last time." With a kiss, he's off to finish the work portion of the day. Too bad I think the work is only beginning, at least as it pertains to Tess.

CHAPTER TWENTY-SEVEN

THOMAS

"This place is fantastic, Dad!" Ellie croons when I join them near the exit. Her words and her body language don't match. Her shoulders are slumped again, her gaze anywhere but directly at me, and she's clenching her jaw.

Ellie should never feel anger so fierce she loses a moment of her childhood. I don't like to say I'm keeping score, but since Tess married Michael, there have been more than a few days where Ellie is upset, which is absolutely unacceptable. A confrontation with Ellie and Frankie at a soccer game even more so.

"Here, Ellie. I'll meet you at the car." I toss my keys into the air in her direction.

"K."

I walk Frankie to her truck. "Will you follow me?"

"Anywhere."

Despite my anger at Tess and the difficult conversation the three of us need to have, she calms my heart and mind. "Short Sands, then I don't know, dinner maybe?"

"Of course."

I open her door, and she settles in. "I don't know all the details of this morning after I left, but I do know without a doubt, you made it easier

for Ellie. I'm grateful for you and your loving, patient, and giving heart."
I lean down and skim my lips across hers. The gnawing ache in my body
only she can soothe will have to wait.

Ellie is silent the entire ride to Short Sands. Only a few people know
about my affinity for the shoreline, namely Tamara, Ellie, and now
Frankie.

"Walk or sit, Ellie?"

"Walk."

Ellie hooks one arm around mine, and Frankie links our fingers. We
start at the parking lot end of the beach and walk. The silence hasn't
broken pertaining to Tess and her behavior this morning. The beach is a
calming force for me, but the deeper I fall for Frankie, the more she
calms me too.

"I don't know what to say other than I'm angry," Ellie mumbles after
a third pass along the sand. "She was rude and wanted me to go with her.
Mom even got upset I spent last weekend with you. It was her choice not
to come home on time. I shouldn't have to give up this weekend because
you got an extra one. Does that make me horrible?"

"No," both Frankie and I reply emphatically. I tighten my hold on her
hand.

"You—"

"Ell—"

"Go ahead," Frankie urges.

"Ellie, you're entitled to feel however you feel about all of it. Michael, the move to Connecticut, Mom's behavior lately, this morning, and Frankie. If you're happy, pissed, unsure, or calm, it's legitimate."

"Okay," Ellie mumbles and then clams up. Two more passes with the cool, salty water lapping at our feet before Ellie speaks again. "I don't like the motion hanging over my head."

If Tess only knew how she was hurting Ellie. Would it matter? Never once have I said anything to Tess regarding how her choices impact our daughter. "What do you mean?"

"She can refile at any time, so I have to start worrying and trying to hide how angry I am at her for making me choose all over again." Ellie pauses for a few steps and then continues. "I've tried to tell her so many times, but she isn't hearing me. I think she's listening, but she isn't hearing I don't want to move."

"You should keep trying, Ellie. Eventually, your mom will hear you," I suggest.

Ellie nods and walks quietly for a bit before blurting, "How did you do it, Frankie?"

"What, Ellie?

"Be nice to her after the awful things she said."

What the hell did Tess say to her? I feel Frankie take a deep breath before responding.

"At some point, your mom will realize I want to be with your dad. You are a huge part of that. Being rude to her won't make it easier for you, your dad, or me."

"You definitely stunned her."

The corner of Frankie's mouth curves up a tiny bit. "I agree."

After we turn back toward the parking lot, Ellie's stomach growls loudly. She bursts out laughing. "Can we get some food? Apparently, I'm starving."

I laugh softly. "What about pizza and bowling?"

"Can we just bring Chinese home?" Ellie suggests quietly.

"Sure, whatever you want. Why don't you and Frankie go home, and I'll follow with the food? It'll give you time to clean up before dinner."

"Sounds good to me. Frankie?"

"Sure."

I lean down and kiss Ellie on the top of the head and lightly kiss Frankie. "I'll be there in a little bit."

The two most important women in my life walk away with their arms linked, and Ellie's laugh floats back toward me. I'll always be grateful to Tess for Ellie. Even without talking to Frankie and hearing the specifics, I have no doubt Tess was obscenely rude. Before I get too deep into my thoughts, I order our dinner and take another few passes on the sand.

There's nothing else I can do except advocate for Ellie and build my relationship with Frankie. Frankie and Ellie seem to be finding their way. Frankie handled Tess satisfactorily, at least as far as Ellie is concerned.

Ellie has been clear and vocal about her approval of Frankie. While I didn't need it, it's helpful to know my daughter likes my girlfriend too.

With piping-hot takeout in hand, I step through the front door. Ellie hurries downstairs, freshly showered, grabs the bags and spins toward the kitchen.

"Careful, Ellie!"

"Don't worry, Dad. I'm starving. I won't drop it!" Ellie slides the bags onto the island and takes a bow.

Frankie laughs and hands Ellie a plate as I approach. I kiss her, take a plate, and grab some spicy chicken for myself.

We grab seats outside around the firepit and enjoy our dinner. Ellie is talked out about today's events, at least for tonight. After eating, my daughter clears her plate and curls up with a book in her room. I refill our wine and rejoin Frankie on the porch.

I sit in the corner of the couch, and Frankie sidles against me. "Do you want to talk about it?"

"Nothing really to say. Everything Ellie shared with you was accurate. Tess was rude, and I didn't respond how she expected."

"How did you respond?"

"Despite how I met Tess initially, I would hope she's changed. I told her I want to be with you, and Ellie is a huge part of you. I offered to be friendly with her and be there for whatever Ellie needs from me. I told Ellie I would be willing to listen and offer advice. If she wants to take it and use it, that's up to her. I also indicated how Tess handles her relationship with Ellie is between them. I don't want to replace Tess, but I want to be part of Ellie's life in a way that suits her."

Now I'm stunned speechless. I look over at Frankie. She's resolute in her position and how she wants to handle Tess and Ellie. I'm the luckiest man on the planet to have found a woman willing to be with me, my daughter, and handle my crazy ex-wife. *I'm falling hard for this woman.*

I take her glass and set both on the edge of the firepit. Gliding my hand along her jaw, I lower my mouth to hers. The moment our lips meet, it's only us. Her kiss consumes me. I get lost in her every time we touch and hope it's the same for her. My feelings for her are beyond anything I've ever experienced before. She climbs over me and settles into my lap. I dip my hands beneath the hem of her hoodie and caress her back.

"You're freezing," she mumbles against my mouth.

"No, you're hot."

She rolls her eyes and draws back with my lower lip between her teeth. Containing my reaction is impossible as a low growl catches in my throat.

"You like that?"

"Hell yes. Exactly how I know you like this." I skim my fingertips over the outside of her breasts, intending to pinch her through her bra. Instead, I find a satin bow. With a quick glance around and behind me, I arch my wrists and bare her to me. "You weren't kidding." This lingerie is unlike any I've ever seen. There are satin ribbons tied over her nipples.

"No, not even a little bit."

She drags her teeth over her lower lip and attempts to squeeze her thighs together. "Let's go inside." With my hand in hers, she scoops up her glass with her other hand while I grab mine, and we walk straight upstairs. As we pass Ellie's room, I note she's already asleep.

"How quiet can you be?" I whisper in her ear as we continue down the hall.

"Me? I'm more worried about you not being able to contain yourself."

I close and lock my bedroom door. "You were the loud one the first time. Did you just challenge me?"

She winks at me and tugs off her hoodie and top in one motion. While she wiggles out of her jeans, I strip down to my boxer briefs. Drawing her against me, I set her on the dressing bench and kneel between her thighs. After one tug with my teeth on the ribbon, I suck her peak into my mouth. Her head drops back, and she arches forward. I nip her with my teeth, then soothe with my tongue, and repeat until her pleasured moans near a volume too high for our situation. I reach up and put my fingers against her lips to remind her.

Drawing her panties to her ankles, I cast them aside and push my boxer briefs off as well. I wrap my arm around her waist and set her on the edge of the bed. Kneeling on the dressing bench between her thighs, I drag the head of my length down her seam before one thrust deep into her center. Frankie's ankles are crossed behind my back, and her heels dig into my ass as we chase our release. Her body pulses around me as I harden and lengthen even more. Each muscle tightens as I get closer to exploding inside her.

A muffled, "Tommy," falls from her lips.

Opening my eyes, I look up and see her hand clasped over her mouth and her eyes pinned on me.

"Let go, Sunshine."

With two more hard thrusts, Frankie arches forward and shudders around me. I empty into her until I'm replete. Once I regain control of my body, we move as one to the center of the bed.

"See, I can do quiet."

She laughs softly against the crook of my neck. I kiss up her neck to her lips. Once we clean up, we slip beneath the sheets until morning.

CHAPTER TWENTY-EIGHT

FRANCESCA

Early on Sunday morning, I slip out of bed and pull on shorts and my hoodie. As I pass Ellie's room, I notice she isn't in bed anymore. Panic grips my chest. Before I jump to any conclusions, I tiptoe downstairs and search the living room and the basement. He wasn't joking about the full gym down there. When I reach the kitchen, I find it empty as well.

Then I hear it. The telltale sound of the inside of a foot against a soccer ball. I glance outside and find Ellie doing drills in the backyard before seven on a weekend. Temporarily relieved, I make a cup of coffee, slide on my shoes, and step onto the porch.

Ellie dribbles through the gates she set up on the lawn and then shoots into the goal with her left foot. She follows the same path but this time with her right foot. When she turned around after the second one, she sees me standing on the porch.

"I'm sorry. Did I wake you?" Ellie mumbles as she approaches.

"No, not at all. Do you want to talk?"

"No, this helps me clear my head. Thank you."

"Of course." All I want is for Ellie to know she can come to me. It's not my place to push her to talk. That's on Tommy and Tess.

"Will you defend though?"

I smile. "I won't go easy on you." My words are in jest because I'm not in soccer shape at all anymore.

"Can't get better if you go easy on me."

"Game on, Ellie."

Ellie clears the gates and passes the ball to me. We move along the thick grass at least ten times before either of us take a shot on a goal. Ellie is up by two goals after fifteen trips across the yard. It isn't until near trip thirty I see Tommy sitting on the top step of the steps watching us.

"Morning, Dad."

"Hi, Ellie. Morning, Sunshine."

"Morning." We continue until I trip over the ball and land on the ground in a heap of laughter. Once the laughter subsides, I see blood running down my ankle. There's a cut on my shin from a pointy rock.

"I'll get you a towel." Ellie runs inside as Tommy races to my side.

"I'm fine. It's just a little scratch."

"I missed you when I woke up. Then I heard you two out here. Thank you."

"You're welcome, but you don't need to thank me. I want to spend time with both of you. She didn't share anything else, but she seemed to relax a bit more since I got out here. Just so you know, I won't share anything she asks me to keep in confidence unless it's about her safety."

"Fair."

Ellie is back with a towel and some water.

"Thanks." I take the towel and pour some water over it.

"Let me." Extending his hand with the wet towel, he cleans up my leg and adds a bandage to cover it before hauling me to my feet. "What do you want for breakfast, Ellie?"

"Pancakes." She shouts from behind the workshop where she's putting the goal away.

"You got it. Ready, Sunshine? You have some coffee and side dishes to prepare."

"I'm in."

He kisses my temple as we head inside. The three of us move around the kitchen and prepare breakfast. We eat outside on the patio. Soon the weather will be more seasonable, and it'll be too cold. Ellie rushes up to her room to talk to Kylie on the phone after breakfast. While I prepare fresh coffee, my phone chimes on the island.

"It's a text from Luca," Tommy informs me.

I set a cup in front of him and check my messages.

Luca: You are coming today, right?

Me: Yes, Luca. The three of us will be there.

Luca: Three?

Me: Yes, Tommy has a daughter.

Luca: Cool. See you then.

"He making sure we're going to show this time?"

I shrug. "Yeah. Sorry."

"Nothing for you to be sorry about. It was Tess, and I'll share the truth myself if it comes to it. Should I bring a bottle of wine or flowers for your mom?"

"It would be nice of you but unnecessary."

"Either way, I want to do it."

My phone chimes in my hand. Lily this time.

Lily: See you later.

I know the rest of my siblings will message me too. Whether Mama put them up to it or not, it's annoying.

In our group chat, I add, *"We will be there for dinner. Please stop with the guilt trip messages."*

Lina: Good.

Lia: Sweet. You guys beat me too it.

Lily: Love you more.

Me: Love you all most.

"Are you worried?" Tommy pulls me in close.

"Not at all. The two of you are amazing, and my family will see it too. The only thing I need to do at some point soon is tell Lina about Tess. I don't want her to be blindsided."

"Makes sense. Your parents are Luciano and Rosalie. To clarify in my mind, the birth order is Lina, Luca, you, Lily, and then Lia, right?"

"Yes, and correct."

"Lina is divorced, and her kids are Antonio and Emilia. Luca is married to Willa. Everyone else is single."

"Yes. Perfect. We should get ready soon."

After we dress, Tommy selects a bottle of Tramin Pinot Grigio. As we make our way to the front door, Ellie falls in beside us.

"Can you tell me more about your family, Frankie?"

"Sure." On the car ride over, I fill her in on the details Tommy already knows. It shouldn't surprise me that, when we pull up, my sisters are pacing the front porch.

"Don't worry about them, Ellie. They're harmless though they might hug too tight."

Ellie giggles and hops out of the car. Emilia runs down the steps and throws her arms around Ellie.

"Hi, Ellie! I'm really excited you're here."

"Hi, Em. How are you?"

"I'm good. Your card has a soccer ball on it with glitter. Lots of glitter."

"Thank you."

"I'll show you." Emilia drags Ellie into the house.

"About time you brought him over," Lily states.

I shake my head.

"Hi, Lily. Nice to see you again." Tommy extends his hand to her.

Lily pulls him in for a hug. "I'm glad she didn't run away from your first date."

"Me too," Tommy replies. He greets Lia and Antonio before Willa joins us on the porch.

"Tommy, this is my sister-in-law, Willa."

"Pleasure to meet you. I warn you though, the girls are easy to impress. My husband, not so much."

"You as well. Thank you for the warning."

As if on cue, Luca appears in the doorway. "Thornton?"

Willa simply shakes her head.

"Your brother is Sprinter?" Tommy turns to face me, our fingers laced together. A sense of impending dread flows through me.

"Um, you two know each other?"

"Yeah. I don't know how I didn't put it together before. We were on the same relay team for two years in high school. I ran second, and Luca ran anchor." Tommy lifts my hand to his lips and kisses the back.

"Let's get you inside and meet everyone else so we can catch up over dinner," Luca ushers us inside.

As much as I've been dreading introducing my boyfriend to my brother, it seems to be turning out fine. I completely understand why Lina is worried about which cop friend of Luca's she's into. Maybe it won't matter.

"Who's left?" Luca asks me.

"Lina, Mama, and Papa," I reply.

"Lina is in the playroom, Papa in the office, and Mama in the kitchen," Luca shares.

"I've got this." I all but drag Tommy to the playroom. Lina hovers as Em shows Ellie her place card making materials. "Hi, Lina. Tommy, this is my sister, Lina."

"You were married to Tess Kohl?"

"Yes."

Damn it! I didn't know she knew Tommy from high school too. I should have, but I didn't make the connection. I see the concern etched on her face, considering Emilia and Ellie are thick as thieves already.

"My daughter is nothing like my ex-wife," Tommy assures her, looking over at Ellie and Emilia.

"I appreciate your reassurance. It's a pleasure to see you again." Lina excuses herself to the kitchen.

We continue down the hall to the office.

"Papa."

"La mia bellissima figlia. So happy you're here." He rounds his desk, kisses both cheeks, and pulls me into a tight hug.

"Papa, this is Tommy."

Tommy extends his hand to my father. "Pleasure to see you again, sir."

My father looks puzzled but takes his hand anyway. I fill him in. "Tommy ran track with Luca in high school. I'm guessing you have met before, although I didn't recall myself."

"Frankie is correct. We met at the year-end banquets."

"Welcome."

"Thank you, sir." Tommy exhales.

"You're doing fine. Honestly, I thought Luca would be the tough one," I offer as assurance.

He kisses my temple, and we enter the kitchen. I'm floored with what we find.

Ellie is wearing an apron and stirring a pot of sauce on the stove while Mama adds a dash of this and a dash of that.

"Hi, Dad. Mama Cappelli is letting me cook with her," Ellie exclaims.

"That's fantastic, Ellie. Mrs. Cappelli, pleasure to see you again." He sets the bottle of wine on the granite island.

"This bottle will go well with dinner. Thank you. I remember you, young man. Please call me Rosalie. Welcome to our home."

"Thank you for having us."

I squeeze his hand to make him look at me. "Drink?"

"Sure."

I release his hand and grab two waters from the fridge. "Will you be good here? I need to talk to Lina."

He leans in to kiss me but doesn't. We probably should have discussed PDA before we arrived. Instead, he leans near my ear. "I'll be fine. I hope she isn't too upset."

"I didn't recall the track angle. I wanted to tell her in person. Now it seems like it might have been a misstep on my part."

"I'll be fine, Sunshine."

I notice a coy smile on my mother's face when she hears him call me Sunshine. Making my way through the house, I locate Lina in the backyard.

"Hey."

"I'm sorry, Lina. I wanted to tell you in person. I didn't know Luca already knew Tommy or you would recognize him."

"Initially, I was concerned for Em, but Tommy is right. Ellie is nothing like Tess. It was obvious in how they were interacting."

"No, she isn't."

"I'm happy for you, Frankie."

"Thanks. Why are you upset then?"

Lina pushes out a harsh breath. "I'm upset I don't have the courage to bring a guy here for dinner."

"You went out with him? I'm so happy for you choosing you, Lina." I hug her.

"Yeah, we had lunch twice this week. He's… sweet, has a stable career, and he knows about the kids, my ex, and he doesn't seem bothered at all."

"You deserve to be happy, sis. If you think G is the guy, let him chase you. Let me know when you need a babysitter in the evening."

Her mouth is agape. "I didn't tell you his name. How do you know?"

I smirk at her. "Process of elimination. Davis is still hooking up with Tabi. I've seen Scarlett leaving Smithson's early in the morning. Plus, you know I live across the street from him. That leaves only two, and Craven joined right as Luca was leaving YPD."

"Please don't say anything, especially to Luca," Lina begs.

"I won't, but you should if you think it's going somewhere."

She nods as Lily calls us in for dinner. Once inside, we take our seats at the table. Emilia's place cards are super cute yet again. When Willa came to her first dinner, Em made a card for her on the fly. On the same day, Willa made a template that made it easier for Em to make the cards. Mine has a flower on it, Tommy's says, "Mr. Ellie's Dad," and Ellie's has a huge soccer ball with so much glitter. The cards are perfect.

As usual, Mama cooked more food than we could possibly eat. Ziti, manicotti, chicken parmesan with nuggets and fries for the kids. We dig in and chat about everyday things. Tommy's left hand is crossed over his lap and intertwined with mine beneath the table.

Not once does the conversation stray to the fact Tommy and Ellie are here for the first time. I'm grateful. I want them to be comfortable and willing to come back as many Sundays as possible. The sense of dread never came. It's a stroke of sheer luck Luca already knows Tommy and didn't have to play the overprotective brother card to interrogate him. I'm thankful. Luckily, Lina sees with her own two eyes Ellie is nothing like Tess. I'm grateful to Tommy for bringing her up well despite his ex-wife.

Overall, family dinner is a success. After dessert and Ellie schooling Antonio at soccer in the backyard, we head to Tommy's.

"Thank you for inviting us, Frankie. Your family is awesome! Grandma T never lets me help in the kitchen. It was fun to help out."

"You're welcome. I'll be sure to tell my mom you had a wonderful time."

When we arrive home, Ellie hurries to her room to call Kylie. We also turn in early as well. We're in the bedroom—sleeping, not so much.

CHAPTER TWENTY-NINE

THOMAS

Family dinner with the Cappelli's was remarkably similar to my family. There's a lot of food, inside jokes, and laughter. I can't wait to bring Frankie to one of ours—hopefully, at the end of this month.

"Sunshine, I'm home," I call out as I step into her townhouse midweek.

I can hear her laugh from her office. We have been insanely busy working on the long-term plan for the remaining hotels and the budget and layout for the Boston location. Lately, we've been working out of her office mostly. Today though, I went to my office to meet with Linda and the other board members to smooth some edges between the timelines we recommended and the failure of the construction crew to meet them.

Frankie and I have been spending time at both of our places. When Ellie is with Tess, we stay at Frankie's. When Ellie is with me, we stay at my house. It's been working well for the past few weeks, but I want to wake up with Frankie every day in a place that's ours, not her place or mine. Ellie seems to have adjusted fine to having Frankie in our life. I want to provide stability for Ellie, especially in light of Tess refiling her relocation motion.

"Hi, how was the meeting?"

I pull her close and kiss her breathless. She is air for me. There isn't any issue we can't work out together. I'm wrestling with how soon is too soon to tell her I'm in love with her. "The meeting went fine. Our timeline for the installations were generous. The construction team is going to increase their staff to meet their deadlines so ours can be met as well."

"Good."

"Will you go slip into the sexy dress you planned to wear on our first date and let me take you to *Château Franc* for a proper date?"

Her eyes widen. "Definitely." She kisses me softly and hurries up the stairs.

I call after her, "Sunshine, please wear panties so we can actually make it through dinner." *File that statement in the 'things I never thought I would say' category.*

"No promises."

I grin. She's a constant surprise, and it keeps me on my toes. I grab a water from the kitchen. Less than thirty minutes later, my gorgeous girlfriend descends the stairs wearing the same dress but with different shoes. It doesn't matter. I'm rock-hard recalling the vivid details of the last time she wore that dress. Each time since has been more than I could have imagined.

"You look sinfully sexy once again. Let's get out the door before we don't make it to dinner."

"Thank you. As long as you promise to unzip the dress again later."

"Is there any doubt?"

Her cheeks flush as I offer her my arm. The glimpse of her toned thighs as she sits in the passenger seat has me adjusting myself as I round the car. I want the partnership with her as well as the amazing sex. Dinner is part of our relationship. I can behave myself for a few hours.

We're seated at a table near a wall of windows overlooking an inlet. I sit beside Frankie instead of across from her. My need to touch her increases daily the longer we're together. I never want it to end. Our server shares the specials and leaves our table with our drink and appetizer order.

"What are you nervous about?"

I realize my hand is shaking. "I... would you—"

"Whatever it is, we can handle it." Her confidence in us is comforting. I never had that with Tess. Even though she was my wife, I never had the same confidence we could weather any storm like I do with Frankie. Part of me wishes I saw it earlier, but then I wouldn't have Ellie.

I kiss her softly and whisper, "Move in with us. I know you love your townhouse, but—"

She sets her index finger over my lips. "Do you want to talk to Ellie first?"

I'm floored. She would wait for Ellie to be comfortable. Isn't she already though? "Not really. She's home on the days you stay at my place. Why would it be different on the days she's with Tess?"

She's quiet for a few moments. The server brings our drinks and a bread basket, giving her even more time to stew on my offer. Doubt is creeping in the longer it takes her to answer me. Have I misread us? My chest tightens at the thought she may turn me down.

"I'm crazy about both of you. Yes, I'll move in with you."

I exhale sharply.

"You thought I was going to say no?"

"Honestly, before I said anything, I was confident, but when you took time to answer me, my nerves got the best of me. I'm crazy about you too."

"You can't shake me so easily." A smile spreads on her gorgeous face.

"I don't want to shake you ever," I reply without a second thought. I've fallen for Francesca Cappelli. Hopefully, she heard the ever part of my reply and realizes I'm in this with her.

We enjoy the rest of our dinner and take dessert to go. I buckle my seat belt and notice Frankie's dress is even higher than before, though likely unintentional.

I set my hand on her thigh as we leave the restaurant and skim my fingers inward and outward on her inner thigh as I drive. Goose bumps rise with each pass, and Frankie is vibrating with need. She slides her arm beneath mine and works my belt open. Her soft skin encircles my length as my hand inches higher up her thigh. Her grip tightens around me in measured strokes.

"Did you do what I asked?" I whisper and attempt to focus on the road.

"Sort of." Her voice rises in response.

I raise an eyebrow. Frankie lifts her hips as I push her dress higher. It's difficult to focus on her naughty panties, the building of my climax from her hand, and the road at the same time. We're closer to my house than hers. I turn into my neighborhood and reach higher between her legs. The tips of my fingers meet her hot, wet core. I plunge two fingers into her as I near my own climax.

"Frankie, push the button."

She reaches over and opens the garage door. I pant, trying to keep my composure long enough to park in my garage before we climax. After I pull into the garage, Frankie closes the door while never faltering in her even, tight strokes.

"Move your seat back as far as it will go," Frankie demands and slows her strokes to stave off my orgasm. It's an exquisite type of torture. She brought me to the cusp of bliss and then slowed down.

I drop my hand and move the driver's seat back as far as it'll go. Reluctantly, I withdraw my fingers from her core and lift her to hover over me. She aligns us and sinks down, taking me as deeply as possible.

"You feel…."

Frankie drops down as I thrust upward. I explode in hot bursts as she pulses around me. We continue our back and forth until she screams my name and collapses against my chest. We're both gasping for air.

Once our breathing regulates, she adds some space between us before taking an all-consuming kiss. "You can't touch me like that and not expect me to respond."

"I'm still learning you, but damn, woman, that was hot as hell."

"Don't you worry. I'm feisty, and I'll keep you on your toes."

"I wouldn't have anything less. Let's go inside and clean up; then we can head back to your place." I press a kiss to her head and open the door.

We clean up, head back to her place, and slip into bed with two spoons for our chocolate soufflé.

CHAPTER THIRTY

FRANCESCA

It's been a week since I moved in with Tommy and Ellie. Talia is considering moving into my place. It's paid for, and the market is down right now, so it isn't wise to sell it. I was worried about not having enough space, but Tommy rarely uses his office.

I rearranged it, and there's plenty of space for my drawings and the plans for the Cooper Hotels. Currently, the Boston project occupies the rolling board while the Portsmouth plans are spread on the credenza.

"Frankie, we're here," Ellie shouts when she arrives.

"I'm in the office." *We're here?* I leave the office and meet them in the kitchen.

"Hey, Frankie. This is my bestie, Kylie. Ky, Frankie, my dad's girlfriend."

"Hi, nice to meet you. I'm not opposed to more time with you, but it's Wednesday, shouldn't you be going to your mom's?"

Kylie is shorter than Ellie and has long, blonde hair tied into a ponytail at the nape of her neck. She's wearing jeans, a graphic tee, and a flannel shirt that is three sizes too big. If I had to guess, it's probably her dad's and she swiped it because it's her mom's parenting time. It accomplishes two things: she has something of her dad's and it pisses off her mom.

"We came here to work on a project for school because the supplies are in the workshop. Mom is going to pick me up later."

"Oh, no problem. Want me to fix you a snack or something while you wait for your dad?"

"No need. We can fend for ourselves. Dad should be here soon. Thanks, though," Ellie answers.

"You're welcome. I'll be in the office if you need anything."

"Thanks," the girls say in unison.

I barely refocus on the plans before Tommy gets home.

"Sunshine, Ellie, I'm home."

I hear chuckling from the kitchen. "Awww. So cute," Kylie shares with Ellie.

"Yeah, they are. It's pretty awesome."

My heart squeezes in my chest. While I didn't really hesitate to move in, I was a bit worried about Ellie's reaction. I'm glad she's okay with me living here.

I greet Tommy with a chaste kiss and follow him into the kitchen.

"Hi, Ellie. Kylie. Give me about fifteen minutes to change and we can finish your project for school."

"Okay. We'll be right here," Ellie answers and the girls continue eating their snack.

I turn to head back into the office.

"Frankie, could you join me upstairs?"

"Sure." I follow him upstairs as he removes his tie and starts unbuttoning his shirt. "Everything okay?"

We step into our room. I'm still getting used to that. "Yes, I needed a proper kiss after being away from you all day long."

"Aww. I missed you too."

We spend most of his fifteen minutes kissing and stripping off the rest of his work clothes. Unfortunately for both of us, the girls need assistance.

"Can you meet me back up here, say ten tonight, so we can finish this?"

I laugh. "Definitely."

Tommy changes quickly, and we hurry back downstairs. The girls are completely oblivious twenty-five minutes have passed. Tommy and the girls head out to the workshop, and I head back into the office. I send an email to Macy and Eric and finish up for the day.

In the kitchen, I rummage through the fridge for the ingredients for dinner. Tommy and the girls have been outside for about an hour. As I chop and dice the vegetables, the doorbell rings. With a calming breath, I answer the door.

"Hi, Tess."

"Hello, Frankie. I wasn't expecting you to be here."

Don't engage. "Tommy and the girls are in the workshop. Would you like to go back or would you like a drink while you wait?"

"A drink, thank you." Her words are said through gritted teeth. Tess takes a seat at the island. Even now, at the end of the day, she's perfectly coifed down to her luxury high heels and handbag.

"We have water, iced tea, or milk," I offer.

"Iced tea. We?" Her tone is becoming increasingly agitated.

I didn't think to ask if Tommy or even Ellie shared with Tess I moved in with them. I fill her glass and set it in front of her. "Yes." I don't expound on it anymore.

"Unacceptable," Tess states.

Keeping my cool is getting more difficult the more she speaks. "How so?"

"It's unacceptable you're living here in sin with my daughter under the same roof."

I see Tommy approach out of the corner of my eye, but Tess doesn't. He nods to let me know he's here for backup.

"Did you live with your husband before you got married?"

"Yes, but that's different." Her voice falters because I found the flaw in her assertion.

"Why?" I'm not going to back down.

"You're not her mother. I am. She doesn't need another mother. It's my job."

My blood is boiling, but somehow I manage to keep my cool. "As I tried to explain at the field, I know you're her mother. I'm willing to be supportive of Ellie and assist her if she needs it. More people in Ellie's life who are willing to support her and help her thrive is a good thing."

"It won't matter. My daughter is moving to Connecticut with me soon enough."

"No, I'm not!" Ellie storms into the kitchen. Kylie stands beside Tommy silently.

"Ellie, this doesn't concern you," Tess states.

"Really, Mom? It absolutely concerns me. It's only about me. Since it doesn't appear you hear me when I tell you how *I feel* about this, I'll say it again. This time with witnesses. I don't want to move to Connecticut. I don't want to live in a massive house and spend all my time in my bedroom. I like my school. I have great friends and teammates. It isn't hard to be nice. Frankie is pretty cool. She doesn't try to be my mother because she respects you. It sucks you don't feel Frankie deserves the same in return."

Oh, Ellie. My heart breaks for her.

"Language, Ellie," Tommy warns.

Tess turns toward his voice and sits up straighter, as if his presence will temper anything she chooses to say.

"When I went to your house and the place was trashed, I was scared for you," Ellie admits. "When you didn't answer, I went to Frankie's office because it was the closest. She was there for me when you didn't come home from Connecticut. She was here for me when you didn't show up for court. Frankie cares about me and supports me when you screw up."

"Don't talk to me like that, Eleanor. I'm your mother."

"You are, but lately you haven't been acting like it. I realize you think I'm just a kid, but it's hard enough now going between the two of you. It's great you're civil to one another and he shows up at my games and events when it's your time, but he won't be able to if I live in Connecticut. I'm happy for you and your new start with Michael, but I don't want to start over too."

"I want what's best for you, Ellie."

"You say the words but you aren't hearing me. I love you, Mom, but I don't want to keep doing this." Ellie throws her arms around Tess and squeezes her tight.

Tess flinches and tries to recover, but I saw it. Tommy too. He glances at me to see if I noticed it as well. Kylie silently follows Ellie out of the kitchen.

"I won't withdraw my motion. I don't like that you moved your girlfriend into my daughter's home without consulting me."

"I will not argue with you about this. The truth is you didn't consult me about Keith or Michael. There's no reason for me to consult you about Frankie. This is my home I share with our daughter. If you feel the need to keep your motion in place, we will let the court decide. Please understand, Tess, I will fight your motion, not only because Ellie wants to stay here but because I think it's the best choice for our daughter."

"I hope she makes enough money to support you. I'll fight until I get what I want." Tess's perfectly manicured finger pointed in my direction.

"This isn't about you, Tess. It's about Ellie and what she needs," Tommy states.

"We will let the judge decide. Ellie, let's go. I've had enough." Tess pushes away her untouched glass of iced tea and storms to the front door.

Ellie brushes past her and throws her arms around me. "Thank you for standing up for me, Frankie."

"I always will," I whisper and hug her back.

She hugs Tommy and whispers something I can't make out. Reluctantly, she follows Tess outside.

"Kylie, are you ready to go home?" Tommy calls out to her.

"No worries, Mr. Thornton. My dad is on his way to pick me up. I texted before we came inside."

"Would you like a drink, Kylie?" I ask her.

"Sure. Thanks."

I set a fresh glass of iced tea in front of her.

"I hope when my parents start dating seriously again, they each find someone like you," Kylie mumbles.

"Thank you, Kylie."

She takes a few sips of her tea before her father arrives. Tommy returns to the kitchen after showing her out and hauls me into his arms. His kiss starts off hard and possessive and shifts to reverent and sensual. I melt into him until we're both breathless.

Tommy adds a sliver of space between us and cups my face. "I have been searching for the right time, but I realize there isn't one. Never once have I felt as much for a woman as I do for you. You fiercely and willingly went toe to toe with Tess for Ellie and me. I love you, Sunshine."

"I love you both."

Dinner forgotten. We dance upstairs and tangle up our sheets for the rest of the evening. At least momentarily, it allows us to forget the threats levied by Tess regarding relocating Ellie.

CHAPTER THIRTY-ONE

THOMAS

Over the next two weeks, Tess seems to straighten out a bit. She's home when Ellie arrives from school and is cordial when I speak with her. Although she hasn't budged on her relocation motion. We're scheduled for a mediation today. I'm not hopeful, but for Ellie I'll try. I sincerely hope Tess shows up this time.

Ellie has already stepped out the front door with my keys.

"Sunshine, I need to go," I call upstairs to Frankie.

"I'm coming."

"No, you're not!"

She laughs as she lands before me in the foyer. "You're right, but there's always time later. Good luck. I'll be here all day in case you need to go to court. I love you."

"I love you." I kiss her goodbye.

When I arrive at Antionette's office, I can tell she's already irritated when her assistant escorts me into the conference room.

She's on the phone with someone. "No, Pat. It's unacceptable. I don't appreciate the games your client is playing with her daughter's life. I'll speak with my client and get back to you about our course of action."

"Tess isn't coming. What are my options?" *I'm done with this back and forth.*

"Good morning. You could go to court and get her motion dismissed again. She'll likely refile it. We could go to court and request a hearing as soon as possible for the court to hear the parties, considering it's impossible to come to an agreement if Mrs. Spears refuses to show up. If she fails to show up, we could ask for sanctions if she files again and fails to pursue the motion."

"Can I ask for sole custody?"

My attorney whips her head up. "I didn't know sole custody was something you wanted to pursue."

"I'm not sure I do. The last thing I want to do is cause more strife, but my daughter needs stability. She needs a resolution."

"You can certainly file a motion making that request. Will you be successful? I'm not sure. At this point, Mrs. Spears' behavior doesn't rise to the level of harm, at least harm we can prove. Does her attentiveness need work? Yes. Should she be more mindful of the impacts of her actions on your daughter? Absolutely. In my experience, a judge may order a refresher parenting class at first. If the problem persists, then you might be able to make a case for shifting to sole custody."

"I appreciate your candor. Please see if we can go before a judge today to request a hearing as soon as possible."

"Of course."

"I'm going to make arrangements for after school. Please call me when you have any information," I inform her.

"I will. Hopefully, I'll see you right after lunch."

"Thank you."

I leave her office. I would like to say I'm surprised. At this point, nothing Tess has done rises to the neglect level. I'm prepared to expect nothing from my ex-wife in regard to our daughter. Part of me would like nothing more than for Tess to drop her motion and move to Connecticut. We could work out a visitation schedule around school vacations and holidays. It isn't ideal for Tess, but it might be for Ellie.

Me: Can you meet me at your rock?

Frankie: I'm on my way.

After a short drive, I park along the curb at Hartley Reserve. I consider waiting for Frankie, but I decide against it. As I near the edge of the grass, I remove my shoes and socks to walk along the shore. A few minutes after I pull myself up on her rock, Frankie slips beneath the wrought iron arch at the entrance.

"Thank you for coming." The weather is overcast today, much like my mood now.

"All you have to do is ask." Frankie sets her palms beside me and joins me perched on the large, flat rock. "Do you want to talk or just be?"

"Just be for now." I lift my arm and tug her closer while her arms clasp around my waist. A decent amount of time passes in silence. The only sounds are our breathing, the waves crashing against the shore, and the occasional seagull. "Thank you again for coming. I'm sure it set back your progress on the Cooper plans."

"You and Ellie are more important than work."

"I would have gone straight to my workshop if it weren't for you."

She lifts her eyes to mine. "I meant what I said. I'm here for both of you. I would rather you talk to me and build for pleasure, not because you're sorting through something."

"I know. It's why I called. My attorney gave me a few options. None are sufficient in my opinion. I even asked about filing for sole custody." I pause, expecting Frankie to say something, she doesn't, and I love her for it. "I don't want to take Ellie away from Tess. I want Tess to step up and act appropriately for our daughter. For now, I opted for the less-nuclear option, even though nuclear might be what Tess needs to get herself together."

"What exactly does that mean?"

I push out a breath I didn't know I was holding. "Hopefully, we're going to court later today to ask for a hearing on the motion."

"Can't you just ask for it to be dismissed again?"

"It's an option, but we'll be right back here again after Tess refiles. Ellie needs a resolution to this issue. This takes away Tess's ability to prolong this anymore."

"Makes sense."

My phone ringing breaks into our conversation.

"Hello."

"Mr. Thornton, this is Cammie from Attorney Kramer's office. The court scheduled your hearing at one this afternoon. Will the time be a problem?"

"No. Thank you, Cammie. I'll be there." I end the call, kiss the top of Frankie's head, and slide off the rock. After guiding her to the ground, we walk to the grass and put our shoes back on. "Will you be home this afternoon for Ellie?"

"Yes, I'll be there."

This woman has no idea how much she means to me. No other woman was ever as forthright about Ellie and followed through. Once this relocation issue is settled, I'm going to make her mine for the rest of our lives. After an all-too-brief kiss, I drive to the courthouse and Frankie goes back home. I love that. *Home. Our home.*

I enter the courthouse and locate Attorney Kramer in the corridor outside courtroom two.

"There are two more cases before ours," she informs me.

I nod and take a seat on the bench.

"Contessa Thornton, now known as Contessa Spears, vs. Thomas M. Thornton," the bailiff calls my case a bit later.

We move into the courtroom and take our places at the counsel tables.

"Pasquale Lucci for the petitioner, Your Honor."

"Antionette Kramer for the respondent, Your Honor. Mr. Thornton is to my left."

"Good afternoon. Mr. Lucci, where is your client?"

"My client was unable to join us this afternoon." His tone is clipped and angry.

I glance at Tess's attorney. Even he is fed up with her no-shows.

"Very well. Miss Kramer, you requested this hearing, please proceed."

"Thank you, Your Honor. My client requests a date certain in the near future for the pending motion regarding relocation of the minor child. This is the second time Mrs. Spears has failed to appear when mediations have been scheduled, and her notifications are always last minute."

"Mr. Lucci, your response?" the judge directs him.

"Given the circumstances, I have no objection to a hearing being set for this matter."

If my attorney is surprised, she doesn't show it. I know I am.

"Excellent. Madam Clerk, please provide the soonest morning hearing for this matter. Mr. Lucci, if your client is not present, I will dismiss her motion."

"Understood, Your Honor."

"Please see the chief clerk for your date assignment. The parties are dismissed."

We leave the courtroom and walk directly to the clerk's office. After a short wait, she provides a hearing two weeks from now.

"I'll be in touch to prepare before the hearing," my attorney informs me.

"Thank you. Have a nice afternoon."

"You as well."

I leave the courthouse and hurry home. I may even beat Ellie there. She knows we were scheduled for mediation again today, so I'm sure she'll have questions when she gets home.

"Sunshine." She doesn't answer me. I set my keys in the bowl and lay my jacket over the banister. I pass through the kitchen, nothing. Dismissing the bedroom without checking, I lean against the doorframe of the office. Frankie is marking up a landscaping plan with colored pencils. She's mesmerizing when she's focused. No, she grabs my attention the moment we're in the same room. Even when we aren't, she's on my mind. It isn't until she turns to check something behind her I noticed the AirPods in her ears.

Rounding the desk, I set my hand around her wrist. She looks up at me. I seize the opportunity and kiss her slowly and deliberately. Once I'm temporarily satisfied, she pulls one of the earbuds out. "Hi. How did it go?"

"Hi. This is amazing. Boston or Mystic?"

"Thanks. Mystic. I finished Boston a few days ago. That bad or that good?"

"We have a hearing set. The judge told Tess's attorney, if she doesn't show, he'll dismiss her motion."

"Progress, I guess."

"I didn't know what else to do. I don't want to make it worse, but this is the last chance I'm giving Tess."

"What does it mean, Dad?" Ellie is standing in the doorway of the office.

"Hi, Ellie. Let's talk in the kitchen."

I follow Ellie with Frankie out of the office. "How was school?"

"Fine. Please explain what you just said."

"What do you want to hear?"

"The truth," Ellie answers emphatically.

"Mom didn't show up again. My attorney gave me a few options. One would be to ask for a dismissal again, but she could refile. Second, would be to ask for a hearing, which would require Tess to show up or something even more drastic."

"You went with option two?"

"Yes, but I'll choose the drastic option if she doesn't show up at the hearing."

"Okay. We need to get moving to practice. Big game this weekend." Ellie hurries upstairs and dresses for practice.

"Do you want to stay here and finish or come to the field?" I ask Frankie.

"Do I get a walk and kisses behind a tree?"

I grin at her. "Without question."

"I'll get a hoodie and pull on some shoes."

We are off to practice within thirty minutes. It seems like we have been doing this together longer than we have. I plan to keep it that way.

CHAPTER THIRTY-TWO

FRANCESCA

The plans for the first four hotels are coming along. Portsmouth is complete. Boston and Mystic are ready for review by the board and the franchisee. Even though it's easier to work on the plans at home, I need to go to my office today. Eric is on vacation, and Macy is scheduled to be off this morning.

"Ellie, are you ready?" I call up to her.

"Almost," she replies from upstairs.

"Thank you for bringing her to school. Linda is on vacation, and I need to be at the office early."

"No problem. It'll give us some girls-only time at Sweet Face."

"I need to go. Dinner just the two of us tonight?"

"Yes. I love you."

He kisses me again. "I love you. Bye, Ellie. Love you most."

"Bye, Dad. Love you more."

Tommy leaves, and Ellie hurries down the stairs without shoes.

"I think you need shoes."

She shakes her head and runs back upstairs. With shoes and her backpack, we head to Sweet Face.

"Morning, Tal." My bestie looks distraught this morning. "What's wrong?"

"Morning. Hi, Ellie. What can I get for you?" She's purposefully avoiding my question.

"I'll take a chocolate chip muffin and a water."

"Your usual, Frankie?" Tal asks.

"Sure."

Ellie walks over to my usual spot by the window.

It gives me the chance to grill Talia. "Spill, Tal."

"Holden is getting released in two weeks, and I'm freaking out."

"We have been here at least once a week. Why didn't you tell me?"

She looks pointedly over at Ellie. "I didn't want to intrude on your newfound happiness."

"You're my best friend. I'm never too busy for you. You should have called me."

She shrugs and hands me a tray with our breakfast. "Where's lover boy?"

Her description isn't even close to apt. "He needed to get to work early. Just us girls today. You should join us."

"Thanks, but I don't want to unpack my concerns with Ellie around. She has enough going on in her own life with her mother."

"Okay, please promise me you'll meet me tomorrow for lunch."

"Deal."

I take the tray and sit with Ellie. "Anything big going on at school today?" I ask her.

"Nope."

"Do you have classes with Kylie?"

"Nope, only lunch."

I know better than to read into her demeanor. I have no doubt it has to do with going to her mom's after school today. Only crumbs remain of my muffin, and my coffee is empty. "I'll be right back." I order a second coffee while Ellie picks at her muffin.

We head out the door with my second coffee in hand toward Ellie's school.

"Have a good day, Ellie."

"Thanks, Frankie."

"I'm here if you want to talk about not wanting to go to Mom's later."

"Thanks. I don't want to, but it's the right thing, so I'll go. I appreciate your offer though."

I nod, and she draws me in for a hug.

"See you Friday." She exits my truck and hurries into the building.

I pull away from the curb. Ignoring my strong urge to drive to the shoreline, I park at my office. From the moment my butt hits my chair, the phone is ringing off the hook and the scheduling software I use is acting strange. Call after call comes in, requesting quotes. We get calls daily but not this many. So many in fact, I'm concerned my current team can't handle the workload for the spring. I dig a little deeper with the next caller.

"Good morning, Sunshine Landscape. How can I direct your call?"

"I need to set up a contract for lawn maintenance and new plantings for the spring. Our current company folded, and I saw your information in the announcement for the Cooper Hotel in Portsmouth. Your plans are gorgeous."

"Thank you, Mrs…?"

"Sorry, Mrs. Lennix. I'm sure you're busy but an appointment to chat would be wonderful."

"Of course. I have an opening on Friday morning at ten. Beforehand, could you email me pictures of your current landscape, so I have an idea of the space before we chat?" I provide her with my email address.

"No problem."

"May I ask who referred you?"

"When I reached out to schedule my yearly review, I was informed Greenthumb folded."

"I look forward to seeing the photos. Have a great day, Mrs. Lennix."

Liam's company folded. Clearly, I've missed some major industry news. Without a second thought, I google his company. The website is the first link. As indicated, a banner across the page indicates the company is closed indefinitely. Digging a bit deeper, I find an article that implicates Liam through his company and personally in defrauding dozens of his clients over the last few years. It might explain his desperation in landing the Cooper project. It's a lucrative contract. It would've covered his losses.

Given the number of calls I've received today and the emails in my inbox, I can only assume Eric's looks similar. I pick up the phone and place an ad for experienced landscapers. I thought hiring Macy would be enough given the time needed for the Cooper project. I need to crunch some numbers and focus on keeping all aspects of Sunshine running while I crush the Cooper Hotels project. Promoting Eric will likely be the best option and finding at least one additional foreman, perhaps two, especially considering there are ten voice mails and fifteen inquiries flooding my inboxes in the last thirty minutes.

Thankfully, Eric will be back on Monday. Until then, all I can do is plug away at these inquires and work on hiring the people I need to make it happen. The good news is the design aspect falls on me and will be during the slow winter months. With Eric's help pricing the projects, we should be set for the installation season in the spring with a large enough crew.

The next time I take a breath and look away from my screen, Macy is knocking on my door.

"Afternoon, Frankie."

"Hey. Everything good?" I ask without pushing for details.

"Yes, what can I do?"

"Please contact the scheduling software company and try to figure out what is going wrong. If necessary, please get a technician here. With the number of inquiries, I'm going to need it functioning properly and be using the design software frequently in the next few weeks."

"Right away."

With Macy here to answer the phones, I tackle the inquiries from oldest to newest. Over the next two plus hours, I schedule appointments over the next two weeks for twenty new clients. My inquiry for a new foreman has already yielded some interested applicants. I reach out to the job board and schedule three interviews for next Wednesday after Eric gets back. I value his opinion, especially if he is going to manage these new workers. I'm so deep in the influx of new contacts, I haven't had time to share with Tommy.

Me: Are you free?

Tommy: I'll call you in a few minutes.

I review, respond, and forward to Eric another three inquiries when Macy buzzes me.

"Mr. Thornton on line two," Macy informs me.

"Thanks."

"Hi, babe. How is your day going?" I ask.

"Dreadfully slow. I'm merely here because Linda isn't. They want a senior staff member on the premises daily. Today was my day this week. What about you?"

"It's craziness here. My phone lines and inbox have been flooding with new inquiries and requests for quotes."

"Fantastic."

"Apparently, the announcement about Cooper came out today as well as fraud charges against Liam Samuels and Greenthumb."

"I'm so happy for you," Tommy croons.

"Thank you. We can celebrate tonight." My response comes out a little more sultry than I intend. "I'll see you at home in a little while. I need to get through a bunch more of these before I leave."

"No problem. I'll start dinner. I love you."

"I love you."

I turn my attention back to my work and plow through until I get a text from Ellie.

Ellie: Can you come pick me up at Mom's? She isn't here.

Ellie: I have too much stuff to walk.

Me: Give me the address. I'm on my way.

I check in with Macy and hurry toward Ellie. The trip to Tess's is nerve-racking. I don't know how Ellie will respond this time. Frankly, she has been through enough in my opinion. When I pull into the driveway, I see relief on Ellie's face as she rises from the top step.

"Thank you for coming. I don't know what to do. My mom isn't here, and I don't know when or if she will be back, so I don't want to wait alone."

"I meant what I said, Ellie. I'm here for you."

"I'm grateful I can rely on you too now." Ellie hands me a bag, and I put it in the back of my truck. She adds another and opens the passenger door.

A sleek, red SUV parks beside me in the driveway.

Tess whips open the driver door and starts shouting. "Where do you think you're going with my daughter?" Her words and her tone are unnecessary.

I focus on remaining calm in the face of her angry words. "Hi, Tess. Ellie was worried you weren't here, so she called me to pick her up. Tommy is stuck at the office this afternoon."

Her anger doesn't decrease at all. "Eleanor, bring your things back inside. It's my parenting time today. You don't get to decide where you go and with whom."

Ellie shudders but does what Tess asks. She pulls her bags from my truck and sets them on the grass behind her. One of the times she reaches back in, I catch her wiping a tear from her cheek. My heart breaks for her, and there's absolutely nothing I can do but leave her here.

"Tess, there's no need to be angry. Ellie was worried and she reached out to me. Now you're here. All it means is I took a ride to keep Ellie company."

Tess isn't happy about my presence in her driveway one bit.

Ellie breaks her silence. "Mom, I texted you first, more than once, and waited almost a half hour before contacting Frankie. This isn't the first time you were late or didn't show up. If you had just answered me, we could have avoided this unnecessary confrontation."

Ellie's words strike Tess, but she recovers quickly. "Either way, please go inside and get ready for dinner," Tess instructs Ellie.

Much to my surprise and Tess's displeasure, Ellie rounds my truck and hugs me close. "Thank you for coming. I'll be okay here. Once we're done eating, I'll hang out in my room until school tomorrow, especially if Michael comes home. I love you more, Frankie."

A heaviness clutches my heart. I tighten my grip and whisper, "I love you most, Ellie. Please call again if you need us anytime, day or night."

She nods against my shoulder and discreetly wipes her tears on my shirt.

"I'll see you on Saturday at your last game of the season." Those words are said a bit louder for Tess's benefit. I want her to know I'll be there to support Ellie even if she simply drops her off.

Tess hasn't uttered another word, but her heeled boots are tapping on the cobblestone driveway. She simply stands watching as Ellie makes two trips to the porch with her school project pieces. Once they step inside, I back down the driveway and head home.

Me: Are you on your way home?

Tommy: Yes. Is everything okay?

Me: No. I'll be there soon.

CHAPTER THIRTY-THREE

THOMAS

There's only one possible explanation for the change in Frankie's attitude—Tess. As soon as I arrive home, I drop my keys in the bowl and tug off my tie. I'm waiting on the front porch when Frankie arrives.

"I'm sorry. I thought I was doing the right thing. She called, I went—"

"Slow down, Sunshine. I'm confident you didn't do anything wrong."

She explains the last hour of her day, including the call from Ellie after she texted Tess twice and the words she exchanged with Tess. "When I was leaving, she rounded the car and hugged me in front of Tess. She told me she loved me."

"Breathe, beautiful. Of course she does. You're amazing, and you were able to find the right balance without forcing a relationship."

"You're not mad?"

"Why would I be mad? You went to my daughter when she called you. You held your ground against my ex-wife despite her venom, and you did the correct but the hardest thing of all—you left Ellie with Tess. I love you, Sunshine, and I'm so happy you're mine." I kiss the tears from her cheeks and draw her into my arms.

"I love you most."

I take her hand, lead her to the chaise, and curl up with her in my arms. My phone chimes in my pocket, but I ignore Tess for right now. Frankie did everything right, and if Tess can't see that, that's on her. I whip up grilled cheese with bacon and tomato for dinner. It isn't what I initially planned, but it works out fine. After clearing the dishes, we curl up on the couch in our bedroom. While Frankie checks her email and sorts through her texts, I do the same.

Tess: Your girlfriend can't just show up at my house when Ellie calls.

Tess: It's my parenting time today.

Tess: You need to choose. Your daughter or your girlfriend.

Generally, I don't engage Tess, but this is over the line. She answers right away.

"About time you called me back," she roars into the phone.

Beside me, Frankie stiffens at her loud response through the phone.

"Tess, I'm going to be clear with my words. I will not choose between my daughter and Frankie. There's absolutely no reason for me to do so. I'm entitled to have a personal life like you. Frankie is amazing with Ellie. When Ellie called, she went to check on her. You can't dictate what Ellie does or doesn't do when you aren't at home when you should be. Ellie acted responsibly today and should be praised, just like a few weeks ago when you weren't there and your home was trashed."

"A few weeks ago isn't at issue right now. I don't want your girlfriend near my daughter."

I intertwine my fingers with Frankie's. "Demands and requests about Frankie aren't how this works, Tess. You get to choose who you spend your time with, and so do I. You chose Michael. I choose Frankie. It doesn't in any way impact Ellie negatively." In fact, having a confident, successful businesswoman around my daughter is beneficial. "Tess, you've moved on, and so have I. This is about me, not Ellie. Until Frankie, no other woman was willing to be there for Ellie. Most of them ran away when they learned I'm a father. I'm glad your status as a single mom didn't hinder your dating life before you married Michael. Being a single dad hindered mine. I won't walk away from the best woman I've met in a long time because you're threatened. I've dealt with Ellie having Michael in her life. You need to deal with Frankie all the same. It isn't going to change. I'll see you on Saturday at Ellie's last game of the season. Good night, Tess." I end the call before she has a chance to respond again.

I lift Frankie's hand to my mouth and kiss her fingertips.

"Was today the first time she reacted like that?"

"To you? Yes."

Frankie buries her head into my chest for a moment. "I didn't mean to cause problems. I went for Ellie."

"Stop. Do not even think you did anything wrong. You didn't. Instead of shying away, you went straight to Tess's without a second thought because Ellie needed you. You're beyond what I could ever ask for a role model and bonus mom for Ellie."

"Thank you. Considering how Tess is reacting to this, should I ask my family not to come to her game on Saturday?"

"You invited them?" This woman crushes every quality I was looking for in a partner and mother figure for Ellie.

"Sort of. Emilia asked to come to a game, and then it kind of snowballed from there. Within a few texts, the entire family penciled it in."

"No, they're more than welcome. Ellie's personal cheering section will be huge then. My entire family is coming as well."

"Sweet. I'm looking forward to meeting the rest of them. Hopefully, Tess will stick around for this one."

"I hope so too. Let's get some sleep, gorgeous."

The rest of the week flies by for both Frankie and me. She's uber-busy fielding inquiries and setting up appointments with potential clients as well as working on the fourth hotel plan in the evenings because Eric is on vacation.

"Mr. Thornton, Tess Spears on line three for you."

"Thank you, Melissa."

I take a deep breath and prepare myself for the letdown on behalf of my daughter my ex-wife is about to drop. "Hello, Tess. How are you?" My tone is slightly short of cordial.

"I'm fine, but I need you to take Ellie this weekend. Michael has a function with the board of directors. I tried to wiggle out of it, but I failed. Spouses are required to attend. I'm sure Ellie will understand." Her voice is clipped and her words staccato like she's reading from something rather than speaking for herself.

As much as I would like to remind Tess her relationship with Ellie is crucial, I don't. "Sure. I'll contact the school and let her know I'll pick her up today. Do you have an issue with her going into the house? She may need things for the weekend."

"No, you can take her to the house if she needs her uniform. Thank you."

"Are you sure you're okay, Tess?"

"Yes, I'm fine. Goodbye." She ends the call.

At one point, I thought I was in love with Tess. While it wasn't the case then and certainly isn't now, she was my wife. I know something is going on with her. She may not have been a fantastic wife, but she was a good mother. At least she was until she married Michael. Like Frankie said, it doesn't add up to anything actionable. All I can do is protect Ellie and cushion the blow when Tess lets her down each and every time.

"Melissa, can you get me the number for Principal Mulier please?" I pull out my phone and text Frankie.

Me: Hey there. Tess called. I'm going to pick up Ellie first.

Me: Love you more.

Frankie: Poor Ellie. Love you most.

After Melissa provides the number, I call the school and pack up for the day. I spend the ride to the school going over what to say to Ellie.

Even if I plan the right words and execute them perfectly, it won't be enough to soften the blow of disappointment she's bound to feel from Tess letting her down once again.

I pull up in the pickup line and wait for Ellie.

"Hi, Dad."

"Hey. What do you say to an extra movie night?"

"She flaked again?" My daughter's voice comes out resigned and slightly ticked.

"Not exactly. She called this time. Do you need anything from her house?"

"Yeah."

I drive to Tess's and park in the driveway. "Do you want me to come in with you?"

"Yeah." My daughter's one-word answers increase my concern.

"Do you want to talk?"

"Not now."

"Okay. When you want to talk, we're ready to listen."

She nods and keys open the front door. "I'll be right back." About ten minutes later, Ellie comes back downstairs, sets a bag at my feet, and goes back up. She returns twice more, each time with an overfilled bag in each hand.

"What's wrong, Ellie? This is a lot of stuff for a weekend."

"Most of Mom's clothes are gone. I'm preparing in case she doesn't come back."

"Come here." I wrap my daughter into a hug until my heart stops breaking for her. I don't know if it ever will regarding the unnecessary pain Tess is causing her. "Is there more?"

"Nothing I need."

"Okay, let's go home." I make a trip to my car and back to the porch while Ellie moves the bags outside. After the last bag is in my trunk, we both hop into the car. As I shift into reverse, a police cruiser pulls in behind me and another alongside the curb.

"Eleanor, stay in the car," I demand.

I open my door and close it. I haven't done anything wrong. "Can I help you, Officer?"

"Are you Michael Spears?"

"No."

"Can I see some identification?" Officer Tremont requests.

I make a mental note of his badge number and hand him my driver's license. He steps closer and peers into my car.

"Thank you. This is 18 Maple Lane, and the homeowners are Michael and Contessa Spears, correct?"

"Correct. I'm Thomas M. Thornton. My daughter needed some things for the weekend. My ex-wife, Contessa Thornton Spears, gave me permission to escort our daughter here after school today. Our daughter has a key. Can you tell me what this is about?"

"We have some questions for Mr. Spears regarding an altercation earlier today."

"Should I be concerned for my daughter?" I knew Tess sounded off, but it doesn't necessarily have anything to do with the police showing up at her home. Right?

Officer Tremont pauses a bit too long for my liking. "I don't have any information I can share with you other than what I already have, Mr. Thornton. Have a nice day."

"Thank you." I get back into my car, turn over the engine, and wait for the cruiser to move.

"What is going on?" Ellie demands.

"I'll tell you, but we need to drive away first."

She nods and continues to fidget with the hem of her hoodie. We make it to the stop sign at the end of the block before Ellie inquires again.

"Is Mom okay?"

"They were looking for Michael, not your mom. The officer wasn't very forthcoming with any additional information."

"Can I call Mom?" Ellie whispers because she's worried.

"Ellie, you can call your Mom whenever you want or need to. As I said before, I care about your mother because she gave me you, even though I'm building a relationship with Frankie."

She nods and texts Tess. I can't read the words. I don't need to. She's worried. I hope Tess responds. I doubt she will, but for Ellie, I hope so.

We pull into the driveway, and my sunshine is waiting on the porch. She wraps Ellie into her arms and holds her close.

"I'm scared, Frankie. Mom was fine until she married Michael. Her behavior keeps getting increasingly strange, and it usually means she isn't with me."

"I know, sweet girl. All we can do is offer her help and hope she takes it." Frankie wipes the tears from Ellie's cheeks, and they walk inside arm in arm.

When I return from bringing Ellie's bags to her room, my ladies are sharing a drink at the island.

"I'm going to empty a bag or two while we wait for dinner to arrive. Then I'll pick a movie. Frankie took care of dinner already."

Ellie runs upstairs, and she appears to be at least momentarily settled about Tess.

"The cops are looking for Michael? Ellie said they didn't share very much information."

"No, and Tess hasn't answered her yet to my knowledge, and it makes her nervous," I share.

"It would make me nervous too."

Our conversation is interrupted by the doorbell. I follow Frankie to the door.

"*Cugino*. Thank you so much!" Frankie exclaims.

Her cousin Matteo is a celebrity chef. Not only does he prepare personalized meals for our soccer-playing cousin, Marco, but many of his teammates and the football team who shares the stadium.

"*Felice di aiutare*. Look at you, always gorgeous."

"*Molte grazie*! Come in, come in."

After he sets the bags on the island, Frankie introduces us. "Tommy, this is my cousin Matteo. Matteo, my boyfriend Tommy." Ellie steps into the kitchen. "This is Ellie. She may be as talented as when Marco was her age."

"Pleasure to meet you, Tommy, and you as well, Ellie," Matteo greets them.

"Likewise," Tommy replies.

"Whatever is in those bags smells delicious," Ellie admits.

"*Grazie, bella.*" Matteo spreads the dishes I requested on the island.

"Thanks, Matteo. I appreciate it on short notice," Frankie thanks him.

I consider thanking him too, but I should try his food beforehand.

"*Sempre siamo una famiglia.* Pleasure to meet both of you. I'm sure we'll see each other again."

"Bye, thank you," Ellie states.

Frankie escorts him to the front door as he hurries to his next delivery.

"I have so many questions," Ellie states, shoving a sliver of garlic bread into her mouth.

Me too. She never mentioned her cousins. She speaks Italian?

Frankie laughs. We plate some of Matteo's dishes and curl up on the floor in the living room, using the ottoman as a table. Ellie selects *School of Rock* with Jack Black.

"Frankie, this is ohmygod fantastic!" Ellie compliments Matteo's food.

"Thanks. I'll make sure to share with Matteo. He's gifted. His client list exemplifies his skill level. It's a veritable who's who in professional soccer, football, and a few A-list actors sprinkled in."

We finish the movie, and Ellie is ready to go to sleep. The last game of the season against the second-place team is tomorrow.

"Please verify your uniform is clean. I know it's been a bit inconsistent lately." I don't say it out loud, but Ellie knows I mean Tess.

"I'll check. Good night." Ellie runs upstairs. Less than five minutes later, Ellie returns with an armful of clothes. "I'm sorry."

"Not your fault. I'll take care of this for you."

"Thanks, Dad. Good night."

I throw in her laundry and cuddle up with Frankie on the porch until it finishes.

"You amaze me more and more each day."

She wrinkles her nose at me. "Doubtful."

"No, seriously. I merely mentioned I needed to pick up Ellie on Tess's weekend, which also happens to be right before the last and biggest game of the season, and you went to work. Not only did you come home early, even though I know you're crazy busy at work right now with Eric on vacation, you managed to order a gourmet dinner from your chef cousin who has some serious skills. You put my daughter at ease the moment we arrived. As if all those things weren't enough, hearing you speak Italian is sexy as sin."

A fierce blush creeps across her skin. "I'm taking care of you and Ellie. Lean on me. Let me stand beside you and slay the dragons you're facing and the ones facing Ellie too."

"I would love nothing more, Sunshine. I love you, and I'm crazy excited you love us too."

"I do with all my heart."

I tug her closer and drop a kiss to her forehead. *I do too. I plan to for the rest of my life.*

CHAPTER THIRTY-FOUR

FRANCESCA

Game day for me was always my favorite of the weekend. I'm sure it is for Ellie as well. Tommy is finishing his workout, and Ellie is buzzing around the kitchen looking for breakfast.

"Slow down, Ellie. Save some of this energy for the game."

"Don't worry, Frankie. I'm ready. The Renegades won't know what hit them today. This game is for the league regular season championship. It's a must win."

"I remember vividly being in the same position. It's an amazing feeling to play and win as a team."

"Morning. How are my girls doing today?" Tommy appears in the kitchen. He's drying his face with his shirt. Pulling my tongue back in my mouth is harder than I anticipate. *Sweet mercy!* He's gorgeous and mine.

"Good," I reply.

"I'm crazy hyped. Is it too early to leave?"

Tommy laughs. "Yes, plus I'm not going out without a shower. Make sure you eat well, Ellie."

"On it." Ellie pulls out the ingredients for an egg and cheese burrito. "Want one?"

"Sure," Tommy replies.

"Frankie?"

"Sounds good, thanks. I'll be right back." I join Tommy in the bathroom.

"Hey, do you think Ellie would be interested in going to a soccer game?" I'm working hard to avoid ogling him while he dresses.

His forehead wrinkles in confusion. "A professional soccer game? I'm sure she would, why?"

"I'm considering reaching out to Marco to see if he could get us tickets for a game, but I wanted to check first."

"You're full of surprises, Sunshine. Not only is your cousin a celebrity and sports chef, but your other cousin is *the* Marco Cappelli?"

I chuckle. "Yes, why?"

"He is Ellie's favorite player."

"My cool factor increased a 1000 percent with that tidbit, huh?"

Tommy laughs. "Yeah, if not more. I'm sure she would love it. Now go, so we don't mess up Ellie's breakfast."

I steal a kiss and hurry out the bedroom door. Ellie is finishing up the food.

"Could you make coffee for you and Dad?"

"Sure, Ellie." I make two cups for now and set it up for travel cups for the game.

She sets out the food as Tommy reenters the kitchen. We take our seats and dig in.

"Great job, Ellie!"

"This is tasty," I state.

"Thanks. It was super easy."

We take a bit too long enjoying Ellie's breakfast and have to hurry out the door to get her to warm-ups on time. On the way, my phone is chiming incessantly. Once she hops out, I check my messages.

Lina: We'll see you soon. Em is so excited.

Lily: Cool if I bring Leo?

Lia: Scarlett is coming too.

Willa: We're on our way.

Mama: We're leaving now.

I send off a quick reply to Lily.

Me: Leo is always welcome.

Lily: Thanks. Love you.

Tommy is also checking his phone.

"Your family too?"

"Yeah, Ellie's cheering section is going to be enormous today."

"Lily asked if she could bring her best friend, and Lia is bringing hers. It's pretty awesome."

We grab our chairs and move toward the field. Thankfully, we have enough time to secure space for Ellie's cheering section.

Once we set up, Tommy's family starts to arrive. This is probably Tim, the brother I haven't met yet. He looks exactly like Tommy, just a bit shorter and less fit.

"Frankie, my brother Tim. Tim, my girlfriend Frankie."

"Pleasure to meet you. Ellie and Tam have been talking about you constantly."

"Good things, I hope."

Tim smiles. "All good things."

The next twenty minutes are a flurry of introductions and greetings. Kylie arrives with her mom. Toby arrives at the same time as Lia, Scarlett, Lina, and the kids. Tommy introduces me to his parents, Tommy and Gloria. His dad is an older version of Tommy. My Tommy seems to be more outgoing than his dad though. Gloria, on the other hand, seems to be a social butterfly chatting it up with everyone from my family as well. When she isn't chatting, they're as cute as my parents, holding hands and leaning into one another. I greet my family as well and introduce everyone around. I only have time for a quick side hug to Lily and Leo when the game starts.

The first half of the game is a defensive struggle. The Renegades clearly recall Ellie from their first meeting this season. They are clogging up the passing lanes around her. At the half, the game is scoreless.

Luca and Willa move beside me. "She might be better than you were, even Marco."

"She might be. Ellie is doing everything she can. She trains hard and shows up every game and every practice, despite the upheaval in her life. How's newlywed life?"

"Pretty awesome," Luca chimes in.

"What he said." Willa laughs. "Seriously, though I fought so long to avoid seeing he was perfect for me. In the end, giving Luca a chance was the best thing to ever happen for me, other than Dad adopting me."

Luca kisses Willa's temple while drawing her closer. Leo and Lily return after a trip to the restroom.

"Hey, Frankie. Ellie is pretty amazing," Leo offers. He towers over me with his hulking frame. Once upon a time, Leo was an all-state defensive lineman and played at a division one university too. In college he switched to center. He was drafted and played a few years in the league at nose tackle.

"She is." It isn't until I turn completely to face them I notice Lily's arm linked with Leo's. I raise an eyebrow, and wordlessly she tells me we'll talk about it later. Interesting. Lily truly should give him a chance.

As the players take the field for the second half, Ellie notices her huge fan contingent, and an even bigger smile breaks out on her face. I'm glad she's still happy, even though Tess hasn't shown up for her.

Ellie's first time with the ball in the second half she dribbles forward from midfield, passes it to her striker, who then crosses it to the wing who pushed up. The wing shoots, and it hits the back of the net for the first goal of the game. In the next minute, Ellie takes the shot herself and buries it in the back of the net. Her entire family and mine erupt in applause and shout her name.

She may not realize it yet, but not only does Ellie have me in her corner now but my entire family too.

The Renegades make a few lineup changes and momentum shifts their way for some of the second half. Ellie's team holds up well, and the goalie saves at least four good shots on goal. As the game nears the three-minutes-remaining mark, the Renegades score on a rebound off the goalie. The goalie hangs her head briefly.

Ellie shouts, "Forget it, Sarah. We've got this!" Ellie is an excellent leader on the field.

Sarah air fist-bumps Ellie and settles back into the game. For the remaining minutes, Ellie and her teammates effectively keep the ball on their half of the field. When the referee blows the final whistle, the entire sideline erupts in cheers.

Ellie runs across the field and leaps into Tommy's arms once the team postgame chat ends.

"I'm so proud of you," Tommy shouts.

Ellie pulls me in too.

"Thank you for working with me. The moves you taught me really helped." Ellie smiles.

"You're welcome."

Tommy sets her down, and Emilia circles her arms around her waist.

"Ellie, you were awesome!" Sheer admiration shines on my niece's face.

"Thanks, Em." Ellie high-fives the rest of her massive cheering section. "Thank you all so much for coming to my game." I see the slight flicker of disappointment pass through her mind. Everyone in her life is here except Tess. No matter how hard she tries to mask it, it hurts. My parents never once let me down so significantly and repeatedly, but I have plenty of life experience to equate to it.

Our family members each congratulate Ellie and head home.

"Dad, will you cook for us?"

"Absolutely, but we need groceries first," Tommy offers.

"Deal. Can I sleepover at Kylie's mom's tonight?" Ellie asks.

"Sure. Get me all the details, and we can make it happen."

An evening at home alone with Tommy? Yes, please. I squeeze his hand in mine, and we walk toward the car. After a whirlwind trip around the grocery store with Tommy and Ellie adding so many things into the cart I lose track and hope we got everything we need. The next thing I know, we're putting it away at home.

"Why don't you go clean up, Ellie? I'll get started on lunch."

"Okay."

Once I hear her door close, I turn to Tommy. "What might we do tonight all alone?"

He grins. "I have no idea what you're suggesting, Sunshine. I'm sure we can find *something* to do."

I laugh and scroll through my texts.

Lina: You guys are so cute together.

Lia: Thank you for the invite. We had fun.

Lily: It isn't what it looked like, not exactly.

I reply to Lina and Lia and then focus on Lily.

Me: It looked like you were arm in arm and leaning into Leo.

Lily: Okay, so maybe that's accurate. It doesn't mean anything. We're just friends. He isn't single.

Me: Do you want him to be single?

"Who are you texting with?" Tommy inquires.

"Lily."

"Is she interested in Leo?"

"I'm not sure. They have been best friends since elementary school. As far as I know, nothing has ever happened between them."

"Huh, they looked like more than friends this morning."

"Exactly what I just said to her."

Lily: Yes. No. Maybe. Yes.

Me: Oh, Lil. You should tell him how you feel.

Lily: Nope, I'm not going to break up his relationship. If they breakup, I'll tell him, and not a moment sooner.

Me: Okay. Love you.

Lily: Love you more.

Ellie is ready to head off to Kylie's the moment we finish our sandwiches. Once Tommy confirms the details, he drops Ellie off for the night.

"What shall we do?" Tommy asks as soon as he returns. He stalks toward me like a lion ready to pounce. "Will I find any lingerie beneath those clothes?"

My eyes widen as I reply, "You should come even closer and find out."

Tommy spends the rest of the afternoon and into the evening exploring after he finds not a shred of lace or satin anywhere beneath my clothes.

CHAPTER THIRTY-FIVE

THOMAS

After our eventful weekend, it's back to insanely busy for Frankie at work. Eric is back from vacation today, but this week will be packed with appointments. As far as my schedule, it's similar. While Frankie is handling the landscape design for the hotel and her company contracts, I'm responsible for the other contractors as well.

"Melissa, can you schedule a meeting with the electrical and plumbing contractors for the Boston and Mystic locations at some point in the next two weeks."

"Right away," she replies.

"Also, can you get me the number for the florist again. I need to send flowers to my daughter and my girlfriend."

Melissa smiles. "Of course." Until Frankie, my personal life and my professional life didn't overlap at all. Other than she's diligent and does her job well, I don't know much about Melissa, like my lack of information about Linda and her custody issues.

I settle into my office chair again and cull through my inbox. Once complete, I order flowers and tickets for Ellie's end-of-the-season banquet for soccer. Not sure how it will go, I order four tickets in case Michael and Tess are able to join us.

"Mr. Thornton, Tess Spears on line two for you," Melissa states through the intercom.

"Thank you." With a deep breath and an internal reminder to remain calm, I lift the receiver. "Hi, Tess."

"Hello. Please listen and don't ask too many questions. I need you to keep Ellie for a while. I don't know when I'll be able to come back. There are things for me to wrap up here. I'm trying to protect Ellie."

"Tess, are you okay? Whatever it is, we can help." Probably shouldn't have said "we" there, but it's true. We're a team, and despite her distaste for how Tess has been treating Ellie, Frankie is in this with both of us.

The line is silent. "I will be. Please trust me and take care of Ellie."

The line goes dead. I consider calling her back, but I have no doubt she won't answer. Rising from my chair, I step out near Melissa's desk. "Could you stop in when you have about fifteen minutes?"

"Sure."

I walk around her and straight outside to call Frankie.

"Hey."

"Hi. What's wrong?" Frankie's voice is laced with concern.

"Tess called. She asked me to keep Ellie for a while. She doesn't know when she can return."

"Oh no. Is she okay?"

I scrub my free hand down my face. "She said she will be, but I don't know what it means. I'm also not sure I completely believe her."

"What can I do?"

"I wanted to hear your voice and tell you I love you. I'm meeting with Melissa to rearrange my schedule so I can pick up Ellie from school. Mostly, it's our meetings for Cooper she'll need to move."

"Okay, whatever we need to do for Ellie, we will, even if it means we work at home in the evenings."

"Thank you, Sunshine. I love you more."

"I love you most. I'll see you at home."

I contact the school and set a few surprises for Frankie into motion with a few more calls. After requesting the changes to my schedule and the blocks of time that need to be kept open, I head to Ellie's school.

It's a little early. I enter the building and have the school secretary call Ellie down for dismissal.

"Hi, Dad. I didn't expect to see you today. Is Mom okay?" Ellie asks.

I hate her mom's well-being is in the front of her mind constantly. "Hi, Ellie. We can talk about it on the way home."

We exit the building. I settle into the driver's seat and pull onto the street toward home. "Is there anything at Mom's you might need?"

"No, I took everything that is important to me. What's going on?"

I push out a deep breath. "I don't know exactly. I'm going to tell you straight, Ellie. Your mom called and said she needs me to take care of you for a while. She didn't say how long, and she didn't tell me why. When I asked if she was okay, she said she would be and ended the call. I know it isn't helpful, but it's the truth."

"Okay. It's what I want anyway. This means you're picking me up from school for the near future?"

"Yes, it does."

Ellie shrugs and looks out the window.

I can see her slump deeper into the seat and her face fall. "What, Ellie?"

"What about the banquet? It's in two weeks. I need a dress, and Mom was supposed to take me on Wednesday after school. Will Frankie take me?"

I smile inwardly. "You should ask her when we get home."

Ellie nods and glances out the window again. Once I park, Ellie rushes into the house. By the time I gather my bag and get inside, I hear Ellie and Frankie giggling. Ellie rushes out of the office toward the kitchen and nearly knocks me over.

"Dad! Frankie said she would take me shopping." A huge smile is on her face.

"Great! Homework?"

"Ugh! Yes, I'll get started on it." Ellie scoops up her bag and dumps the contents onto the dining room table.

I step into the office, close the door, and properly greet my woman. After an all-consuming kiss, I add some space between us. "Hi, how was the rest of your afternoon?"

"Not too bad. Yours?"

"I told Ellie the truth, pretty much word for word what Tess told me. Other than dress shopping, she isn't overly upset. She would prefer to be with us anyway, her words. Thank you for agreeing to take her."

"I'm happy to help and ecstatic she asked. When is the banquet and is it something we're attending as well?"

"It's in two weeks. Yes, we're going."

"Are you sure you can handle me wearing a dress again?"

My mind flashes with the last three instances Frankie wore a dress. "As long as you wear a different dress, I will be fine."

She feigns pouting and then smiles. "Deal. I'll have to find one equally alluring for the banquet."

"It wasn't a challenge, Sunshine."

"I took it as one. I have a few emails left, and then we can cook dinner."

I press a tender kiss to her lips and walk out of the office. I pass Ellie hard at work in the dining room and move upstairs to change. Within twenty minutes of me starting dinner, both Ellie and Frankie join me in the kitchen. Ellie sets the table while Frankie prepares a salad.

"What kind of dress are we looking for, Ellie?"

"Something comfortable and cute."

Frankie smirks. "Okay, a cocktail dress. Short or long?"

"I don't have a preference."

Ellie isn't very helpful with her responses, but Frankie doesn't seem bothered. We gather at the table and eat dinner as a family. Ellie doesn't seem overly affected by Tess's absence. I wonder if I should be comforted or worried. Unfortunately, the answer is both. I appreciate Ellie's comfort level with Frankie, but Tess repeatedly letting her down worries me.

My girls are chatting about colors, lengths, and cuts of dresses with huge smiles on their faces. I have no clue what any of it means as far as the dresses. Their expressions and laughter only make me fall deeper in love with Frankie.

CHAPTER THIRTY-SIX

FRANCESCA

The past two days have felt normal. It's certainly something I want going forward. The three of us working and acting like a family. After Ellie's fun practice last night, which was more the girls hanging out at the field and playing a scrimmage, we all turned in early.

I've been in the office this morning since Tommy went downstairs for his workout. I need a head start on today's work to take Ellie to So Elegant after school today. Clearing the inquiries from overnight, I forward the necessary ones to Macy for invoicing and Eric for planning. Macy is handling the office well and seems like a great fit for my company.

Our interviews last week went well. With Eric's input, I hired two assistant foremen, Tanner and Jude. Both have three years' experience. We also added two more crew members. Eric will train his assistants and oversee the two teams. If necessary, we'll add more crew members based on the workload.

"Morning, Sunshine." Tommy steps into the office freshly showered with a cup of hot coffee.

"Morning. Thank you." I take a sip of the coffee and attempt to hand it back to him.

"That's for you. You're going to pick up Ellie from school and then shop, right?"

"Yup. What's worrying you?"

He checks behind him to see if Ellie is ready to go yet. "Honestly, even though having Ellie here is her preference and mine, I don't like how it happened. The motion is still pending, and the hearing is in ten days. What does 'a while' mean to Tess? Will she be finished in time with whatever it is she's doing?"

I set the cup down and wrap my arms around him. "I can't answer any of those questions. Ellie is safe and happy here with us. Whatever happens with Tess or doesn't happen with Tess is on her. If she returns in time, we can handle it. If she doesn't, we'll figure out what's best for Ellie. It may mean arguing for full custody. Our focus is, has been, and will continue to be Ellie."

"I love when you use that word," he murmurs.

"What?"

"Us."

I smile. "I'm much more confident using it now than I was the first time."

"As you should be. I need to get Ellie to school and then to work. I love you more." He kisses me and hurries out of the office.

"I love you most." I'm flopped back into my chair when Ellie pops her head into the office.

"Bye, Frankie. I'll see you at pickup. Love you."

My chest tightens. I was hopeful for Ellie's acceptance eventually. I'm glad it didn't take as long as I thought it would. "I'll be there. Love you more, Ellie."

Before I forget, I call Marco. Surprisingly, he answers.

"Hey, *cugino*. How are you?"

"I'm well. Your stats are insane this season and on par to beat last season."

"Thanks. I hear there's a new man in your life."

"Matteo ratted me out, huh?"

"Of course. Want to impress him with tickets?" Marco asks.

"Not him, his daughter. She's apparently a huge fan of yours.

Marco laughs. "Does she know we're related?"

"Nope, she hasn't put it together yet. She has skills, Marco."

"I'll send four to will call for this Saturday. Can she walk in with us as well?" Marco offers.

"Seriously? You can make that happen?"

"For you, I can. Stef will send you the details. Please give her your new address and sizes, especially for… what's your daughter's name?"

My daughter. My heart tightens in my chest. She is in all the ways that matter. "Ellie. Thanks, Marco."

"We're family. We should set up a cousin reunion when the season is over. I know Marcella, Milana, and Mila would be on board for a raucous bash."

"The five of you are a trip, and we have so much fun together. Let's do it!"

"Perfecto! We'll start planning in a few weeks. I'll see you guys on Saturday."

"Thanks, Marco."

Before I turn back to the Mystic project plans, I text Tommy.

Me: We're set for a game on Saturday.

Tommy: She'll be so excited. Are you going to tell her or surprise her?

Me: I'm leaning toward surprise.

Tommy: Okay. Love you more.

Me: Love you most.

I slip in my AirPods and get back to work. Near eleven, I take a break and answer my morning texts.

Lina: Morning. Em is asking to see Ellie soon.

Me: I'll try to find some free time.

Lina: She'll be very excited.

Me: What about G?

Lina: We're taking it slow.

Me: Happy for you.

Lina: Thanks. Me too.

I read the next one from Lily.

Lily: You were right.

Me: About Leo?

Lily: Yes! Now I'm miserable.

Me: Sorry. You're a nice person. I understand why you want to wait.

Lily: It's a curse. Love you more.

Me: Love you most.

The last one is from Talia.

Talia: How is this going to work?

Me: It's going to take time and effort. Do you want him back?

Talia: Maybe. Probably.

Me: Be there for him and then see if you still work as a couple.

Talia: Love you, bestie.

Me: Love you too.

I return to my office and work until it's time to pick up Ellie from school. We make a quick stop at Sweet Face before I park near So Elegant.

"Is this the same place my mom was going to bring me?"

"I don't know. It's owned by a friend of mine. Want to share what's bothering you?"

Ellie faces me. "I really like spending time with you, but it feels like… like I'm cheating on my mom."

I suppress the laughter at her comparison. "I understand why you feel that way. I'll be here for you however and whenever you need me. I won't try to replace Tess but be another adult you can lean on."

"Thanks."

"Let's go find a dress."

Ellie smiles and hops out of the car. I ring the bell and the door swings open.

"Can I help you?" a petite woman with a pink pixie cut asks.

"We have an appointment with Kelly." I met Kelly when I was younger. She and her family vacationed here. When she got older, she moved here and opened her dream store. Now, she not only designs couture dresses for everyday people, but she also designs costumes for A-list productions. It's how she met her actor and director husband, Ellis.

"Hi, right this way." The woman leads us into the showroom and disappears.

Kelly comes out from behind a white curtain and hugs me tight. "It's so good to see you."

"You too. Kelly, please meet Ellie."

"Nice to meet you, Ellie. I understand you need a dress for a soccer banquet."

"Yes." Ellie's voice cracks.

"What are you thinking? Straps or strapless? Short or long? Floral or plain? Sparkle or no sparkle?"

"Whoa! Short, please. I think, honestly, I'm not sure. I'm not against flowers. Limited sparkle. Straps or Dad will go nuts."

"Okay, give me ten minutes and I'll bring you some options to fitting room four."

"Thanks, Kelly," I state as she walks away.

"She's awesome!" Ellie exclaims.

"She is. She designed Willa's wedding gown and bridesmaids' dresses."

Ellie peeks through the racks until Kelly returns. There's a lot of color in the pile of dresses.

"All set, Ellie."

A few minutes later, Ellie steps out of the dressing room in a tea-length dress with thin straps crossed in back. The fit is okay.

"What do you think, Ellie?" I ask.

"Too bright."

Interesting considering she's the star player on the team. "No problem. Try the next one."

"You look happy, Frankie," Kelly states.

"I am. Tommy is… he knocks me off my feet but doesn't let me fall. I'm sure it doesn't make any sense."

Kelly smiles. "It makes perfect sense. I knew Ellis was for me the second he held my hand and admitted he couldn't cook worth a damn. I knew then he would change my life."

Ellie steps out of the dressing room in a floral, floor-length maxi dress. It's beautiful on her.

"How about that one?"

"It's closer. I like the length and the floral pattern, but it's heavy," Ellie shares. "It's a maybe."

I nod. "How are the kids?"

"Nick is growing fast, and Elena has her daddy wrapped around her pinkie."

Ellie steps out of the dressing room in a burgundy off-the-shoulder dress with lace panels at the waist, midthigh, and the hem. It's perfect.

"What's your opinion?" I ask with a smile.

"I love it, and Dad won't freak because it has wide straps."

The three of us laugh.

"Perfect. What size shoe do you wear, Ellie?"

"Six."

Kelly produces a few pairs of shoes with low to medium heels. Ellie opts for the black sparkly slingbacks with the smallest heel. Ellie steps out of the dressing room with the dress on the hanger.

"I'll bag this for you along with the shoes."

"Thank you," Ellie replies.

"You're welcome."

We meet Kelly at the counter, and I pay for her dress and shoes. After a quick hug with Kelly and a promise to set up a dinner out with our other halves, Ellie and I head home.

"Shopping with you was so much fun! Thank you!" She croons as we pull into the driveway.

"You're welcome."

Ellie takes off into the house. With her dress and shoes in hand, I follow.

I lean against the doorframe of the kitchen while Ellie chronicles our outing for Tommy.

"It was awesome. The store is super cute. Kelly, the dress designer, was really nice. I tried on a few other dresses, but this one is perfect!" Words flow from Ellie's mouth as fast as she can say them.

"I'm glad you found something. You should get cleaned up for dinner," Tommy informs her. "Thank you for taking her. I don't know if I would've handled it well. Let me know how much for the dress and I'll get it to you."

"We had a great time. Don't worry about the dress. We should talk about expenses though."

"Meaning?" His tone is one I've never heard before. It's difficult to discern at first, but then it hits me. Tess never worked, so she couldn't contribute to the household finances.

"I moved in, and we really haven't talked about me contributing to our household."

He looks surprised and confused. "I asked you to move in, not pay for anything."

"I appreciate your position, but it won't work for me. I want to be your partner, not someone you have to take care of financially."

He shakes his head and draws me close. "Okay, we can talk about it more over the weekend. There truly aren't a lot of expenses though. I think I mentioned, this house belonged to my grandparents. I bought it from my grandmother about six months before she passed away. I paid Tess from my investments. I don't have a mortgage."

"Thank you."

Ellie spreads out her homework on the dining room table while we cook dinner. We have a relaxing dinner and sit outside until we turn in for the night.

CHAPTER THIRTY-SEVEN

THOMAS

The rest of the work week flies by with a flurry of activity to finalize the Portsmouth installation for lighting and flooring. The Boston and Mystic projects are well underway too. Friday night at the movies on my couch with my girls is the perfect way to end the week.

When I crest the stairs after my workout on Saturday morning, Ellie is waking slowly while Frankie can barely contain her excitement. Once I down a second water, Frankie moves into the office and carries a huge box into the kitchen.

"Ellie, this came for you yesterday," Frankie informs her.

Stef, Marco's assistant, went overboard I'm sure. Ellie tears into the package. Inside she finds an envelope containing the tickets and field passes for today as well as five jerseys.

Frankie waits patiently for Ellie to read the note and follow what is going on. By patiently, I mean only her foot is tapping incessantly.

"Wait, we're going to the game today?"

"Yes," Frankie replies.

"These are field passes for the game and this is a handwritten note from my favorite player of all time, Marco Cappelli."

Frankie reaches out, and Ellie hands her the envelope. "Yup, looks like his handwriting."

"Wait, you know what Marco Cappelli's handwriting looks like?"

"Well, yeah, he's my cousin."

Ellie's mouth drops open. She's speechless. Frankie has the biggest grin I've ever seen on her face.

"No way! Are you joking?" Ellie's tone indicates it would be an awful prank to pull on her.

"Not even a little bit. Ellie, did you finish reading the card?" Frankie asks her.

She shakes her head furiously and refocuses on the card. "I get to walk in with... OMG! Ohmigod! Thank you so much! When do we leave?"

I laugh along with Frankie. "I think you should finish looking in this package."

Ellie sifts through the rest and pulls out five jerseys. "Why five?"

Frankie lifts them one by one. "This one is for you." She hands a jersey to me. "Then there's one for me and your dad and Kylie."

A loud shriek comes out of Ellie's mouth. "There's one more, for who?"

Frankie lifts the jersey and turns it. Now the back is facing Ellie. "Read it, Ellie."

"Ellie, Congrats on your soccer championship." Ellie takes a deep breath. "Is that an autographed jersey? This is crazy! Thank you so much! Are we picking up Kylie on the way?"

I simply nod my head. "Yes, we need to leave in a little over an hour."

Ellie rounds the island and hugs Frankie tight. "I'm so freakin' excited! Thank you so much!"

"You're welcome. Go get dressed," Frankie instructs.

I sidle next to Frankie and lean closer. "I love you, Sunshine, for being exactly who you said you were."

"I love you for letting me."

With Kylie and Ellie laughing in the back seat, we drive down the highway toward the stadium. When we arrive, we're directed to a small lot right near the player entrance. All the laughing and talking from the back seat has ceased.

"Are you okay, Ellie?" I ask my daughter who is suddenly ghost white.

"Uh-huh."

Frankie turns in her seat. "Ellie, to you, Marco is this huge superstar. To me, he's family. He's a normal guy who has abnormal skills on the pitch. No need for you to be nervous."

"Will you stay with me?" Ellie's voice cracks.

"As long as I can."

I hear Ellie exhale sharply before we're whisked into the tunnel and she meets her soccer hero. I have no idea how Frankie set all this up, but I'm floored, and so is my daughter.

Marco Cappelli jogs toward Frankie and lifts her into a hug. "It's so great to see you! It's been too long!"

"You too. Marco, please meet Tommy, his daughter, Ellie, and her bestie, Kylie."

Marco reaches out and shakes my hand and Kylie's. Then he extends his hand to Ellie. "Hi, Ellie, Frankie has told me so much about you. Congrats on your club championship. Like Frankie, I played for the same club as well."

She takes it. "Hi. Thank you for the jersey and being here today. It's amazing!"

"You're welcome. Follow me and we'll get you situated until it's time to go onto the field." Marco turns to lead the way.

Ellie can't contain the grin on her face. Ellie and Kylie shriek in silence like tweens do and execute an insanely cute happy dance while his back is turned. Frankie simply shakes her head and follows her cousin.

I slide beside her and thread my fingers through hers. "I can't thank you enough for today," I whisper so only she can hear me.

"No thanks are necessary. Not only will I do anything for you, but her too."

"I love you more, Sunshine."

"I love both of you most."

I kiss her cheek, and we wait near the field entrance to the stadium.

Once we are near the entrance, Marco turns back to us. "Stef will be here in time to assist Ellie in lining up. Then she will escort you to the spectator area behind the bench. She will also bring Ellie to you after the national anthem."

"Great. Thanks, Marco." Frankie hugs him again, and he runs off.

"This is insane!" Ellie mutters to Kylie. "I can't believe this is really happening. I'm sure this is a dream."

Kylie pinches Ellie's arm.

"Owwww!" Ellie bellows.

"Not a dream! Go have a great time." Kylie brings Ellie back to earth.

Ellie hugs her bestie and smiles. "Thanks, Ky. I'll be back soon."

Stef joins us and hugs Frankie. After introductions, she escorts Ellie to the front of the line to meet Marco. Once the final bars of the national anthem play, she escorts Ellie back to us.

"This is the best day ever!" Ellie exclaims and jumps up and down with Kylie.

The match is exciting, and Ellie is rapt watching the action on the field. At the half, the score is tied at zero. In the second half, Marco scores one goal and assists on another to secure a win for his team.

As we walk back through the tunnel, Stef hurries to join us. "Ellie, Marco asked me to get this to you. It was a pleasure meeting you." Stef hands Ellie a ball autographed by Marco's entire team.

"Wow! Thank you so much! Please thank him for me," Ellie states.

"Of course," Stef replies. After a brief hug with Frankie, she's gone.

We walk toward the car. "Are they a couple?" I whisper.

"I don't believe so. They've been besties since high school I think," I reply and settle into the passenger seat. The drive home is much quieter than to the stadium. Within fifteen minutes, both Ellie and Kylie are sound asleep in the back seat of the car.

No one has ever taken care of Ellie like me, not even Tess. I'm not suggesting Tess is negligent, at least not until recently. However, no one has ever risen to the level of care I provide my daughter until Frankie.

CHAPTER THIRTY-EIGHT

FRANCESCA

We arrived home very late last night after the game. The postgame traffic was certifiably over the top. A drive that should've taken under two hours topped out near four. It doesn't matter I'll need a bucket of coffee to get through today due to lack of sleep, the sheer excitement on Ellie's face was priceless.

When I roll over in bed, Tommy's side is cold. I'm not surprised; he's dedicated to his workouts. I tug on a hoodie and pad to the kitchen for my first cup of the day. As I pass Ellie's room, I peek in. The girls are still sound asleep.

With coffee in hand, I tiptoe down the stairs into the basement. I don't intend to interrupt, but he isn't there. I slip on his slides near the back door and wander out to his workshop.

He finishes sliding a piece of wood along the guide of the table saw, removing a two-inch piece on the edge. "Morning, Sunshine." Tommy's shirt is covered with sawdust, and there are shavings on the tops of his shoes.

"Morning. Need to talk about something?"

"Nope. I'm fine. I'm better than fine. I haven't been this happy… ever before, and I owe it to you."

"I feel the same way about you and Ellie." I move beside him and wrap my arms around him, knowing I'll be covered in sawdust too.

He lifts me onto the saw table and kisses me boneless. Sex with Tommy is... the best I've ever had. Yet making out is equally as fulfilling on most days. I would want to spend time with him even if those things weren't on the table. He's my biggest supporter, willing to handle my crazy family, and like me, is fine with movie nights at home.

The telltale sound of the sliding door has me righting his shirt and Tommy setting me back on the floor.

"What are you working on?" I ask.

"A new desk for you."

The workshop door creaks open.

"Morning, Dad. Frankie."

"Morning, Ellie," we reply together.

"We're starving. Can we cook breakfast?" Ellie asks.

"Sure, I'll be right in to get started," I answer her.

Ellie takes off back to the house.

"You're building me a desk?"

"Sort of. I'm adding to the one already in the office."

Oh this man. "There's nothing wrong with the desk."

He looks over at me. "You need more space. You have papers hanging on boards, papers piled for the next two projects on the floor beside the desk, and even more stacked on the built-in bookcase on the back wall." He isn't wrong.

"Thank you."

"You're welcome. When I'm finished, you'll be able to fold it down when you don't need as much space. It'll be a while though since you're working on plans for ten hotels."

I've never met anyone like him. He's an amazing man and an even better father. I'll thank Talia each morning for selecting the right name for my coffee cup. "Are we still going to family dinner?"

"Yeah, we are going to drop off Kylie on the way."

I lean forward and kiss him softly. "I'll start breakfast with the girls. Thank you for knowing I need something before I do."

"You're welcome. I'll be in as soon as I finish this piece and clean up a bit."

I nod and walk toward the house. After a small breakfast of French toast and sausage, the girls hurry away to hang out a bit longer before we need to bring Kylie home.

We pull up in front of his parents' home. It's a sprawling colonial with a lush, green lawn to die for.

"I'm afraid to ask, but who does your parents' lawn?"

Tommy and Ellie laugh. "I planted it, but Tim maintains it."

"I'm impressed."

Tommy smiles sheepishly. "Thank you. It's a huge compliment coming from you."

Ellie hurries out of the car once her grandparents step onto the wrap-around porch. Once tight hugs finish, Ellie rushes inside. We follow her after greeting Gloria and Thomas on the porch.

"It's great to see you again so soon!" Gloria speaks first.

"I agree. Come in, come in," Thomas urges us.

We're greeted by the rest of his siblings, who are assembled in the living room. Each greets us and continues talking with Ellie and one another. It strikes me Ellie is the first and only grandchild.

"Is there anything I can help with, Gloria?"

A look of surprise crosses her face. "I knew you were different the moment Ellie shared you were there for her when Tess wasn't at home. Those real smiles have been missing for quite some time. Thank you for loving my son and granddaughter so well."

"Thank you for sharing them with me."

Gloria hugs me and sends me into the living room with the rest of the family. When I step into the room, I hear Ellie recounting the game and meeting Marco.

"Then I walked onto the field with Marco and stood for the national anthem. It was so freakin' amazing! I will never forget it. I can't believe you didn't tell me he's family."

"I didn't know he was your favorite player of all time until I suggested going to a game. So I think it's partially your fault."

"Oooh, Ellie. I think she got you there," Toby states and high-fives me.

"Thanks, Toby."

"Merely stating the truth, Frankie."

"Fine. Frankie, are there any other celebrities who you're related to by blood?"

"Maybe. Depends on how you define 'celebrity.' Marco's sister was a model when she was younger."

"Frankie, do you know any other celebrities in real life?"

"Yes."

Ellie's eyes go wide. "Who?"

"Do you remember Kelly from So Elegant?"

"Of course. She was awesome."

"Her husband is a celebrity, and Kelly is too but more in a behind-the-scenes kind of way," I respond.

"Wow! I'm going to need details upon details."

Everyone laughs. Thankfully, I'm saved by Gloria calling us to the table. We dine on wonderful food and share a few laughs. Being here with Tommy's family is strikingly similar to mine. They are honest with one another and genuinely seem to care how the rest of the bunch is doing. I'm crazy grateful for Jimmy Delano right now. If I hadn't flattened him in Tal's defense, I may not be here and found my forever person and his beautiful daughter.

CHAPTER THIRTY-NINE

THOMAS

"Any chance you're willing to skip your regular workout this morning?"

Frankie's tongue is travelling down my flank. My muscles contract when her hair skims my rock-hard shaft. Tightened abs seem to push Frankie forward.

"So?"

"An exception can certainly be made this morning."

She doesn't acknowledge my words but continues down over my hip. Settling between my thighs, Frankie draws her tongue along my inner thigh and then up the seam of my leg. I never knew that feels good until this moment. A low growl falls from my lips.

"You like that?"

"Yes, didn't know until this moment." I feel her smile against my leg before she licks the same seam again.

Her tongue follows the vein along my length and up and down in a zigzag pattern before she takes me into her mouth. Hollowing out her cheeks, she takes me even deeper, moving her fist tight around my shaft in time. As if that weren't enough, which it is, with her free hand, Frankie skims her fingernails along my inner thigh at the same time.

"Sunshine, I need you to stop if you—"

Her response vibrates around me, and I pulse in her hot, wet mouth until I'm replete. With my hands wrapped around her upper arms, I haul her up and kiss her hard.

"Good morning to you too," I murmur against her lips.

"Morning. Time to get moving or you'll be late for your meeting with your attorney."

"Fine. What would be next if we didn't have to get out of bed?"

A twinkle gleams in her chocolate eyes. "I'm sure we could come up with something to do. Can we make that happen soon?"

"A day with only us and nowhere to go unless we choose to?"

"Yes."

I lift my head and brush my lips across hers once more. "I'll see what I can do." Reluctantly, I release Frankie and she moves off the bed. Pushing the ideas about time alone with Frankie aside for now, I dress for the day.

My focus now is on the hearing set for today. I've worked hard to balance being an amazing dad to Ellie and, as Frankie would say, walking the tightrope between her and Tess. Honestly, I'm done.

I haven't heard from Tess since she called and said she needed me to care of Ellie. It doesn't appear Tess is going to show up, and I don't know how the hearing will go this time.

"Ellie, we need to get to school."

"Coming," she calls from upstairs.

I stop in the kitchen, and Frankie hands me a cup of coffee to go. "You're fabulous."

"I try."

"I think you more than try, especially that thing you did this morning with your tongue."

"Oh really? You liked that?"

"It wasn't obvious?" My voice rises in question.

Frankie bursts out laughing so hard tears fall from her eyes.

"What's so funny?" Ellie steps into the kitchen.

"Nothing." Our reply is instant.

While Frankie composes herself, I grab a bagel from the counter. "Ready, Ellie?"

"Sure. Can this be the last hearing, Dad?" Her voice is soft and low.

"I hope so." Truly, I do. I don't know what Tess is up to or why she needs Ellie to stay with us, but since her polite demand, our little family is doing well.

"Me too. Bye, Frankie. Love you more."

"See you after school, Ellie. Love you most."

Hearing my daughter and my girlfriend care for one another so deeply makes my heart swell. I know, regardless of the outcome of today, I'll spend the rest of my life making these two ladies happy and any other tiny humans Frankie and I create.

Cammie greets me as I enter my attorney's office. "Good morning, Mr. Thornton. She'll be right with you."

"Thank you." I take a seat in the lobby and thumb through an outdated magazine.

"Tommy, please come in."

I step into my attorney's office and notice she looks more relaxed today. "I gather from your demeanor Attorney Lucci hasn't called yet to say Tess won't be present."

"He did call, but this time he proposed a solution. When did Mrs. Spears leave Ellie with you?"

I probably should have informed my attorney Tess left Ellie with me. "Almost two weeks ago. I may not be married to Tess anymore, but I know something is going on with her, and I think it involves her husband, Michael. She would leave Ellie with me if she had any concerns about our daughter's safety. I didn't question her. I rearranged my schedule and made it work."

Antionette nods. "Attorney Lucci has informed me his client is willing to withdraw her motion and agree to not filing any motions for the next calendar year."

I try to mask my shock. It kicks the can down the road, but at least Ellie won't have to move before the end of middle school. "I would agree to that."

"I thought you would. We're scheduled for midmorning."

"I'll be there. Thank you for your patience with Tess. Before she remarried, she wasn't flaky and irresponsible."

"You're welcome. I'll see you at the courthouse."

Instead of heading home, I drive to Short Sands despite the overcast sky. I only have twenty minutes before I will need to leave for the courthouse. Pulling into a spot, I step out and take a seat on the bench. Within minutes, Frankie sits beside me with a fresh coffee from the Perk.

"How did you know I would come here?"

"I didn't. I need pencils and drafting paper, so I parked here so I could get a scone before going home. I saw you park while I was returning to my truck. Is it bad news?" She offers me her coffee.

I take a heavy, satisfying sip before answering. "No, not really. Tess agreed to withdraw her motion and not file anything new for at least a calendar year."

Frankie tilts her head. "Not terrible. What time do you need to be there?"

"I need to go in the next ten minutes."

"Okay."

"Do you have any idea how much you being here settles me?" I ask.

"Impromptu seems to be what we do best. I understand, it would be the same for me."

She offers me more coffee. "Are you going to the office?"

I take a sip then reply, "No, I'll work from home after court."

"Perfect. Think I can use your skill set for lunch?" Frankie whispers despite the fact we're alone.

A grin breaks out on my face. "Which one?"

"Both."

I shake my head, kiss her softly, and we walk to her truck. "Love you more, Sunshine."

"I'll see you at home. Love you most."

Feeling the slightest bit lighter, I get through the hearing and the judge enters an order pursuant to our agreement. Through her attorney, the motion is withdrawn and Tess agrees to refrain from filing any motions for a calendar year. I don't know what's behind her change of heart. I'll take what I can get for Ellie's sake.

The moment I step foot into the house, I'm immediately calmer. Simply knowing we have a reprieve and Frankie is here makes me lighter. She greets me at the door and leads me upstairs. I don't make good on my promise of specialty grilled cheese, but we spend the next few hours painstakingly exploring one another from our toes to the tops of our heads and every pleasure-inducing spot in between.

CHAPTER FORTY

FRANCESCA

Since the court hearing, both Tommy and Ellie seem happier and more settled. Tommy shared the outcome of the hearing with Ellie. At first she seemed angry there wasn't a definite resolution. Her anger fades with each day she's with only us. Frankly, the possibility of Tess filing another motion even in a year will be in the back of my mind. I'm sure Ellie misses her mother, but the stability and consistency of knowing where to go each day after school and what to expect when she arrives has improved her attitude and mood. Today might be the exception though.

Something about attending the banquet is flustering her. "Ellie, we need to leave for the salon in ten minutes."

"I'll be right down," Ellie replies from her room.

"Thank you for taking her," Tommy murmurs to me.

I can read between the lines. This is something Tess would've done if she were here or even in communication with Ellie. "I meant what I said."

"I know. I'm thanking you for her. Handling her feelings for you and her mom has been difficult for her. She feels like she's being disloyal to Tess because she cares about you."

Oh, Ellie. "I appreciate you sharing."

Ellie joins me in the foyer. "Let's go get pretty."

Tommy and I laugh. "You already are. We're merely adding sparkly nails."

A flicker of uncertainty passes over her face. "True. See you later, Dad." Ellie laughs, grabs my keys, and steps onto the porch.

"Love you more, Ellie," Tommy calls after her. "See you in a few hours. I love you most, Sunshine."

I slide my hand along his strong jaw and kiss him softly. "I love you more, Tommy. Be back soon."

The ride to the salon is silent, aside from Ellie's keystrokes on her phone.

"Kylie?"

"No. It's Jamie."

I wonder if I should push and quickly decide to see how it goes. "Is Jamie a boy or a girl?"

"Boy. He lives a few houses away. His parents have been fighting a lot. He texts me when it gets bad."

"You're a great friend, Ellie. If he needs somewhere to hang out, he's welcome at the house."

She nods. "Thank you for acting more like my mom than she is."

My heart hurts for her and swells because I love being there for her. "I'll always be here for you, Ellie. However, whenever, and wherever you need me."

"I knew you were different from the day we met. I appreciate you coming through for me over and over."

"You're welcome." I decide to leave it there. Her conflicting feelings about me and her mom are hers to handle. I don't want to add my opinion into the mix. In my opinion, Tess has failed Ellie more than once since I met her. I refuse to share my feelings with her no matter how hard it is to keep my thoughts to myself.

Just over an hour later, our fingers and toes are sparkling in the late fall sunlight.

"Can we stop and get something for Jamie?" Ellie asks quietly.

"Sure, what are you thinking?"

She shrugs. "A few cookies from the Perk."

"I'm always up for some of Kelsey's treats."

We take the short drive to the Perk and step inside. The aroma in here gets me every single time. I could only want coffee, yet I buy a sweet treat or two as well.

"Hi, Scarlett. How are you?"

"Hi, Frankie. Good to see you."

"You too. Ellie, this is Lia's friend and classmate, Scarlett."

"Hi. Love your nails."

Ellie smiles. "Thanks." She places her order for Jamie.

I add coffee for me and Tommy, as well as some scones. With our spoils, we bid Scarlett goodbye and head home. "Do you want to stop by his house or invite him over for a little while?"

Ellie faces me. "Do I have time?"

I mentally calculate the time she needs to get dressed and travel time. "Sure. Invite him over and you can hang out for at least an hour before Lily will be over to do our makeup. Even more if you want to go second."

"Thanks, Frankie. I'm sure he would love to get out of the house for a bit." She sends off a text.

When we pull into the driveway, a tall, lanky boy is walking down the street.

"Hi, Ellie. Thanks for the invite. It's pretty tense." He hugs her and promptly releases her when he sees me.

"I'm Jamie," he extends his hand to me.

"Frankie. Please come in. I can get you some drinks if you want to hang out on the patio."

"Thanks." Ellie and Jamie walk through the house. Ellie freezes when Tommy steps into the kitchen.

Jamie saves her. "Hi, sir. I'm Jamie. Thank you for letting me hang out with Ellie." Tommy shakes his extended hand, and the kids continue out the French doors.

He looks directly at me. I talk to him without words as the kids pass. Tommy only contains himself for the slimmest of minutes. "What's going on? Who is that boy? Did you say it was okay for her to have a boy over?"

"Breathe. They're just friends. He lives a few doors over, and he needs some space. Ellie was texting him on the way to the salon. His parents are considering divorce. I apologize if I overstepped, but she was visibly upset for him."

He slides his arms around me and presses a kiss to my temple. "No, you didn't. I'm not used to having another responsible person around for Ellie. Let's get those drinks."

With two glasses of iced tea and the cookies on a tray, we bring refreshments to the kids on the deck.

I overhear Jamie say, "They argue about every little thing. Who cares what color their coffee mug is? It doesn't make sense. Okay, you don't want to be together anymore. Try to be nice while you figure out your plan."

Ellie's hand is covering his between them on the couch. I set the tray on the table, and Ellie thanks me. We slip back inside.

We sit on the couch. "I hope we didn't make Ellie feel that way," Tommy murmurs into my hair.

"Probably not like that. It hits differently at twelve. Jamie is more aware and hears more than a six-year-old girl."

"I hope you're right."

I do too. "Have you heard anything from Tess?"

"No, not a word. I assume she hasn't contacted Ellie either. She would've mentioned it to one of us."

"I agree." I snuggle deeper into his arms on the couch until Lily knocks on the door. My time in his arms will never be enough.

"Hi, Lily. Come in."

"Hey, sis. Hi, Tommy. Your home is beautiful."

"Thank you. It's mostly Ellie's handiwork."

Lily smiles. "Where is the soccer queen?"

"I'll let her know you're here. She's hanging out with her friend on the porch."

When I get to the door, I note Ellie and Jamie are passing a soccer ball back and forth and laughing. I step outside and let her know Lily arrived. "Hey, Ellie. Lily is here. You have thirty minutes or so until it's your turn."

"Thanks, Frankie."

I slide the door closed. "They're fine, Tommy. They're passing a ball. He seems calmer now." I can only imagine what has been going through his mind in the last hour. It's been a while since I was her age, but Ellie has a good head on her shoulders.

He seems to relax a tiny bit. "I have been freaking out this entire time."

"Have a little faith in Ellie and your parenting skills. Please send Ellie up after Jamie leaves." I press a kiss to his lips and lead Lily upstairs.

I take a seat on the dressing bench, and Lily gets to work. I'm sure I could pull off simple makeup, but Lily is more proficient and definitely faster. "How are things with you?" I ask.

"Same. As much as it hurts, I won't share my feelings with Leo while he's with Danica. It isn't right."

"You're stronger than me. It would kill me to finally know my feelings and not share them."

"Leo has been part of my life since elementary school. I know how he earned each and every scar on his body. I know how he pulled off his senior prank and somehow didn't get caught like his buddies. Just like he knows almost everything about me. He's my person. I have to wait to tell him."

"I'm sorry, Lily."

"Me too. Enough about my love life, how's yours?"

A huge smile materializes on my face. I couldn't stop it even if I wanted to. "They're pretty amazing! I'm happier than I've ever been, and it's because of them."

"Blissfully happy looks good on you, big sister." With a flourish, Lily finishes my makeup with some light powder.

"Thanks. You and Leo will find your way—eventually."

"I hope so. I'm miserable and faking it. When he's around is more difficult than I anticipated. Yet I refuse to skip the time I get with him even though he's dating someone else."

"Nor should you."

Ellie knocks lightly on the door. "Hi, Lily. Thank you for coming."

"Hi, Ellie. Are you kidding? I love doing this. At least someone is going out on a Saturday night."

Ellie laughs. "Is Leo busy?"

Lily is speechless. Even Ellie can see her feelings for Leo. "Lily and Leo are best friends, not dating," I supply.

"Oh, sorry. You seem so happy and comfortable. I thought you were a couple," Ellie states.

"No problem." Lily lets out an exhale to regain herself. Ellie won't notice, but I do.

I stand up, and Ellie takes my place. Within thirty minutes, Lily has given Ellie age-appropriate makeup and created ringlets in her hair. The only thing left is to slip into her dress.

"I'll come help you get dressed after I walk Lily out."

"Okay. I'll be in my room. Thank you, Lily." Ellie throws her arms around my sister.

"Anytime." Lily smiles at me over her shoulder.

I'm sure she left off the "once you're invited to family dinner, you're considered family" on purpose given Leo has been numerous times. After walking Lily out, I help Ellie into her dress.

"We'll meet you downstairs in about fifteen minutes."

"Thank you for all of this." Ellie gestures over the dress.

"You're welcome."

I return to the bedroom in time to watch Tommy cover his washboard abs with his dress shirt. I frown.

"I saw that," he says from the bedroom.

"Wasn't trying to hide it. I'll rip the shirt off later." I slither into a navy sheath dress with a two-strand back necklace. With a few spritzes of perfume, I'll be ready to go.

"Do you have any dresses that don't make you look sexy as sin?" He slides his hands around my waist and grips my ass.

"Is there such a thing?"

"Are you wearing panties this time?" His question comes out more like a rumbling growl.

"You'll just have to wait to find out when we get back home." I wink at him and head downstairs. Ellie is not-so-patiently tapping her foot in the foyer.

"A little excited, Ellie?"

"Yes. You look pretty."

"Thanks. So do you." Maybe a bit grown-up for Tommy to handle as well.

When Tommy finally makes it downstairs, he stares at the two of us. His words stick in his throat for a few extra seconds. "How did I get so lucky? I have not one but two beautiful dates for this party." Tommy threads his fingers with mine and kisses Ellie's head.

Ellie smiles and shakes her head. Once we arrive at the banquet hall, Ellie is off to her seat with her teammates. Three long hours and a not-so-great meal later, we head home. It takes all three of us to carry Ellie's awards and trophies to the car, including Player of the Year, a sportsmanship trophy, Excellence in Leadership, and most assists and goals for the season.

"We're crazy proud of you, Ellie."

"Thanks, Dad and Frankie. I wasn't expecting all of this. I play because I love it, not for the trophies and awards."

Marco says something similar every time he receives an award. Interesting.

"You're welcome," Tommy replies.

"Can we get something to eat on the way home? Dinner wasn't very good."

"You can be honest, Ellie," Tommy states.

"Dinner was terrible. Not even the cake was tasty. I mean, baking a cake isn't difficult. If I can bake an edible cake, it can't be too hard."

We laugh. Then drive through one of the many chain restaurants and eat on the way home. With our help, Ellie adds the trophies and plaques to the shelf in her room and turns in for the night.

I intertwine my fingers with Tommy's and lead him to our bedroom.

"Can I check now?" A devilish gleam shines in his eyes.

"Yes, as long as you promise you can be quiet."

Tommy locks the door with his free hand. He skims the fingertips of both hands up my outer thighs, bunching my dress as he rises. Even before he learns I'm not wearing panties, he's straining against the zipper of his pants.

"What am I going to do with you? You're full of surprises every day."

"You can do whatever you want. I like keeping you on your toes. Being with me will never be boring," I murmur near his earlobe.

"No, it won't."

As quietly as possible, we spend the rest of our Saturday night searching for spots to coax shudders of pleasure from each other.

CHAPTER FORTY-ONE

THOMAS

"Ellie, time for school."

"Coming," she replies from her bathroom.

The past month with Ellie here has been wonderful. Ellie is happy and calm. She trades off spending time with Jamie and Kylie, but never both, most days after school. Soon she'll start indoor soccer, but for a few more weeks, she's free after school. While I hope Tess is fine and able to handle whatever it is she's doing, part of me hopes Ellie can stay with us permanently even when Tess finishes her mysterious mission.

I peer into the office, and my gorgeous girlfriend lifts her head from the report she's reading. She's ahead of schedule on Mystic and needs to take a trip to Montauk, but she's expanded her business here and almost doubled her staff for the spring. I'm crazy proud of her.

"We're headed out. Ellie wants to try Thai food for movie night tonight." I round the desk and draw her up from the chair to kiss her properly. Once she's flush against me, I lower my mouth to hers. Even now her kiss makes it hard to breathe. I can't imagine my days without her, and I don't plan to ever find out. "Love you more, Sunshine."

"Sounds good to me. I've never had Thai food. Love you most."

I drop Ellie off at school and hurry to my office. Melissa packed my morning with meetings so I can adhere to picking up Ellie each day. It isn't a complaint, but it makes for busy mornings.

I have successfully fixed a problem with the inspector for the Portsmouth property and met with the electrician and painting contractor for Boston with barely enough time for a bathroom break before my next two conference calls.

Just before lunch, Melissa informs me there's a call for me waiting on line one. The caller indicates it's urgent. Panic courses through me for Ellie and Frankie.

"Mr. Thornton speaking. How can I help you?"

"Thomas Thornton, Jr.?" the caller asks.

"Yes, what is this in regard to?"

"My name is Joan. I'm calling from Greenwich Memorial Hospital. You're listed as an emergency contact for Contessa Thornton in our system."

Tess. Despite my intention to spend the rest of my life with Frankie, fear grips me on Ellie's behalf. "Is she okay?" I manage.

"Mrs. Thornton was brought in unconscious after falling down a flight of stairs. She has a broken arm, broken wrist, and a serious concussion. There's as also older bruising and her records indicate other injuries consistent with domestic abuse."

"Tess is my ex-wife."

"I apologize, sir. She's in surgery to set her wrist. It's protocol we reach out to the emergency contact when they arrive unconscious."

"I understand. I'll be there as soon as I can, but it will take at least four hours," I inform her.

"I'll let her know when she wakes."

"You indicated domestic abuse. I have no personal knowledge one way or the other. However, her husband's name is Michael Spears in case you need it for your records." In sharing the information, I hope he's kept away from Tess if the allegations prove to be true.

"Thank you, Mr. Thornton. When you arrive, have reception call the patient desk so they can properly direct you."

"I will."

Frankie was right! Part of me is glad Luca made his sisters aware of the signs and how to protect themselves.

"Hi, Tommy," Frankie answers my call with a smile in her voice.

"Hi, Sunshine."

"Is Ellie okay?"

My heart is pounding in my chest, but those three words decrease the pace a bit. "Ellie is fine. It's Tess. She's in the hospital in Greenwich. I'm still listed as her emergency contact. Her injuries are suggestive of domestic violence."

I hear Frankie exhale sharply. "How can I help?"

I love this woman deep in my bones. "Can you pick up Ellie and be as vague as possible until I get more information? I don't know when I'll be back."

"Of course. Call me when you can. I love you more, Tommy."

"I will. I love you most, Sunshine."

I settle my warring thoughts and buzz Melissa. "Can you come in here for a moment?"

After I speak with Melissa to reschedule my single afternoon meeting, I head to my car and drive toward Tess. While I have some information pertaining to her injuries, the fact my ex-wife and the mother of my daughter who had a stiff backbone and sharp tongue didn't stand up for herself makes utterly no sense.

On the outside, it looked like Tess got everything she wanted when she married Michael, including luxury clothes, spa treatments, house, car, and even their vacations. There will never be a time where I can afford to take Frankie to Fiji on a whim. The irony is Frankie would never ask for a trip to Fiji or any other outlandish place unless she could afford it herself. Considering her work ethic, if Frankie wants something, I'm confident she would earn it on her own. It only makes her more attractive to me.

I make a stop near the border of Connecticut for some coffee and continue the rest of the drive to the hospital. I park in the closest lot I can find and speak with the receptionist as Joan recommended. She directs me to the correct floor.

"I'm here for Tess Spears," I inform the nurse near the entry door.

"I don't have a patient named Tess Spears."

I shake my head. "Contessa Thornton."

"Right this way." She leads me down a narrow hallway and points to Tess's room. "Her nurse should be in shortly to update you."

I look over the woman who used to be my wife lying in a hospital bed. Her face devoid of makeup. Bruises, new and old, in varying colors evident. The exposed portion of her upper arm is marked with what looks like fingerprint bruises. Her left arm is in a cast up to her elbow. I surmise the rest of her is battered as well considering she fell down a flight of stairs.

Joan appears in the doorway and motions for me to join her in the hallway. "Mr. Thornton."

"Tommy, please. As I mentioned on the phone, Tess and I aren't married anymore. I don't know if you should be sharing her medical information with me despite what the computer says."

"I understand your position. You're welcome to wait with her until she wakes. They gave her a sedative for the pain."

"Thank you." I fall into the sturdy chair in the corner of Tess's room.

Me: I'm here. Tess is sedated. I'll let you know more when I do.

Frankie: Thank you. We're fine. Love you more.

Me: Love you both most.

The nurses have been in and out of the room twice since I arrived. Ideally, Tess will wake soon. I can't imagine Tess was talking about domestic violence when she indicated she had something to wrap up. She did say she was protecting Ellie though.

Tess shifts in the bed, and her eyes flutter a few times, but then nothing. It isn't for almost another forty minutes before Tess wakes.

"Tommy? What are you doing here?"

"I'm still listed as your emergency contact."

A few tears stream down her face. She winces when she lifts her uninjured arm to wipe them away.

"Why didn't you take our help when I offered it?"

More tears fall before Tess composes herself enough to speak. "My family won't speak to me because of my marriage to Michael and my treatment of you and Ellie. They accused me of moving on and putting my marriage to Michael before my daughter."

"You didn't answer my question, Tess. I offered to help. Why didn't you take it?"

"Mostly to save face. I didn't want to look like I failed at another marriage, and I'm embarrassed… I'm stronger than this."

"How long has this been going on, Tess? Has he hurt Ellie?"

A renewed flood of tears stream down her cheeks. "No, he never hurt Ellie. It's why I sent her to bed so early. To shield her."

I nod.

"It has been escalating since about a year into our marriage. At first it was nasty comments, then a slap here or there. Ever since the promotion, his stress level is insane, and he grows violent when his trades don't pan out and he loses money. The more he loses, the more violent he becomes. Only recently was I unable to cover my injuries with clothes or makeup. When Ellie walked to Frankie's office, I was at a local hotel recovering from his latest round of losses."

Damn! Frankie was right. "He's violent when things don't go well at work?"

"Yes. Please know I turned him in and I'm going to press charges this time."

"Meaning?"

Tess sighs. "I downloaded a copy of his hard drive and delivered it to the FBI field office. Apparently, he has some software that tracks keystrokes. After assaulting me again, he pushed me down the stairs when I wouldn't admit it was me who turned him in. I need time to take care of my situation and protect Ellie. Where is Ellie?"

"She's with Frankie."

"What did you tell her?"

"I asked Frankie to avoid giving Ellie any details considering I didn't truly have any to share with her. I won't ask Frankie to lie to our daughter. You should tell her the truth, Tess."

"Why?"

"Your recent actions hurt Ellie profoundly. She's concerned you dislike Frankie and feels like she needs to choose between the two of you. Your insistence Frankie is not good enough to be around her didn't help. Frankie and I are together and will be for a long time. Ellie deserves the truth about all of it, from Michael's crimes to his physical abuse."

"As much as I would like to say something negative again, she's good for you. You were never as happy as you are with her when we were together. Perhaps I should have listened to my sister when she told me not to marry you."

"I'm glad you didn't listen," I respond.

An incredulous look crosses her face as she winces.

"If we didn't get married, we wouldn't have Ellie."

"You're right. Our daughter is amazing, and I'm glad you found someone to love you like I couldn't."

I'm floored. "I'm sorry you haven't."

"Thank you." Silence settles between us. I never wished Tess ill will. I wanted her to be happy like I do for myself. Maybe taking my time and protecting Ellie led me to Frankie, maybe not. I wouldn't have it any other way.

A different nurse enters the room. "Good, you're awake. What can I get for you?"

"Some water would be great. When can I get out of here?" Tess replies.

"I'll check with the doctor, but the police are here to talk to you, if you're up for giving your statement," the nurse shares with Tess.

"Send them in. I need to get my statement over with so I can leave."

The nurse nods. A few minutes later, a uniformed officer and a plain-clothed FBI agent enter Tess's room.

"Mrs. Thornton, I'm Officer Delgado, and this is Special Agent Moira Stillman."

"Thank you for coming. My name is Contessa Spears."

"And you are?" Officer Delgado inquires of me.

"Thomas Thornton. I'm her ex-husband. I was still listed as her emergency contact. Tess, I'll be outside while you speak with them."

Tess nods, and I leave the room.

CHAPTER FORTY-TWO

FRANCESCA

Tess may not be my favorite person on the planet, but I truly didn't want my hunch to be correct. My run-ins with Tess haven't been pleasant, but I know even the strongest of women could fall victim to an abuser who continually promises them the world. Especially someone like Tess who desires the world.

"Ellie, are you ready to pick a movie?"

She rushes back downstairs. "Do you want to order from one of our normal places and save the Thai for when Dad is back?"

"Sure. Chinese or pizza?"

"Chinese," she replies. "Can we get some of the moo shu pork Dad hates?"

I laugh. "Absolutely."

Ellie flops down on the couch with the remote in her hand. "I'll find a movie. Maybe something a bit more girly than normal since it's just us girls tonight. Does that work?"

"Definitely." After placing our dinner order, I grab drinks and join Ellie in the living room. She momentarily pauses on *Sixteen Candles* but then chooses *Sweet Home Alabama.* Both excellent choices.

Ellie starts the movie and curls up in the corner of the couch. "Have you seen this one before?"

"Not the entire movie. Bits and pieces when I catch it on cable."

"Cool."

Ellie is silent for most of the movie. We take a break and spread our dinner on the coffee table.

When things start to fall into place for the main character, Ellie pauses the movie. "You're kind of like Melanie, except you didn't run away to another city. You don't leave when it gets tough."

I don't miss the "like her mother" she didn't say out loud. After a deep breath, I reply, "I can see where you would draw the comparison."

"Is my mom going to be okay?"

"All I know is your mom is injured, and Tommy went to assist her. I don't know the extent of her injuries or how they happened."

"Is it weird to be here with me while Dad is taking care of his ex-wife?"

"No. I trust Tommy. I believe in what we're building, the three of us." There's plenty of reasons that Tommy and Tess are divorced, but I'm not going to share them with Ellie. I'm sure he still cares about Tess as Ellie's mom and nothing else.

"After they got divorced, at least initially, I didn't want Dad to find someone. I didn't want to share him. I needed at least one parent to be always available for me. Even when they were married, it was always Dad. He would stay home from work when I was sick, even though Mom was home. I cherish my time with Dad, especially when I had to go to Mom's. Since he met you, I realize he was probably dating but some of the women didn't want me. Mom was dating as best I can remember almost immediately."

"While that may be true, it's in no way your fault. My sister Lina is a single mom, and the reason isn't her fault. To me, Lina is as worthy as I am to share her life with someone. It shouldn't matter her first marriage ended in divorce or Em and Antonio come along with the deal. Some women want to start a relationship with no potential drama. I'll admit it has been a bit rocky with Tess, but it doesn't impact how I feel about you and your dad. From the beginning, I saw you as another person I could love and guide as much as you would let me."

"Thanks, Frankie."

"You're welcome. When I know more, I'll share with you."

Ellie restarts the movie, and I finish my lukewarm pork fried rice. After Melanie and Jake finally have an appropriate wedding reception, Ellie clears our dishes.

Once everything is loaded into the dishwasher, she hugs me tight. "How is this going to work when Mom gets home?"

"What do you mean?"

"Does it go back to the way it was before when I go between the houses every other day and every other weekend?" Her tone gets increasingly upset.

"I don't know. I suppose that's between your parents. You could also tell them how you feel." My tone is even and flat in the hopes my anger doesn't come through. Ellie doesn't deserve to feel caught between her parents. Yet both deserve time with her. "What would it look like for you? I know it's a hard question to answer."

"So like, bigger chunks of time at each house, I think. I don't know if it could work, but... I don't like the going back and forth every other day."

"Thank you for sharing, Ellie. You should probably share your feelings with your parents."

"I'll think about it. If I decide to, will you be there with me?"

It'll be difficult, but... "Yes, I'll be there."

"Cool. I'm going to call Kylie and then maybe Jamie."

"Okay. Good night."

"Good night. Thank you for choosing us."

"Thank you for letting me. Love you more, Ellie."

"Love you most, Frankie." Then she disappears up the stairs.

I push out a harsh breath. Not only does my heart beat for Tommy but for Ellie too. I rummage through the drawer in the kitchen and locate Tommy's keys. Other than our bed, this is the closest I can be to him right now. I hurry across the grass and throw open the workshop door. The smell of the wood and varnish assail my senses.

I completely understand Tommy's love of this space. My skill level doesn't come close to his, but I feel him in here. As if he heard my heart searching for his, my phone rings.

"Hi."

"Hey, Sunshine." He sounds upset. "How are things there?"

"Ellie is fine, but she's going to need some information soon. In my opinion, it should come from Tess."

"What did she say?" Worry laces his tone.

"Nothing for you to be worried about until you get home. How is Tess?"

"You're remarkable, Sunshine. I have never met anyone as selfless and loving as you. Not only am I in an awkward and impossible situation, but you could also see it that way too. Yet you step in and support me and Ellie."

"As are you, going to Tess despite everything she puts you and Ellie through," I add.

"I think you're forgetting what she's done to you as well."

No, I didn't forget, don't think I ever will. "No, but you and Ellie are more important than my feelings toward Tess. I tolerate Tess because she will always be a part of your life and Ellie's. Hopefully, she'll see I follow through and I'm not going anywhere." Silence runs through the phone line.

"Tommy?"

"I'm here. Where are you? Can Ellie hear you?"

"No, I'm sitting in your workshop."

"Why, Sunshine?"

"I needed to be closer to you, and this is the best I can do right now."

"Is it working?" His response comes out low.

"A little bit." *I would prefer to curl up in your arms where I feel loved and protected.* "Don't worry about us. We're fine."

"I worry about both of you constantly when I'm not with you. As far as Tess, you were right. Michael is abusing her."

"Oh. Of all things to be right about, I wish I wasn't."

"I know. She is being released in the next hour or so. My plan is to drive back home overnight."

"Okay. Does she have somewhere safe to go? Will she need a grocery delivery?"

"Every hour she needs to be checked on for tonight and through the day tomorrow. I would prefer to be home with you and Ellie, not somewhere else with Tess."

I will do this for them. Tess will always be part of this family too. "I'll fix up the guest room for her."

"There are no adequate words to explain what this means to me. Thank you. I'll be home as soon as I can. I love you most, Sunshine."

"I love you more." With a deep breath, I lock up the workshop and get to work. Within an hour, I've changed the sheets, found extra pillows, and freshened the towels in the guest bathroom. I check on Ellie and fall into our bed.

CHAPTER FORTY-THREE

THOMAS

"Tess, we're here." She slowly opens her eyes from her latest nap.

"You truly don't have to do this."

"Yes, I do. You can't be alone. By your own admission, there's no one else."

She starts to shake her head but stops. "Thank you," she mumbles under her breath.

I cup Tess's elbow and lead her into the house. Slowly, we make our way upstairs and I settle her into the guest room. Frankie is more than I deserve. Not only is the room freshened up and set for Tess, but there are bottles of water and a few bland snacks on the night table.

"You always were a class act, Tommy," Tess mumbles in her half-asleep state.

"This is all Frankie. She beats me in class by miles."

Tess drops her head slowly in acknowledgment. I never expected her words about Frankie earlier tonight. My only goal is civility between them. If they can grow to be friends, even better for Ellie.

After a trip to the car, I climb the stairs again. I slide into bed and curl myself around Frankie. "I love you most, Sunshine," I whisper before falling asleep.

Nearly four hours later, I wake with a start. *Damn it!* I throw the covers back and hurry into the bathroom. When I step back into the master, Frankie is near the door with a steaming cup of coffee.

"Tess is fine. I heard the alarm last night and checked on her. She's in the kitchen."

"I'm so sorry. Exhaustion took over."

She simply shakes her head. "No reason for you to be sorry."

I take the cup, set it on the bureau, and draw her against me. Adequately conveying I can't live without her with my lips will have to do right now. "Let's start some breakfast for Ellie."

We creep past Ellie's door and into the kitchen.

"Morning, Tommy."

"How are you feeling, Tess?"

She shrugs. "Physically, I'm sore, but I'll be fine. Figuring out everything else is going to take some time."

I open our fridge and withdraw ingredients for pancakes with bacon and get to work. Frankie places coffee beside me and starts the bacon.

"Can you give me Tamara's number later this morning? I know she isn't my biggest fan, but she'll be able to help," Tess addresses me.

"Sure. If anyone can find you a suitable home, it's my sister."

When I'm nearly finished cooking, I hear the floor creak in the hallway. "Ellie is awake," I inform Tess.

"I'll talk to her."

"Do you want us to leave?" I offer, despite my concerns.

"No. This pertains to all of us now."

I appreciate her inclusion and acceptance of Frankie, even though I'm still skeptical. I set the food on serving plates as Frankie finishes getting the dishes.

"OMG! Mom, are you okay?" Fear is interwoven with Ellie's words. She takes a seat beside her mom and gently glides her hand over the purple, blue, and yellow marks on her arms and cheek.

"I will be fine... eventually." Tess closes her eyes briefly before speaking again. "I need to apologize to all of you. I was embarrassed and unsure how to accept your help without being weak. I realize now accepting the help makes me strong."

Ellie takes Tess's hand in hers. "We're here for you, Mom."

Tess pushes out a sharp breath and swipes away a stray tear. "Ellie, I'm profoundly sorry for the things I've done over the last few months. Please understand I didn't want you to see me battered and bruised. When I stayed in Connecticut to meet Michael's new bosses was the first time I couldn't cover up the marks he left on my skin."

A tear streaks down Ellie's face. "That's why you sent me to my room when I was with you."

Tess nods curtly. "When the house was trashed, I was at a local hotel tending to new bruises. I was trying to protect you. Well, I didn't want to admit my husband was hurting me. In the process, I hurt you deeply. Eleanor, please know, I love you with all my heart. The choices I made were what I thought best at the time. I never meant to hurt you in the process of figuring out how to get away."

Ellie rises from her chair and delicately hugs Tess. "I love you, Mom."

"I love you too, Ellie."

Ellie retakes her seat but holds her mother's hand. Every action Tess has taken is starting to fall into place. She couldn't find adequate clothes or makeup to hide Michael's abuse, so she didn't show up to the mediations or hearings. A small part of me is wondering if I missed earlier signs before Frankie noticed the makeup and the wincing when she came to pick up Ellie that afternoon.

Tess turns to Frankie. "I never felt threatened before you, and it's clear why. I know where Tommy and I failed, and you don't possess the same flaws. You're perfect for him. I never felt threatened before you as a mother either. My behavior toward you was rude and unacceptable. I'm truly sorry. Thank you for loving Ellie and being there for her when I couldn't. You've never let Ellie down despite my harsh words and actions. I appreciate it immensely. She's lucky to have you in her life."

Frankie takes a moment before replying, "Thank you."

"Tommy, you have never let me down since the day we met. I'm grateful for you and your much more capable parenting skills. I'll be a better co-parent going forward. It's what Ellie needs."

I watch Ellie glance over at Frankie who nods slightly.

"Can we talk about that?" Ellie's voice comes out soft and unsure.

"Talk about what, Ellie?" I ask.

"I assume you aren't moving to Connecticut anymore, right, Mom?"

Tess nods. Frankie's gaze on Ellie screams pride and approval.

"Can we make changes to the schedule?"

"What don't you like about it?" Frankie urges Ellie to continue.

"I don't want to make you mad, but the chunks of time in one place is easier for me." Ellie looks directly at Tess.

"I'm not mad. What are you suggesting?" Tess asks her.

"I'm not sure how it would even work, but maybe a week at each home with Wednesday dinner with the other parent. But…."

"We won't be angry, Ellie," I assure her.

Her gaze turns back to Tess. "I don't want to miss anything. If I have a game, practice, or I want to go to Kylie's, it shouldn't matter where I'm staying."

"I don't see why we can't try it out. However, I need a new place to live first. Can Ellie stay here until I find somewhere to live?" Tess looks to me.

"Of course. When we finish cleaning up, I'll give you Tam's number."

Frankie lifts the pancakes, reheats them in the microwave, and sets the plate on the island. Then she warms the bacon. "Let's talk more while we eat."

Once everyone has food, Tess and Ellie talk about all the things she's missed, including the championship game, meeting her soccer idol in real life, and the banquet. She chooses her words as diplomatically as possible, but Tess's expression shows her realization of exactly how profoundly she hurt Ellie and how Frankie filled in for her. I'm grateful Tess sees and acknowledges her mistakes with Ellie. More importantly, I hope her newfound polite demeanor toward Frankie remains in place.

EPILOGUE

THOMAS

The past month has been filled with changes for our family. Michael was arrested for his assault on Tess. The FBI caught up with him and added a list of charges, including securities fraud and insider trading. Tess sold the house in Maine and purchased a townhouse in the same complex as Frankie's. Ellie can easily go between our homes as necessary. We have been using the new visitation schedule for two weeks. Ellie seems happier and less stressed with moving between the homes less frequently. It also gives Tess time to focus on her healing and moving forward.

"Is it time yet?" Ellie whispers.

"Almost. Your mom is running late. She texted about fifteen minutes ago."

"This is a big deal, Dad."

I smile at Ellie. It's a huge deal. I've been waiting for everything to be perfect, but I'm not worried. I enlisted Ellie, Matteo, my siblings, and even Luca to help pull this off. Right now, Frankie is at Luca's for some phantom family meeting. I don't know how long the ruse will hold.

Along with Ellie and my siblings, we have been hard at work making a romantic setting in the backyard. We erected a tent with string lights and portable heaters. Tim set up a small wooden area so we could dance if we choose.

Tess arrives in a flurry. "I'm sorry I'm late. I wanted to find this for you." She sets my grandmother's wedding band in my hand. I gave it to Tess as a promise ring years before her engagement ring.

"I appreciate you taking the time to find it. I'll hold on to it for Ellie." Everything about Frankie is different. I don't want any overlap from my marriage to Tess.

"Ready, Ellie?"

"Yup. Will you be coming to the party tomorrow or just bringing me there?"

"I'll stay if it's okay with Frankie," Tess replies.

The Cappellis are having a huge family dinner, including all the cousins, tomorrow. "You're more than welcome to stay, Tess."

"Thank you. We'll be there tomorrow. Here, Ellie, get into the car. I'll be right out."

"Everything okay, Tess?"

She smiles. "Yes. You found your true other half. I'm happy for you."

"Thank you. I'm sure this is difficult for you considering you're divorcing Michael."

"Not really. I'm stronger now, and someday I'll find my other half too."

Ellie honks the horn to get Tess's attention as Frankie pulls into the driveway.

"Oh shoot! I'm going. We'll see you tomorrow." Tess hurries out the front door, passing Frankie on her way in.

I kiss her as I close the front door. "Hi, Sunshine."

"Hi. Is everything okay with Ellie and Tess?"

"Yes," I reply.

"Why is she leaving then? What about the party tomorrow?"

"Breathe, Sunshine. We're going on a well-deserved, long-overdue date."

"Oh."

"Please get ready for a fancy dinner. Everything you need is upstairs courtesy of Kelly with Ellie's help."

Sheer glee crosses her face. Francesca Cappelli is a complex woman. She's a successful businesswoman in a male-dominated profession. I understand why men in her field find her intimidating. Plus, the overprotective big brother factor, which luckily doesn't faze me because I already knew Luca. I'm sure it paved the way a bit. The glee she gets from dressing up is icing for both of us. She loves doing it despite her penchant for planting beautiful landscapes, and I love how high heels make her legs look sexy and a mile long. "How much time do I have?"

"Your sisters will arrive any minute, but Lily only has an hour for you to get ready."

"I have no words. I love you more." She throws her arms around my neck, nestles her curves against me, and sets her lips on mine.

I'm going to kiss this woman for the rest of my life starting tonight. Waiting until tonight wasn't the initial plan. I had lunch with her father to ask for her hand about a month ago. Then I had to push it off because her ring wasn't finished on time. "I love you most."

The Cappelli sisters arrive and whisk Frankie away. I scan my texts to verify everything is set. Matteo is set to arrive with our dinner in about two hours. The flowers arrived while Frankie was gone, and Tam set some up outside. The rest are in the office. I sneak out to the workshop and set one of my gifts for Frankie under the tent as well.

When I step back into the house, laughter floats down the stairs. I grab a water and make my way to the guest room. I change into a suit and return to the kitchen. Lia and Lina come downstairs first.

"The dress is beautiful," Lia states.

"The shoes are spectacular. Lie to her when she asks how much they cost," Lina adds.

I smirk. "That was all Ellie."

"Are you kidding? We love that we know something she doesn't. Can't wait to share tomorrow with everyone. Prepare yourself, it will be crazy."

"Understood."

Lily joins us in the kitchen too. "She should be down in a few minutes."

"Thank you for coming, ladies. I want this to be perfect."

They all smile and hug me. "It will be. Even if it isn't, she'll be ecstatic."

Once they're out the door, Frankie descends the stairs. The dress Ellie picked is a deep maroon color. It has lace along the hem and the entire back. The shoes are peep toe with a high heel.

"You look gorgeous."

Her flawless skin turns pink. "Thank you. Ellie picked well."

"You don't think I could've picked this outfit for you?"

"Maybe, but I know it was Ellie. She left a cute note. It said she picked the dress so you wouldn't take credit for her work."

"She's clever."

I take her hand in mine, press a kiss to the back, and lead her into the kitchen. Dropping her hand, I scoop the roses from the office and present them to her. She kisses me in thanks before reaching for the vase. I intend to look away. However, the absence of a panty line has me watching her hemline creep up the back of her thighs instead of offering my assistance.

"Tommy?"

"Uh-huh."

"What's wrong?"

"You're tempting. I was distracted by your dress revealing the back of your sexy legs while you reached for the vase. Almost tempting enough for me to forget our date, throw you over my shoulder, and carry you upstairs." I pull myself together. I will have every evening for the rest of my life to be with Frankie. "Right this way." I offer her my arm and lead her out the French doors.

We made an aisle lined with lanterns leading to the tent. The side is closed so she can't see inside yet. When we reach the tent, I reveal the work we did this morning.

"When did you do all this? It's magical. Everything from the lanterns to the lights and the table is perfect."

"I had a lot of help from our siblings and a cousin," I admit with a sly grin. I never asked if Frankie liked surprises. Her reaction would lead me to believe she doesn't hate them.

"You really didn't have to go to all this trouble for a date."

"Trouble, not even close. Planning, sure. I'll do this and so much more for you as long as you'll have me."

"What are you saying?"

"Please sit."

She takes a seat, and I bring my first gift of the night to her.

"What's this?"

"I made you something."

"You made me something in addition to the gorgeous foldaway desk?"

"Yes. I started this first though."

She opens the wrapping. "It's gorgeous. What is it?"

"It's a memento box. I made one for Ellie when she was born. I've been filling it with milestone photos or remarkable events of her childhood. I want you to have one to fill for us." I take her hand in mine and drop to one knee in front of her with the ring box in my hand. "You're willing to love not only me but my almost teenage daughter. Without hesitation, you accepted us both. I knew the qualities I needed in my partner, and you exceed them beyond measure. I have been searching for you my entire life. When I am with you, the only place I want to be is closer. Francesca, will you spend the rest of your life with me?"

"Yes, absolutely yes!"

I slide the cushion cut diamond ring with micro pave band onto her finger and kiss her until we're breathless. "Shall we eat or go inside?"

"We should eat Matteo's food before it's cold," she replies.

"How do you know Matteo cooked?"

She smiles and brushes a kiss across my lips. "The napkins are folded in the shape of the letter C, his signature. I assume Ellie isn't coming home tonight, so we have at least twelve hours to celebrate appropriately anywhere in the house."

"We better eat quickly then. We have a bunch of rooms to check off the list in one night."

She giggles. "No."

"No?"

"We have a lifetime to complete all the rooms in the house."

"Can we add that to our vows?"

"Yes. I love you more, Tommy."

"I love you most, Sunshine."

Thank you so much for reading *Chasing My Sunshine*!

I hope you love Frankie and Tommy. Find out what happens with her sister Lina.

Pre-Order *Worth the Chase* now so you don't miss it!

A new book in the Blackthorne Security series will be released soon. Pre-order *Protecting Us*. Will Cruz fall next?

You don't have to wait for Cruz and Jillian's. Start the York Beach Series with Genevieve and Joseph's love story *A New Beginning with You*

Did you love *Chasing My Sunshine?*

Thank you for taking the time to read it. I hope you loved it!
If you liked this book or another one of my books, please consider
posting a review.
A short line or two will be perfect!
I appreciate your support and feedback.

COMING SOON

Two new stories are coming soon!

A York Beach Novel

The Cappellis

Worth the Chase

A Blackthorne Security Novel

Protecting Us

MY BOOKS

YORK BEACH SERIES:

A New Beginning with You

Taking A Chance on Me

Just One More

Kiss You Like You're Mine

Only with Him

My Once in a Lifetime

THE CAPPELLIS

Chasing Forever

MORGAN BROTHERS SERIES:

One Unforgettable Favor

Until I Kissed You

Always Have, Always Will

BLACKTHORNE SECURITY

Protecting My Forever

Protecting Our Forever

www.ingramcontent.com/pod-product-compliance
Lightning Source LLC
Chambersburg PA
CBHW072341020726
47506CB00004B/955